MW01146065

POWERHOUSE

DROPKICK
MY *Heart*

WINTER TRAVERS

Sarah,

· Much love!

1

Copyright © 2017 Winter Travers

All rights reserved. Without limiting the rights under copyright reserved above, no part of this publication may be reproduction, stored in or introduced into a retrieval system, or transmitted, in any form, or by any means (electronic, mechanical, photocopying, recording, or otherwise) utilization of this work without written permission of both the copyright owner and the above publisher of this book.

This is a work of fiction. Names, characters, places, brands, media and incidents are either the products of the author's imagination or are used fictitiously. The author acknowledges the trademarked status and trademark owners of various products referenced in this work of fiction, which have been used without permission. The publication/use of these trademarks is not authorized, associated with, or sponsored by the trademark owners.

For questions or comments about this book, please contact the author at
wintertravers84@gmail.com

Also by Winter Travers

Devil's Knights Series:
Loving Lo
Finding Cyn
Gravel's Road
Battling Troy
Gambler's Longshot
Keeping Meg
Fighting Demon
Unraveling Fayth

Skid Row Kings Series:
DownShift
PowerShift
BangShift

Table of Contents

Acknowledgments

My boys and family. I wouldn't be able to do any of this without you.

Lizette. #RideOrDie Did you just pee a little? LMAO

Nikki Horn. Best Street Team Captain ever! Thank you for all you do!

The amazing group of ladies who let me sprint with them, and who are some of the most encouraging people I've ever met. Mayra Statham. Sarah O'Rourke, S Van Horne, Trinity Rose, Layla Frost, and Brynne Asher. You ladies Rock!

All my readers, and fans. You humble me every day.

Dedication

All you need is love, and cookies.

I never imagined when my son started taking karate lessons that it would lead to my mind going crazy with an all new series that bumped everything out of the way, and demanded to be written. It's true that inspiration can come from anywhere.

A huge thank you needs to go out to my son's karate teacher. The man managed to keep his cool, and answer every one of my annoying questions at any time of the day. Thank you, Jefe San!

Kellan

"Left, Ryan." I shook my head and watched Ryan punch to the right. "Your other left, Ryan." In my fifteen years of teaching martial arts, I discovered left and right was a concept that was hard learned by anyone under the age of ten, especially when they were just excited to be punching and kicking the shit out of stuff.

"Okay! Lock it up." I stood in front of my class of twenty-five under belts and watched them all fall to the floor, eagerly looking up at me. I waited for all eyes to fall on me. "Good job today, guys. We need to work a bit longer on delta, but for only working on it one day, you guys are killing it." Clinton raised his hand eagerly, and I tipped my chin at him. "Go ahead, Clinton."

"Mr. Wright, when are we going to get to put all of the combos together?" he asked meekly.

"As soon as we learn them all," I assured him. Clinton asked the same question every class. The kid was the most eager to learn, but he had the attention span of a squirrel. I surveyed the class, then looked over the crowd of parents waiting to pick up their kids. "Now, remember that belt graduation is in three weeks, and you need to have your homework turned in before. Otherwise, you don't graduate." Everyone groaned at the word *homework*, and I couldn't help but smirk. They didn't have any clue how much homework I had done to reach sixth-degree black belt. "Everyone up," I said, motioning up with my hands. "And bow," I ordered, placing my hands at my sides and bowing.

All the kids started running up to me, giving me high fives and then scurrying off to their parents.

"Is Mr. Roman going to be here next time?" Carrie asked me as she high-fived me.

"He should be. He had a couple of things to do today and couldn't make it to class." Like sleeping until noon and screwing me over completely. Thankfully, it was the last class of the day, and I could hopefully find some time to sit down for five minutes.

Finally, the last parents left with their kids, and I locked the door behind them. I loved classes on Saturday, but they were exhausting when I was the only instructor.

The phone rang on the desk, and I knew it was Roman with some lame-ass excuse for why he didn't make it in today. Roman and I were business partners with Dante and Tate, but most of the time, it was all on me to make the school a success.

Roman's name flashed on the caller ID, and I picked up the phone. "So, what's your excuse this time?"

"Ugh, I'm fucking sick, man."

I shook my head and sat down behind the front counter. "That's called a hangover, Roman. Drink some fucking coffee, and get out of bed."

"Nah, man. This is worse than a hangover. I think I got food poisoning from the burger I ate last night at Tig's." Roman moaned into the phone, and I sighed.

Food poisoning from Tig's was a definite possibility. "I guess you should stop eating nasty shit while you're getting shit-faced every night."

"It's not every night," Roman grumbled.

"Sure, keep fucking telling yourself that."

Roman sighed. "Look, I was just calling to tell you sorry about not coming in today. If you wanna take off next Saturday, you can. I'll take care of the monsters all by myself."

"Nah, don't worry about." I made the mistake once of trying to take off a Saturday. Roman had called me halfway through the day, and I could barely hear him over yelling parents and screaming kids. I ended up coming in and spending most of the day putting out fires he had started between yelling at the kids and telling the parents to shut it while he was teaching. "Just get better, and I'll see you Monday night."

"What time do classes start?"

I closed my eyes and counted to ten. "Four. Same as every Monday," I reminded him.

"Got it. I'll be there."

I hung up the phone and sighed. Roman was one of the most talented guys I knew when it came to karate, but his adulting skills were severely lacking. At the age of twenty-eight, he should have his shit figured out.

When Roman, Tate, Dante, and I opened Powerhouse, we expected to help kids the way we were taught when we were young and just starting karate. Roman, Tate, and I began karate at the same time and worked our way through the belts together. Dante was a red belt when we were white belts, but he took us under his wing, and we all became close friends.

While Dante was almost ten years older than most of us, I was the highest black belt. Dante was a second-degree black belt, while Roman and Tate were fourth-degree. I was going for my sixth degree this year.

We all came together to start the school, because we all had our own specialties that, when put together, created a karate studio unlike any around. Dante was an international sparring champion six times over, while Roman and Tate were geniuses when it came to kamas and bo staff. I rounded us out with my expertise in forms and people skills the three others lacked at times.

The school had only been open for six months, but Dante and Tate already thought we needed to open another location. Not only had Roman bailed on me today, but so had Tate and Dante to go look at a space two towns over for a new studio.

I was in the minority when I said we should just focus on the Falls City school. Dante and Tate had decided between themselves that if we were doing so well here, another studio would be a goldmine. I didn't think they were wrong, I just wanted them to slow down, and wait for all of us to agree.

I threw my phone on top of a pile of new student paperwork and propped my arms on my head. I pushed off on the floor and spun around in the chair. Most days, it was hard to believe this was my life, and today was another one of those days. Dante, Tate, and Roman were my closest friends, but sometimes it felt like everything rested on my shoulders, while they were off somewhere enjoying life, and spending all the money we were making.

The days we didn't have classes, I was giving private lessons, or working on lesson plans for each class. Most of the time, the Kinder-kicker class was like herding a pack of cats that were all hyped up on catnip, and the Little Ninja class wasn't much better. Although, I still tried to teach them forms and basic karate to help them get to white belt. Once the kids hit white belt, things became more serious, and I buckled down on the curriculum.

The highest belt level we had right now was an orange belt, but in the stack of paper on the desk, there were three kids wanting to transfer over to Powerhouse. One of them was a purple belt, and the other two were red belts. I was rather shocked the two red belts wanted to transfer schools when they were close to being black belts, but I knew it was because in the short time we had been open, we already had a reputation of being the best.

If you were even a little bit into karate, you would have at least heard of one of us. We were the best, and we had the trophies and medals to prove it. That reputation was bringing in students left and right, but I couldn't keep doing this on my own anymore.

But, I wasn't going to stress about that right now, because a knock on the front door made me jump, and I turned to see my next private lesson through the glass.

My five-minute break was up, and it was back to the grind.

Someone had to make Powerhouse a success, and that someone was going to be me.

****

Molly

"Three vanilla *lattes*, skim, and one *Americano*."

I grabbed the cups Sage set down on the counter and set them next to the grinder. I could make these drinks in my sleep. Some mornings, it felt like I was still sleeping after staying up all night trying to figure out whatever new drink had popped into my head.

"Here, or to go?" I asked while I started the espresso.

"Here. They are for the Moaners," Sage said over her shoulder as she grabbed the pot of dark roast before making her way around the cafe doling out refills.

Ah, my Monday Moaners. Every Monday like clockwork, the Moaners showed up and sat in the same corner and discussed the latest romance novels they had read. When the Moaners first started coming in, they were just a book club, but Sage and I had dubbed them the Monday Moaners after we had heard all the things they discussed. The name fits them perfectly, and it seemed to stick.

"Molly."

"Yes, Frank?" I called as I poured milk into a small metal pitcher.

"When are you going to agree to go on a date with my son?"

And that was how I absolutely knew it was Monday. Frank was here, bugging me about dating his son who, according to Frank, was the right man for me. "I'm kind of busy this week, Frank. Why don't we try next month?"

"It's April first, Molly," he grumbled.

I shoved the pitcher of milk under the steamer. "What was that, Frank?" I yelled over the howling of the machine.

Frank swatted his hand at me and headed back over to his group of retired friends who came in every day.

"Moll!" Sage shouted. "I'm almost out of dark roast. Start me another pot?"

Four drinks and one full pot of dark roast later, I was ready to sit down for five minutes. I had been going since four o'clock that morning, and my feet were killing me.

Sage hopped up on the counter and pointed at the ceiling. "You start a new playlist?"

I slipped off my shoe and flexed my foot. "Yeah, I was getting sick of the same songs playing over and over."

"That playlist had over two hundred songs on it. I don't think I heard the same song more than twice."

"The fact that I'm here every waking second might have something to do with that." I laughed and grabbed my huge coffee cup off the counter. "Did you try the salted caramel truffle latte I made?"

"Yeah, it was delicious like everything you make. You think you could make them skinny though, so they don't go straight to my ass." Sage grabbed her cup and turned it upside down. "You filled my cup up three times today with it. It's a miracle I'm not bouncing off the walls."

I smirked. "That might have to do with the triple shot of espresso I put in them."

Sage laughed and pushed her cup towards me. "Ya think?"

"Refill?"

Sage rolled her eyes. "Yes, but this time, make it two shots less."

"Wuss," I mumbled.

Sage shook her head and glanced at the tables out front that were more than half-empty. "Pretty slow today, huh?"

I started working on her drink. "Yeah, but it is Monday and almost closing time."

Sage smiled. "True, true."

Afternoons normally were slow, but it was also the time I was able to take a breath and just relax for a bit. I've been working my ass off for the past five years to make Java Spot Coffee House a success, and it was finally starting to pay off. I had loyal customers who came in daily and numerous weekly book clubs that were my bread and butter to pay the bills.

Java Spot was the first business to enter the new shopping center, and with each new business that rented space, the more customers I got. The yoga place three doors down brought in the hipster crowd who were always looking for a healthy drink or a crazy tea fad. There was an accountant at the other end who brought in the straight-laced, suit and tie black coffee drinkers with the occasional latte, and the laundromat that brought in an array of strange and weird customers who typically paid with quarters. Those were not Sage's favorite.

The latest addition to the shopping center was the karate place that had taken up residence right next door. On Saturday, I typically saw an upswing in customers from the karate moms and dads dropping their kids off to practice and then dropping in for their daily dose of caffeine. Although, I had yet to meet the new owners of Powerhouse Martial Arts. I've seen them in passing, but they haven't come over to introduce themselves. However, I haven't made an effort to go over to them either, so I really can't call them out on it.

From the flow of traffic going in and out of the place, I could tell business was positively booming for them. And from the looks of the karate moms and dads coming in, I knew karate lessons were not cheap.

"I'm gonna do one more round with the coffee pot before we close." Sage grabbed the pot and meandered around from table to table.

It was almost three—close to locking the doors and cleaning up. I poured Sage's drink into her cup and watched Bess approaching the counter.

"Can I get a to-go cup for my latte?" She set her cup on the counter and smiled up at me. Bess was the head Moaner and one of my first customers.

"You sure can. How's the meeting going today?"

"You know, discussing the mechanics of whether you can actually have sex on a bike while it's moving, and if there really are twenty-something billionaire bachelors out there."

I poured her latte into a to-go cup and snapped the lid on. "You in the market to trade in Joe?"

Bess threw her head back and laughed. "Only if you can promise the new one will be trained already. It took me twenty-nine years for Joe to finally learn how to put the toilet seat down. I couldn't start over from scratch."

I handed her the cup. "Well, I'm sure Joe appreciates the fact that he's not easily replaced."

"Pfft. Half the time, the man doesn't even realize I'm there or gone. Damn model trains consume him since he retired."

"Then, I guess that gives you more time to read, right?"

"I guess you can look at it that way." Bess pointed over her shoulder. "That kung fu place sure is loud today. Sounds like they're actually beating the hell out of each other."

"Really?" Over the banging and clanging I did making drinks, I didn't hear much.

"Oh yeah. It's not as bad as Saturdays, but we could definitely hear them today."

"Maybe I'll have to pay a visit to my new neighbors and have a little chat with them."

Bess waved her hand at me. "Don't worry about it, hon. Like I said, Saturdays are much worse. It just made Regina turn up her hearing aid a bit, and Rach talk a bit louder. No harm, no foul." She winked and headed back to her table.

"Just let me know if you want me to go talk to them," I hollered.

I turned around and leaned against the register. I had heard the karate place before, but that was normally later in the day after I closed. When the grunting and yelling would start, I just turned up my music a bit louder and tuned them out. I didn't like that they were so loud during the day that my customers were unable to enjoy themselves.

"Refills are done; everyone knows last call is up." Sage dropped the empty coffee pot in the sink and turned on the water. She plugged up the sink and squirted in a butt-load of soap. "What's got you looking like a Debbie Downer?"

"Nothing really. Just thinking about the karate place."

"You thinking of joining to learn how to kick some ass?"

"Negative. I'm pretty sure I'd break my whole body. You know I have the grace of a newborn giraffe."

"Then, why were you thinking of the four hunks next door?" Sage wiggled her eyebrows and turned off the water.

"Bess told me that they are really loud over there, and it was messing with their book club today. Hell, not just today. She said Saturdays are even worse."

Sage waved her hand. "Please, those five cackle in the corner and are oblivious to anything except for the scorching hot sex in their books."

Scorching hot sex was a pretty accurate description of what Bess and her group of ladies liked to read. Some of the covers on those books would make even a call girl blush. "Yeah, but still. Don't you think I ought to say something? I mean, I'm sure they would complain if I was making too much noise over here."

"I highly doubt that. From the looks of those four fine specimens of men, they don't complain or ask, they just do and take."

I crossed my arms over my chest. "So then, what do I do?"

"Keep making coffee, and move the Moaners over to the other corner. Hell, put Frank in the corner. Half the time, he forgets to turn up his hearing aid. He won't even hear them over there."

I sighed and started taking apart the espresso machine for its daily cleaning. "How is that fair? They can be loud, obnoxious dill holes, and I have to move all of my customers around?"

Sage shook her head and dunked her hands into the soapy water. "Number one, we need to work on your insults. I'm not sure you calling them dill holes is as intimidating as you think."

I grabbed the towel next to me and snapped it at Sage. "I'll have to work on that. Now, tell me what number two is."

She held up two soapy fingers and smirked. "Number two is, you go make nice with the head kung fu hunk."

"Why?"

"Because if you don't start trying to get laid, Frank's son is going to start looking more and more appealing."

I dropped some of the dirty machine parts into the water and grabbed a dry dish towel. "That is never going to happen, Sage."

"Which one? Frank's son, or the kung fu master?"

"Both. I'm not going to date Frank's son, and I am not going to meet anyone over at the karate studio."

Sage rolled her eyes and handed me a soapy mug. "Mmhmm, we'll see about that."

"What is that supposed to mean?" I set the dry mug on the counter.

"It just means you never know what is going to happen."

I glanced at Sage from the corner of my eye, and couldn't help but feel that she knew something I didn't. Sage always seemed to be one step ahead of me, no matter how much I tried to keep my head up. "I'm afraid," I mumbled.

Sage threw her head back and laughed. "Afraid of what?"

"I'm afraid of the smirk on your face and what you already know that I don't know."

Sage shook her head. "That was a mouth full."

"And now you're ignoring the fact that I know that you know something that I don't know."

Sage laughed. "Say know one more time for me."

"No. And that's not the know you want me to say, either." I tossed the dish towel at her. "Just for that, you can do the dishes on your own, while I take inventory."

"So, just like every other Monday, right?" Sage called.

I pushed open the door to the storeroom and flipped on the light. There wasn't much storage room in the coffee shop, but I had figured creative ways to organize most everything into the small space—the extra bags of coffee beans, flavored syrups, and my overabundance of cups. I had an irrational fear of running out of cups. If I were to actually step back and think about it, I'm sure I had enough cups for at least half a year, lids included.

The storage room butted right up next to the karate studio, and I pressed my ear to the wall. It was quiet, and all I could hear was my own breathing. "You look like a dope right now, Mol," I mumbled out loud. Thank the Lord there wasn't anyone around to see.

I grabbed my clipboard I had hanging next to the door and stood in front of the shelving that stored all of the beans.

This was my Zen time—where I could just take in the fact that everything I wanted for the past seven years was finally mine. Owning Java Spot was something I had dreamed about since I was a young teenager and had walked into the local coffee shop where I used to live. I loved the smell of coffee and the vibe of relaxing and just taking the time to stop, and breath.

At least Java Spot used to be a calm place. Now, with all of the screaming and grunting coming from next door, I didn't know how long it would be until more customers started complaining. I turned to look at the wall and tilted my head. Maybe Bess was just too sensitive. I had never heard any screaming before. Maybe it was all in her head.

"Molly," Sage called. "I'm gonna lock up, finish the dishes, and then I gotta run to pick up Sam from school, okay?"

I peeked my head around the corner. "Leave the dishes, and just lock up on the way out."

Sage took off her apron and draped it over the counter. "You sure? I still have fifteen minutes until I need to get him." Sage had a five-year-old son who I absolutely adored.

"Yes, I'm sure." I waved her off. "I need to work on some new drinks anyway, so you doing the dishes I'm just going to dirty again doesn't make sense. Go. I'll see you in the morning."

Sage hemmed and hawed for a minute before I finally pushed her out the door and threw the lock after her. Now it was time for the fun part of the day—finishing up inventory and then time to experiment.

I really did have the best job, and I couldn't ask for anything more.

****

Kellan

"Dude. How do you not have any furniture yet?"

Roman shrugged. "I got everything I need."

I looked around the small studio apartment Roman moved into over six months ago and shook my head. "You have a TV, recliner, and a lamp."

"Is there something wrong with that, Martha Stewart?"

I flipped him off and collapsed into the lone recliner. "I see you're still in a shitty mood."

Roman leaned against the wall. "I'm fine. Just fucking bored."

"Try coming to the studio and working. You might not be so bored then."

"It was fucking Sunday today. We were closed."

I shook my head. "There is shit to do when we aren't open for classes or lessons, you do know that, right?"

"You know I'm not down with doing fucking paperwork. That's your shit to do."

"So, I assume washing down the mats and mopping the floors is my shit too, huh?" I spent all day washing down the mats while Dante had mopped and vacuumed the floors. I was sorer from crawling around on the mats than after an intense workout.

Roman waved me off. "I didn't know you were doing that shit today."

I sighed. Roman was going to drive me to drink. "What the fuck is your deal, man? You know the third Sunday of the month we clean the studio from top to bottom. Been that way for the past six months."

"You come over here just to lecture me? Because you could have done this shit over the phone instead of sitting in my only chair to do it."

I didn't want to come over here and act like Roman's dad, but he needed to figure out what he was doing. We all agreed six months ago that this was what we all wanted, but now Roman was acting like a sullen teenager who was being forced to do his chores all of the time. I had signed up to start a business, not be his fucking babysitter. "I came over here to try to figure out where your head is."

"What the fuck is that supposed to mean?"

"It means if you wanna be part of Powerhouse, then fucking be there. We decided to do this together, but it seems all you're doing is collecting a paycheck while Dante, Tate, and I do all the fucking work."

"I miss one day, and don't scrub the fucking mats with you, and suddenly you think I'm just there for the fucking money?"

I stood up and paced the length of the living room. "Yesterday wasn't the first day you've missed, Roman. You fucking know that. I know we all don't have to be there every day, but your days off outnumber your days working."

"You want me to start punching the fucking time clock? We'll see how much I really am there then," he sneered.

I ran my fingers through my hair. This wasn't what I fucking wanted. Roman was my best friend, and all I wanted to do was run a kick-ass karate school with three of the best black belts I knew. "Just fucking be there, Roman. And if you don't want to be there, just say it."

Roman pushed off the wall and fell into the recliner. He grabbed the remote off the floor and turned on the TV. "I'll see you tomorrow, three o'clock."

"Classes don't start until five."

"I'll be there at fucking three. I'll do my penance by washing the windows."

I sighed heavily. "That all you fucking got out of this?"

Roman turned up the volume on the TV.

I threw my hands up and stalked out the door. "See ya later, dick," I called. I slammed the door behind me and leaned against the wall outside his apartment.

When did life go from fun and just living, to having to be a fucking boss? I glanced at my watch. It was only half past six, and I knew what I needed to do.

Head back to the studio and beat the hell out of a punching bag. Too bad I was going to imagine it was Roman's head.

****

Molly

"Done," I sang out as I dried the last coffee cup.

It was well past closing time, and I was once again talking to myself. It had been a busy day with Sage having the day off, and I had managed to man the register and the coffee machine with ease. Thankfully, I had an amazing group of customers who were okay with waiting a couple extra minutes to get their coffee.

I leaned against the counter and tossed the dish towel in the laundry basket I had on the floor. I needed to do one load of laundry, but I really wasn't feeling it. I rolled my shoulders and knew a hot bath when I got home was going to be the only thing I would be doing before falling into bed. Laundry would have to wait until tomorrow.

Gavin Degraw crooned from the speakers piped in throughout the cafe, and I looked around, making sure I had finished everything I absolutely had to do.

The specials board was washed clean of last week's specials, and now boasted the all new concoctions I had dreamed up. I knew the Mint Iced Coffee was going to be a big hit with the soccer and karate moms, and the new flavored teas were going to help bring in more of the yoga crowd. I was constantly tweaking the menu, hoping to find that one drink people went crazy for.

I tilted my head to the side and stared at the wall connected to the karate school. "Holy balls."

I heard it—screaming. Although, screaming wasn't the right word. It was more like grunting and weird syllables being yelled. So that was what Bess had been talking about.

Yesterday, I had been so busy that I hadn't been able to hear myself think, let alone listen for strange noises being bellowed. Now that I was all alone, I could hear it loud and clear. I slowly walked into the storage closet and shut the door.

"What in the hell?' I whispered. I could hear the grunting, but now I could also hear something that sounded like pounding.

"Ta, aye!"

Okay, now I was beyond confused. What was going on over there? I was utterly clueless when it came to anything with karate, and well, any sport actually, but I had to wonder, did he have to be so loud? On top of the grunting, and pounding, his music vibrated the wall with its throbbing bass.

I stepped back and clutched my hand to my chest as a loud booming scream ripped through the wall, and I knew exactly what Bess had been talking about.

"Shit." What was I supposed to do now? I couldn't not say anything. Maybe they didn't know they were so loud. I grabbed my clipboard and wrote down the time and date.

I was too exhausted to put any thought into this right now. Maybe today was just a fluke. The grunting stopped, but the pounding bass still shook the walls. I hung up my clipboard and walked out of the storage closet. The music was barely audible by the time I made it to the register. I turned around and jumped when the grunting started again.

Either someone was getting the shit beat out of them, or they were actually working out some frustration right now. A shot of espresso would probably do them some good.

I dropped my dirty apron in the laundry basket, turned off all of the lights, and shuffled to the door with the basket under my arm.

After locking up behind me, I headed to my car. I knew I was going to have to say something to the karate school, but today was not going to be that day.

My bed was calling my name, and nothing was going to keep from sleeping like the dead tonight.

Not even grunting, macho kung fu dudes.

****

Kellan

"One more time. This time, loud and give it everything you've got." I slammed the blockers together, and the three lines of twenty-five kids ran through their delta combo. Tate and Roman wove in and out of the kids, watching each student and stopping where more instruction was needed.

Roman had made it a point to be here every day since I ripped into him on Sunday. Four days in a row where he was here early and didn't bitch about anything was pretty damn impressive.

"All right, take a knee!" I hollered over the excited chatter around the room. "We are two weeks out from belt graduation. I should have a lot more homework coming in than this. The pretest is this Thursday. You *need* to have all of your stripes, homework, and the sheet from your teacher filled out completely if you want to test." Most of the kids groaned except for the few who had already turned in their homework. Tate and Roman stood behind the kids with their arms folded over their chest and shook their heads. "Get it done, or no new belt. Everyone up," I commanded. "And bow."

We all bowed, and after twenty-five sets of high tens and milling around finding coats, shoes, and bags, all the students and parents wandered out.

"You do know if we keep getting new students like we are, we're going to have to start having separate classes." Tate was laid out on the mat, his arms held up as he twirled a kama in each hand.

"We'd have to even if we weren't getting new white belts. Half of the class is moving onto level two this next belt graduation." I grabbed the stack of attendance cards off the small podium in the corner. Each student had their own attendance card that they needed to give a black belt each time they made it to class. Each student had to make it to at least sixteen classes over the course of two months as part of being able to move onto the next belt color. We offered four classes a week, so to make it to sixteen in two months wasn't much of a hassle. It was when they moved onto levels three and four when things got much harder with the requirement of thirty classes.

Tate stopped spinning the kamas and sat up. "Oh shit, you're right."

"How the hell are we going to do that?" Roman asked. He grabbed his bo staff and started doing left-right-lefts, spinning the bo around.

I shook my head. "It's not going to be that big of an adjustment. In the long run, it'll be easier for us. Right now, we really need three of us here for classes."

Tate snickered. "Except when we all bail on you."

"Yeah, except then," I agreed. "After we split the classes, two instructors will be more than doable."

"Until you get ten more white belts walking through the door," Roman mumbled.

Tate resumed spinning the kamas sitting up. "I'm thankful for each white belt that walks onto this mat. Means my electricity bill is going to be paid this month."

"True that," I agreed.

Roman tossed his bo in the air, spun around, and caught it behind his back. "You guys ever miss the tournaments?" He continued throwing and catching the bo effortlessly. Roman had definitely become the man to beat when it came to bo staff.

"What are you talking about? There's a tournament three weeks from today you can enter, Ro." Tate tossed up a kama, pointed over his shoulder with his empty hand, and caught the kama in the air on the kama he had in his other hand. "First place is fifty bucks," Tate snickered.

Roman shook his head. "Anyone ever tell you you're a dumbass?"

Tate stopped spinning his kama and pointed it at Roman. "So, do you store your bo up your ass? Because that would explain the stick you have shoved up there."

Roman tossed his bo on the ground and advanced on Tate. "I'm going to enjoy kicking your fucking ass," he rumbled.

"Knock it off," I called. I turned, bowed to the mat, and walked backward to the office. "I don't want to clean blood off the mat."

Roman growled, clasped his fists at his sides, and glared down at Tate who had fallen back laughing at Roman. "I'll catch you in sparring next week," he warned.

I shook my head and turned into the office. I didn't have time to babysit Tate and Roman to make sure they didn't kill each other. I dropped the attendance cards on the desk and sorted them out into three piles.

"You're gonna have to add orange to that pile in a couple of weeks."

I glanced up and saw Dante walk through the front door with two bags full of fast food in his hands. "Yeah, we were just talking about that." I sat down and grabbed a pen. "About time you fucking showed up."

Dante set a soda down in front of me and tossed a straw at me. "You're welcome."

"And what am I thanking you for?"

"Because I passed on signing a contract with that space Tate and I looked at last weekend." Dante sat on the couch in the corner of the office and started pulling food out of the bags.

I ripped the wrapper off my straw and stabbed it into my cup. "You finally come off your high thinking you were going to be the next huge name in karate."

Dante slid a burger across the desk to me. "Powerhouse *is* going to be the next big name in karate. Once word gets out of how we are running things, everyone is going to be beating down the door to come train with us. There's going to come a time where we aren't going to have to take on any Tom, Dick, or Harry that walks through the door."

I pushed the burger to the side and shook my head. "I'll be happy if things just keep going the way they are."

"Come on, Kel. You're telling me that you don't hope to one day be as well-known as any one of those top five teams out there competing right now?"

I looked up and leveled a glare at Dante. "We were well-known, Dante. We were the top four on the circuit. We opened Powerhouse because we were done with all of that. Now you're telling me you want to go back?"

Dante shook his head "No, I personally don't want to be competing. I want to be the guy sitting on the sidelines, that when someone walks by claps me on the shoulder and tells me how amazing Powerhouse is."

"So, you wanna be Jim. The guy we all grew to hate by the time we left."

Dante ripped off a huge bite of his burger. "In theory. Jim was always an ass, we were just blinded by his sell of becoming famous."

If that wasn't the truth. Jim, the owner of Cornerstone M.A., sold Tate, Roman, Dante, and me a dream that was hard to pass up. But in the end, we had all received what Jim had promised, but it sure wasn't as glamorous as he portrayed it to be. Five years being on top felt like ten years. I pointed at Dante. "Rule number one, don't turn into Jim."

"Ugh, we talking about that asshole again?" Tate leaned against the doorframe. "If I never hear that name again, it'll be too soon."

Dante tossed a bag at Tate. "Word is he's on the prowl for the next big thing. Don't be surprised if you see him sooner than you would like."

"He'll find some young kid to corrupt and start the cycle all over again," I mumbled.

We had all came up under Jim, and while we had him to thank for helping us hone our skills, we also had him to thank for burning us out of competing.

Tate opened the bag of food and pulled out a fry. "I heard he's been circling local tournaments."

"Who?" Roman grabbed the bag out of Tate's hands.

Tate moved to sit next to Dante. "Jim."

Roman's hand stopped mid-air, a french fry inches from his mouth. "You're fucking kidding me. What the fuck is he in Falls City for?"

I went back to checking off attendance cards. "Probably hoping to strike big twice here. This is where he found us." Jim was a piranha. All he cared about was money and being on top. We were all his puppets for five years, helping him to secure that top spot. Now, he was scrambling to find the next karate superstar. As of right now, he was still empty handed.

Roman shoved the french fry into his mouth. "Looks like I'm going to have to enter that tournament now."

Dante smirked. "You lose your mind while I was gone?"

Roman shook his head, and a menacing smile crossed his lips. "No. Just think I need to remind dear Jim what he lost."

Tate shook his head and held up his burger. "As much as I'd love to stick around and plot taking down Jim, I gotta run to the store and then over to Mom's."

"Mom's?" Roman asked.

"Yeah. You coming with?" Tate's mom had become a mom to all of us. Mostly because anytime we would go over there, none of us left with an empty stomach.

"Dude, you got a bag of food in your hand right now," Dante smirked.

Roman grabbed a burger out and tossed the bag at Dante. "This will hold me over until we get over to Mom's house."

Roman and Tate gathered their bags and walked out the door.

"Don't forget pretesting starts next week. Kids are going to be clamoring in with homework and shit. Be here," I called. The front door slammed shut without a response from either.

"They'll be here. I think whatever you said to Roman sunk in." Dante shoved the rest of his burger in his mouth and pulled out another.

"I just told him to get his ass here, or don't show up at all."

Dante shrugged. "Well, it must have been what he needed to hear."

It must have been, but I just wished I wouldn't have had to make the ultimatum. "You up to working out after you stuff your face?" I finished filling out the cards and put them on the edge of the desk.

"That's the plan. I plan on giving you an ass-whopping."

I leaned back in my chair with my arms over my head. "Yeah, we'll see about that. Get changed, Cinderella, and we'll see if you've still got it."

Dante chuckled and tossed the burger back into the bag. "I'll save that for later. It's time for me to remind you why I kicked your ass all the time and have four titles under my belt." Dante tossed the bag of food on my desk, strolled out of the office, and grabbed his sparring gear. "I'm gonna enjoy this," he mumbled.

Dante was going to kick my ass. It was a given, but it was the distraction I needed to not think about Jim being in town. He had made my life hell before I had quit the circuit and was one man I hoped to never see again. My blood boiled at the last words he had said to me. *"You'll never make it without me. You were all nothing before you met me, and you'll go back to being nothing as soon as you open your studio."*

He was wrong, and I was hell-bent on proving it. Powerhouse was going to be a success, and no one was going to stand in my way.

****

Molly

"Are you going to keep staring at the wall all afternoon?"

I glanced over at Sage and grabbed my coffee cup. "Can you not hear that?"

Sage dumped three dirty mugs into the sink and shook her head. "Yes, I can. I don't know how you never heard it before Bess mentioned it."

I focused on the wall, glaring. "It's loud, Sage."

"No, it really isn't. It typically just fades into the background."

"Yeah, if I crank up the music so no one can talk."

Sage stood next to me. "You know, if you're so bothered by it, you need to go over there and talk to them, right? Giving the wall the death glare hasn't been working the last week. It's time to actually go do something about it."

She was right, but it was so much easier to glare at a wall than to have to talk to the jackasses. Yes, they had escalated to jackasses in my book. "I plan on writing a letter."

Sage threw her head back and laughed. "A letter? Are you serious right now? Mol, walk the twenty feet around the corner and just talk to them. They're hot, not anything to be afraid of."

I turned my glare at Sage. "I'm not afraid." I really wasn't. I just knew how I was when I came face to face with a problem. I became a bumbling fool who couldn't seem to put two sentences together. Confrontation was not something I excelled at.

"Then, go over there."

"Hmph, why don't you go over there, and I'll stay here. Someone has to close up." It was five to three, and the cafe had cleared out.

"Pretty sure I know how to close up seeing as I do it every day. Besides, I'm not the one who's been glaring at the wall all week. Their grunting doesn't bother me. If you ask me, it's kind of sexy."

"Sexy?" I scoffed. Low grunting was far from sexy.

"Kind of like a glimpse into the bedroom, you know?" Sage bumped me with her elbow. "Don't tell me you didn't think of that."

"I really think there might be something wrong with you. Might explain why we're both single."

Sage laughed. "What does my being weird have to do with *you* being single? Pretty sure that is all on me."

"Weird by association."

Sage stood in front of me and put her hands on my shoulders. "I'm pretty sure you're just as weird as I am, but that's a whole other discussion. Stop trying to distract me from sexy as fuck kung fu masters."

"Do you think they would appreciate you calling them that?"

Sage rolled her eyes. "Who doesn't want to be called sexy as fuck?"

"I'd like to think I'm quirky."

Sage slow-blinked. "Can you focus for two minutes on the words coming out of my mouth?"

I bit my lip and tried not to laugh. "I can only guarantee a minute since I know that this is going to be a conversation that I don't want to have."

"Too bad, we're having it."

I folded my arms over my chest. "Hit me with it."

"You're going to go over to the karate hotties, and talk to them."

"Why?"

"Because if I have to deal with you one more day longer while you bang and clang around complaining about the grunting, I'm going to lose my shit."

I huffed. "I have not been complaining all week."

Sage rolled her eyes. I think this was the most I had ever seen her roll her eyes in one conversation. "Molly, you have been. Even the customers noticed."

"What?" How would the customers know that I was bitching about the noise?

"I told them."

I pushed her hands off my shoulders. "Why would you tell them that?"

"Blame Bess and Frank. I swear, those two should work for the FBI the way they grilled me until I gave in." Sage wiped off her forehead and sighed. "I needed a drink after they were done with me." She gazed off and frowned.

I laughed and snapped my fingers in her face. "Did I lose you?"

Sage shook her head. "It was bad. I'm pretty sure I would have told them my life story if they had asked."

"I bet."

She waved her hand. "Never mind that. We're focusing on you and the four kung fu masters."

"There is no me and four kung fu masters."

"Yet."

I rolled my eyes. It was apparently catching today. "Your minute was up about two minutes ago."

Sage took a deep breath. "You're going over there, right now, and you are going to talk to them. I'm sure they just don't know that they are loud."

"No, I promise not to complain about it anymore."

"Bess complained to me about it today, too."

"What?" Bess hadn't mentioned anything to me since the first time. I had assumed I was the only one who could hear them since I was closest.

"She told me they were really loud today, and that Sharon left early because she couldn't take it."

"That's not okay, Sage."

She shook her head. "I know it's not. That's why you need to go over there, and have a civil discussion with them, and maybe try to sneak a covert picture of them with their shirts off for me."

I shook my head. "I'm going to ignore that last part because it just proves that you are whacked in the head."

Sage smirked. "That's probably for the best. But any who, you're going over there today."

"And why can't you go over there?"

"Because I need to pick up Sam from daycare in half an hour." Sage untied her apron and tossed it in the hamper. "Go over there, show them who's boss. Shit, maybe even take some of the leftover cookies with to soften the blow of telling them to pipe down."

"I highly doubt they eat cookies."

Sage grabbed her purse from under the counter and slung it over her shoulder. "If they don't eat the cookies, then you know they can't be trusted."

"I don't need to trust them, I just want them to keep it down."

Sage pulled her keys out of her purse and pointed at the wall. "Then, you gotta go over there. Otherwise, they are just going to keep grunting and groaning, and then one day, it's going to get the best of me, and I'm going to have to find out if that's how they are in bed."

"You're going to find out for each of them?"

She shrugged. "Don't make me have to find out, Mol. Go over there and take care of business."

I pointed to the front door. "Go before I question your sanity anymore today."

Sage gave me a salute and headed out the door. "I'll leave it open since all you need to do is grab some cookies, and you'll be following right behind me." The door slammed shut behind her, and I dropped my eyes to the floor.

I heard more grunting and yelling coming through the wall.

Damn it all, I was going to have to go over there.

****

Molly

I knocked.

Hard.

Four times.

Nothing.

I could see two guys beating the crap out of each other if I pressed my face to the glass and looked far to the right. The music they had playing was thumping so loud that I was amazed I didn't hear that more clearly when I was in the cafe.

I pounded hard on the door one last time. "Answer the door, assholes," I mumbled.

It was late April, but there was still a chill in the air. Typical of Wisconsin weather. I should have known to grab my coat on the way out the door, but I had just wanted to get this over and had completely blanked on how cold it was outside.

The song that had been playing ended, and I banged on the door, fearful it was going to shatter.

I smashed my face into the glass and saw they had both stopped and were looking at the door. I jumped back, straightened my glasses, and pushed them up my nose. I didn't bother to look down at my clothes, because I hadn't even bothered to take off my apron. With the box of cookies in my hand, I looked more like a delivery person than someone who was about to have a serious conversation with these guys.

Thank God Sage wasn't with me, because they were both shirtless, and I'm sure she would have whipped out her phone and had a mini photo shoot.

I leaned into the glass and caught sight of one of them moseying over to the door. I couldn't help but thank his mama for building him the way she did. He was covered in sweat, his skin glistening under the glow of the lights, as he unvelcroed his gloves with a scowl on his face. He was sexy but also pissed off.

Whoops, maybe I shouldn't have knocked on the door so hard.

He unlocked the door and cracked it only open a couple of inches. "We're closed, and we didn't order anything."

"I'm not—" He slammed the door in my face and threw the lock. He stared at me through the glass and folded his arms over his chest. Nice, and inviting he was not.

I pulled on the hem of my apron and cleared my throat. Time to be the badass you are inside your head, Molly.

I waved and pointed at the cookies. "I brought you cookies." Oh Jesus, what kind of badass starts off that way?

He shook his head. "We don't want them."

I could only imagine what was going through his head. I looked like a freak standing at his door telling him I brought him cookies. Time to try a different tactic. "I'm Molly."

Tall, sexy, and pissed laughed. "I'm Dante."

Well, I at least had a name to put to the pissed off face. "I own the cafe."

He shook his head but didn't move to open the door.

"What in the fuck are you doing?" I heard but couldn't see who had said it.

Dante turned his head. "Some chick is trying to give me her cookies."

"Since when did you stop accepting chick's cookies?" Dante moved over, and the guy he had been fighting looked out at me. Holy mother of God, the man was gorgeous.

Dante scowled. "I'm not into strange chick cookies."

It was time to start again. "I'm Molly."

Dante threw his head back and laughed. "I'm Dante," he howled.

"I'm Kellan," Tall, sexy, and hot said.

Kellan and Dante. It was worse than I thought. Not only were these guys drop dead gorgeous, and sexy, they had hot names. Sage would have creamed her panties by now and been in full photo shoot mode. "I brought cookies." I seriously don't know what was wrong with me.

"So, I heard. But if Dante doesn't want your cookies, I have to go with him and say we don't want them. Maybe the spa down the street wants them."

Well, Kellan at least seemed nicer than Dante, but that really wasn't much of an improvement. "I brought them for you because I need to talk to you. I own the cafe."

Surprise flashed on his face, and he unlocked the door. "Java Hut?"

"Spot."

"Spot what?" Dante asked.

Kellan opened the door, and I slipped in. "Java Spot, not hut."

Dante and Kellan had only taken half a step back from the door. They were both looking down at me, curiosity in their eyes. "I thought it was Java Hut," Kellan said.

I shook my head. "Nope, always been spot."

Dante pointed at the box in my hand. "Let me see your cookies."

Kellan scoffed. "You generally at least buy them dinner before you ask that."

I rolled my eyes and opened the box. Dante licked his lips, and Kellan inclined his head. I made amazing cookies. Even just looking at them, you could tell that they were going to be good. "Peanut Butter Fudge Chunk, and Lemon Sugar."

Dante grabbed the box and moved behind the desk. "I'm sorry I didn't take your cookies right away," he mumbled. He smashed half a cookie into his mouth and collapsed in the chair behind the desk.

Kellan looked me up and down. "Are you the neighbor welcoming committee? You're a little late. We've been open for six months."

"Um…no. Welcoming committee I am not. I just came over to talk to you guys for a second."

Dante pointed at me. "You can talk as long as you bring more cookies."

I rolled my eyes. "Come to the cafe, and you can buy as many as you want." I was, after all, running a business. The way Dante was putting away those cookies, I knew I would lose money if he expected me to bring cookies over.

Dante tilted his head. "You have cookies every day?"

"Yes, until they sell out."

"You run out every day?"

I dumbly nodded.

"I'll be there at eight."

Well, this had definitely turned in a direction I didn't see it heading. Now I was going to have the broody Dante in my cafe. Sage was going to squeal when she saw him. "And I will be there also." Lame, Molly. Totally lame.

Kellan stepped back and leaned against the front desk. "Are you looking to take some classes?"

I pointed a finger at my chest. "Me?"

"Well, he ain't talking to me, darlin'. I just kicked his ass on the mat." Dante grabbed another cookie out of the box. "You look like you could take some of the adult classes."

I looked down my body and wondered what made him think I was capable of doing karate. Or anything physical. "I'm good, thank you. I just came over wondering if there was a way to keep the noise down."

"Noise?" Kellan and Dante asked at the same time.

I rubbed my hands on my thighs. "Um, yes. The wall of your studio butts up to the cafe. You are rather loud when you are, you know, doing your kung fu."

Dante choked on his cookie, and Kellan threw his head back, laughing. "We don't do kung fu, Cookie."

Cookie? What was he calling me that for? "Well, whatever it is you do over here." I waved my hand, dismissing the fact I had no idea about what I was talking about. "Can you do it without screaming so loud that you make my customers complain?"

Kellan folded his arms over his chest. "We do a mix of Muay Thai and Jiu Jitsu. We *scream* so we know we are breathing."

I pushed my glasses up my nose. "That makes absolutely no sense." Blunt and straight to the point on that one, Molly.

"It makes sense if you know anything about karate."

Dante snickered but didn't say anything.

"Well, do you think you can keep your scream-breathing down a bit?"

Kellan unfolded his arms and pushed off the desk. "Probably not."

"I think you probably can."

Kellan skirted around me and opened the door "No, we can't. I'm not changing how I teach so you can serve coffee and listen to your shit chick music."

"I do not listen to crap music."

"Okay, you don't." Kellan pointed out the door. "Thanks for the cookies."

I huffed and crossed my arms over my chest. "I came over here to have a conversation with you like adults."

"And that is exactly what we did. You told me what you wanted, and then I told you it wasn't possible." Kellan motioned out the door. "You're welcome to bring cookies over anytime you want."

"I brought the cookies to be nice."

"And to soften us up, which did work in your favor since Dante ate all the cookies, and you had to deal with me."

I turned to Dante who was reclined back, watching the show between Kellan and me. "Can you please not scream and grunt so loud?"

Dante shook his head. "Sorry, darlin'. It's all part of karate."

I sighed and stomped my foot. "You are both being ridiculous." I moved in front of Kellan. "I don't want to have to complain to the landlord about you."

"Then don't."

"I won't if you promise to keep it down."

"No, Cookie. This is a battle you aren't going to win."

I growled and moved out the door. "This isn't over."

"Bring it, Cookie." Kellan shut the door and slid the lock. He folded his arms over his chest.

I stomped my foot again because I was frustrated as hell, and spun around. I stalked around the building and wrenched open the door to the cafe, realizing I had locked the door. I dug the key out of my pocket and twisted the key in the lock.

After I opened the door and closed it behind me, I fumbled with the tie on my apron and tossed it on the floor.

I was pissed. Mad. Infuriated. Ready to wring Kellan's neck.

Who did he think he was? I wasn't asking some huge thing. Would it really be that hard for them to grunt quietly?

"Breathing," I scoffed. I was breathing right now, and I wasn't screaming.

I slowly raised my head and glared at the back wall. The grunting and screaming had resumed, but it was twice as loud.

My blood boiled, and I knew I was going to have to do more than asking nicely for them to quiet down.

It was about time they got a taste of their own medicine.

I rubbed my hands together menacingly and knew things were about to get very interesting.

****

Kellan

"You gonna stare out the window the rest of the day, or can we get back to kicking your ass?"

I pushed off the door and turned around to look at Dante. "What was that?"

Dante licked his fingers and dropped the empty cookie box into the garbage. "That was bullshit. That's what that was. Although, she makes a killer cookie."

"What does she expect us to do?"

"I'm going to have to get more."

I scowled. "You think you could not think about your stomach for five minutes?"

Dante stood up and patted his stomach. "You have no idea what I just had in my mouth. It was heaven."

"You've said that about other things too."

Dante smirked. "Those cookies rival the likes of Jill and Diane."

"Can we focus on the chick who was just in here, and not the ones who have been in your pants?"

Dante rubbed his chin. "I might let her in my pants too."

"Jesus Christ." I grabbed my sparring gloves and shoved my hands into them. "You really are a dick, aren't you?"

Dante bounced on the balls of his feet, and hit his hands together. "The ladies usually don't think so."

"Yeah, until you dump them."

He lifted his shoulders dismissively. "They know the score before they fall into bed with me. I'm not looking for that happily ever after shit."

I marched to the edge of the mat, bowed, and walked over to the speaker on the podium in the corner. "I'm just going to forget about that chick." We weren't that loud over here. I didn't know what she was talking about. When we had signed the lease for the studio, the landlord hadn't mentioned anything about a noise ordinance. I was only going to start worrying if the landlord showed up on our doorstep.

"Probably for the best. She seemed pretty feisty when you opened the door for her."

I turned on the music and cranked it a little louder than it had been. If Molly thought we were loud before, I planned on showing her just what loud was.

****

Molly

I put the phone to my ear and waited for Sage's perky hello. "You were wrong. So, so wrong."

"Molly?"

I rolled my eyes and flopped down on my couch. "Were there other people you gave bad advice to today?"

"What are you talking about?"

Mr. Mittens, my calico cat, climbed into my lap, ready for his daily petting. "I went over there."

"Oh, you went over there. Did you take pictures for me?"

Mr. Mittens nudged my hand in my lap. "Yes and no. It was awful. They were asses." I scratched Mr. Mittens behind his ear and sighed.

"Did you bring them cookies? It really is true that the way to a man's heart is through his stomach."

"Yeah, well, I'm not looking to get to their hearts, I just want them to shut up, which isn't going to happen."

Sage sighed. "I doubt it's really as bad as you're saying. I just put Sam to bed, so I'm free to listen without my Mom Tourette's surfacing." It was a running joke because whenever I would talk to Sage on the phone when Sam was awake, every tenth word she was saying something about a toy or telling Sam not to put that in his mouth. "Plus, I'm three glasses into my bottle of wine."

Oh Lord. I could only imagine what kind of responses I was going to get from Sage now. "I stood at their door looking like a girl scout trying to sell cookies, Sage. I looked like a fool before I even opened my mouth."

"I think you need a glass of wine, too, hon."

I looked over at the half-empty bottle on the end table. "We're both three glasses in, except mine isn't having the same effect on me that yours is."

"Well, drink another one and tell me what else happened."

I stopped petting Mr. Mittens and grabbed my glass. "Well," I mumbled into my glass and took a sip. "Dante asked if he could eat my cookies."

Sage sputtered. "Holy crap, woman. I just spit out my wine. You need to warn me before you tell me a hot, sexy man offered to eat your cookies."

I rolled my eyes and downed the rest of my wine. I hadn't imagined Dante ever wanting to see my cookies either, but there it was. "That was the highlight of the whole conversation. After I had asked them to try and keep it down, the conversation was over quick. I was out the door in a minute tops and back to the cafe listening to the music cranked even louder, and I swear they were grunting just to piss me off."

Sage laughed. "So, what are you going to do now?"

I sighed. "I have absolutely no idea, but I know I can't let them think they won."

"Why don't you take it to the business owner committee?"

I set my glass down and shot up. "Why the hell didn't I think of that?" Duh. How did I forget about the committee? Hell, I was the damn vice president of the thing.

"Probably because you guys don't have meetings anymore because you never had any issues. You used to complain about going each month until you made the motion to end the meetings unless there was an emergency."

I smirked and tapped my finger against my chin. "I do believe we have an emergency, Sage."

Sage laughed. "Lord help those poor, sexy men."

Lord help them was right. They didn't know what was about to hit them.

****

Kellan

"Hey, what is this?"

I grabbed my half-empty energy drink and walked out of the office. "What is what?"

Tate held up a piece of paper. "This? Who is Molly Rey, and who peed in her Cheerios?"

I grabbed the paper out of his hand. My eyes skimmed over the brief, but to the point, letter. "This is bullshit."

"What does it even mean?"

"It means that chick I told you about who came over last weekend has bigger balls than I thought she did. She's going to the business owners committee about us being too loud." I balled up the paper and tossed it in the trash.

Tate laughed. "No shit."

Roman walked out of the bathroom pulling his shirt on over his head. "What are you laughing about?"

Tate smirked. "Kellan and the coffee chick are about to go around."

"Oh, yeah? She came over and gave him hell about the yelling again?"

Tate shook his head. "Even better, man. She went to the damn committee about us."

I slammed my drink down and sat in the chair behind the front desk. "She isn't going to get anywhere with this."

"I don't know, man. Maybe she's got this committee in her pocket." Roman grabbed his bag off the floor and slung it over his shoulder.

"I'd say so. Before Kellan threw it away, I saw vice president next to her name." Tate laughed and took a bite out of his apple.

This shit was not going to happen. "I need to talk to her again."

Roman laughed. "Because that worked so well for you last time."

"Dante and his comments about her cookies didn't really help." Dante was still talking about those damn cookies.

Tate pointed at me. "You should totally go over there to talk to her, and come back with some cookies so Roman and I can try them."

I rolled my eyes and grabbed the crumpled paper out of the garbage can. "You're just as bad as Dante."

Roman leaned against the counter and looked at the paper. "So, what are you going to do about it?"

I grabbed my keys off the desk. "I'm pretty sure that should be what are *we* going to do about it."

Roman shook his head. "I got shit to do."

Tate agreed. "Yeah, I got some shit to do, too."

I pointed my finger at them. "You're both pussies." I was going to have to take care of this shit on my own, just like I took care of everything else that had to do with Powerhouse.

"Hey, Dante said you weren't coming in to help clean tomorrow, so you can deal with the coffee chick today." Tate tipped his head at the paper in my hand. "Just turn on the charm, man, and she'll be putty in your hands."

Roman laughed. "Maybe you can find out what her cookies taste like."

I shook my head and pushed open the front door. "Lock up when you leave, and I'll see you assholes Monday."

Roman and Tate mumbled their byes, and I made my way around the building and stood in front of the cafe.

Well, for one, she was right about the name. It was Java Spot, not hut. I wasn't much of a coffee fan, so I never actually took notice of what the name of the place was. Four tables with large umbrellas spanned the front of the store, and four chairs sat scattered around each table. The front of the building was brick like the rest of the businesses in the strip mall, but with one striking difference. Molly had randomly painted bricks bright red. It was odd, but it somehow worked and seemed fitting for a coffee shop.

The windows were painted with swirly shit all over them, and the door had a huge coffee cup, with the words *Java Spot* scrawled on it. She had a prime place in the strip mall and even had a drive-thru on the side of the building.

Powerhouse also had a corner spot, but we were on the back side of the building, opposite from the main entrance. Two of the tables out front were occupied, and from all of the cars parked in front, I knew they were busy.

The instant I opened the door, the warm, robust smell of coffee hit me, and a little bell above the door chimed. To the left and right were small, round tables, half-full with people drinking coffee, and straight ahead was the main counter. There were shelves full of little knick knacky shit that women loved to buy, and even the pictures on the wall seemed to be for sale. I couldn't figure out if I was in a coffee shop or a small flea market.

"Hey, hon." A small, pixie-like woman was flitting around with a pot of coffee in her hand filling up cups as she waved to me. "Molly can help you up front."

Perfect, just what I needed. Directions to the woman making my life hell at the moment. I headed to the front counter and looked for the pain in my ass.

"I'll be right there," she called from somewhere.

I turned around, and leaned on the counter. The coffee shop was the same size as Powerhouse, just laid out a bit differently. The seating area was in the shape of a U, with the counter and bathrooms in the center. She had the coffee shop vibe definitely going for her.

"How can I help you?"

A grin spread across my lips. She had no idea who I was. I slowly turned, and looked her up and down.

"Shit."

"Got your letter, Cookie."

She growled. "My name is Molly."

"I know, Cookie."

"You think you could not call me that? I am, after all, the vice president of the Business Owners Committee."

I grabbed the letter out of my pocket and unfolded it. "So, it says on the bottom of this letter."

"Damn, the post office is quick. I dropped that in the mail yesterday." She wiped her hands on her apron and nervously looked around. "The meeting isn't for another month, though. You're a bit early."

I chuckled and set the note on the counter. "Cancel it."

She looked at me, bewildered. "What?"

"Cancel it. This is bullshit."

She blustered and shook her head. "It's not bullshit. You're disrupting my business with all of your cavemen yelling."

"Look, Cookie. I'm going to have to explain this to you again, aren't I?"

She rolled her eyes and folded her arms over her chest. "This about you being unable to breath with your mouth shut and scream at the same time? You might want to check out the yoga place three doors down. She can help with your breathing problems."

I growled. "I know how to breathe."

"Are you sure about that? Kennedy, the owner, breathes all of the time, and I never hear her doing it."

I took a deep breath, put my hands on the counter, and leaned in. "Stop this nonsense before you regret it."

Molly put her hands next to mine. "And why should I have to stop? If you would just be reasonable, and keep it down, none of this would be necessary."

"I really don't think you should be talking about something you know absolutely nothing about. Breathing and yells are an important part of karate. The fact that you want me to teach people in a sub-par manner blows my mind and shows that you only care about yourself."

She leaned in. "I am one of the most selfless people you will ever meet, but when pushed, I can't help but push back. I'm not asking you to change whatever it is you're teaching, just to not yell so loud that you rattle the coffee cups."

"You're not listening to a word I'm saying."

"And neither are you. You waltz in here expecting me just to drop to my knees and do whatever you ask. Well, that isn't going to happen."

"Cancel. The. Meeting."

Molly shook her head and pushed off the counter. "Not happening. You have one month to learn how to be quiet, or the board will *make* you be quiet."

"The board seems like a pile of shit since you're the vice president. I don't stand a chance in hell."

She shook her head. "That's where you're wrong. I can't just shut you down. If I could, I would have already. I'm just the one organizing the chaos. I need to get at least three other owners to agree with me."

I smirked. "So, that means all I need to do is get everyone on my side."

Molly shrugged. "You can try."

"You think you got this in the bag, don't you?"

"I know every business in this strip mall, and serve most of them every day. I doubt you've got enough time to turn them all on me."

I shook my head. "It's not about turning them against you, Cookie, it's just me making them see my side. Plus, the month also gives me time to make you change your mind."

"Doubtful. You can try, but that's all you're going to do."

I smirked. "You really don't know who you're messing with."

"Hmph, there's nothing you can do about it."

"Oh, but there is, Cookie. Just you wait." I spun around on my heel and stormed out the door.

Molly Rey wanted to mess with me?

I was going to show her just what she signed up for.

****

Molly

"Sweet Jesus, what was that?"

I grabbed a towel off the counter and wiped my hands. That was exactly what I thought was going to happen when I set up the meeting, although I didn't expect him to try to run me off. "That was Kellan. Head kung fu asshole."

"I've never seen him before. Typically, I see the silver fox."

"The silver fox is Dante."

Sage whacked my shoulder. "How do you know these guys names, know which one is which, and not tell me?"

I rubbed my arm and glared at her. "Because it doesn't matter what their names are."

"Please, speak for yourself. Now I have names to go along with the fantasies." Sage's eyes glazed over, and I didn't want to know what was running through her mind.

I snapped my fingers in her face. "Do you think you could focus?"

Sage shook her head. "Yeah, sorry."

"Kellan came over to tell me that he got the notice about the meeting."

Sage bit her lip. "I'm going to assume that he wasn't happy."

"Unhappy would be an understatement. Pissed is more like it."

"What did he say?"

"He said I didn't know who I was messing with."

Sage frowned. "That doesn't sound too promising."

It didn't, but I had no idea what he could do to me. He was right, he could talk to the other business owners and try to get them on his side, but it felt like he wasn't talking about that.

"So, what are you going to do?"

That was the million dollar question. He wanted me to run with my tail tucked between my legs, but that wasn't going to happen. I wasn't asking him something unreasonable. There was no reason why he couldn't just yell a little quieter. "I planned on making my way over to all the other businesses this week, and just waiting until the meeting."

"You really think that's the best, just waiting?"

It wasn't, but I had no idea what Kellan had meant when he said I didn't know who I was messing with. "I think I'm just going to have to play this by ear. I think Kellan came over here thinking he could just scare me into canceling the meeting."

Sage laughed. "Obviously, that didn't work."

"No. I have just as much of a right as he does. I'm sure if I was doing something to piss him off, he would complain too."

Sage grabbed the coffee pot she had set down. "Well, I can tell you that I can't wait to see what he has planned. If it involves him coming in here again, I'm okay with it."

I pointed at her and shook my head. "He's the enemy, Sage. Remember that."

Sage waved me off and moseyed over to refill cups. "He's hot, Mol. I don't know how you don't see it."

I turned around, and leaned against the counter. I knew he was hot, but the problem was he knew it too. I glared at the wall that butted up to the karate studio. Kellan had thrown down the gauntlet, letting me know he wasn't going to lie down quickly.

Now, all I could do was wait and see what his next plan of attack was going to be. He didn't want to listen to me, so I had no plans of listening to him.

Four weeks until the business owners meeting. All I needed to do was keep my eyes open, and make sure to get over to all of the businesses to get them on my side.

I grabbed my coffee cup and continued my stare down with the wall. I had no idea what was going to come next, but I knew I had to be prepared.

Kellan and his kung fu buddies were going down.

****

Kellan

"That was quick."

Tate and Roman were standing next to their cars, and I really wished they had already left. "I said what I needed to say."

Tate leaned against his Camaro. "She cancel the stupid meeting?"

I shook my head. "No, she insists on having the damn thing. Although, I have a plan."

Roman laughed. "You always have a plan, fucker. That's why we keep you around."

I flipped him off and tilted my head toward the studio. "You lock up?"

Tate smirked. "Yeah, we weren't sure how long you were going to be, so I hit the lights and everything."

I spun my keys around my finger. "Good. I think I'm just going to head home and worry about all of this shit on Monday."

"You're not coming in tomorrow, right?"

I was finally taking a damn day off, and there wasn't a damn thing that would make me come in. Even a feisty *barista* who had decided to make my life hell. "Yeah, I'll be in on Monday." I headed over to my Challenger and beeped open the locks.

"You gonna tell us what your plan is about the coffee chick?" Roman called.

I opened my door and slid in. "I'll let you know when I think of one."

Tate laughed. "I thought you said you had one."

"Give me until Monday, I'll have something then." I slammed my door and shoved the key in the ignition.

I was always the man with the plan, but this was one time I really wasn't sure what to do. With Molly being the vice president of the committee, we were already a step behind.

The Challenger purred to life as I turned the key, and I shifted into reverse, ready to just get home. I had told Tate I would have a plan Monday, but as I passed by the yoga studio, an idea hit me.

Dante, Tate, Roman, and I always had chicks clamoring after us when we were on the circuit, and it didn't matter if they were young, old, or in between. We always had women playing out of our hands.

It was about time we pull out all of the stops and meet our neighbors.

Powerhouse was here to stay.

****

Molly

"Molly, I really think you need to give my son a chance. I believe it's just what you are looking for." Frank pointed his finger at me and shook his head. "Just one date isn't going to hurt you."

I smiled at Frank and set his full cup in front of him. "Americano, Frank. Is there anything else I can get you?" The bell above the door chimed, and I glanced over to see Dante walk through the front door. Son of a bitch, what was he doing here?

Frank droned on. "Yeah, I want you to give him a chance." Dante stood behind Frank and folded his arms over his chest. I don't know how he could look so pissed off just standing there. "Friday night, he's free."

I turned my eyes back to Frank and shook my head. "'I'm good, I promise you. If I need a date, I'll let you know, and your son will be on the top of the list."

Frank swatted his hand at me, mumbling under his breath about ungrateful kids, and ambled off to his table.

Dante raised his hand. "I'm Dante."

Jesus. Did I really need to relive my embarrassing moment right now? "I'm Molly."

Dante smirked and eyed-up the pastry case. "You have the best cookies I've ever tasted."

My cheeks heated, and I knew I was blushing ten shades of red. "I'm going to take that as a compliment and move on."

Dante winked. "It's usually for the best to move on after I've had your cookie, but I can't seem to move on from yours."

I surveyed the cafe, praying for Sage to need a refill on the pot of coffee she was carting around. I leaned and whispered. "Are we actually talking about cookies right now?"

Dante threw his head back and laughed. "We sure are, darlin'."

Well, now I really felt like an idiot. For a second there, I had thought Dante was hitting on me. Dream on, Molly. Dante was not the kind of guy who would be interested in me. I grabbed a box from under the counter. "What kind, and how many?"

"Whatever's good."

I nodded my head. "That would be any of them. How many did you want? I'll just give you some of each."

"Make it a full dozen. Tate and Roman are at the studio today."

And now the hot guy circle was complete, and it was confirmed they all had sexy as hell names. "Coming right up," I mumbled.

Dante leaned against the case and watched me fill the box. "You really going through with that meeting?"

I sighed and grabbed three huge chocolate chip cookies. "Yes."

"We're just trying to run a business, just like you are, darlin'."

I dropped three more cookies into the box and looked up at Dante. "I know that. I'm not trying to shut you guys down, but you're disturbing my customers."

Dante looked around. "Maybe they should all turn their hearing aids down. Problem solved."

I rolled my eyes. The clientele was on the older side, but that didn't mean anything. I grabbed six more cookies and closed the box. "Anything else?"

"You got protein shakes?"

I wrinkled my nose. "Negative."

Dante shook his head. "You should get some protein shakes in here. We would be over here every day if you did."

That would be the last thing I wanted. Especially if I ended up getting my noise ordinance approved. The boys of Powerhouse were not going to be fans of mine if I got my way. "Eight ninety-nine."

Dante pressed a ten into my hand. "Keep the change, darlin." He grabbed the box out of my hand and sauntered out the door.

Bess bustled over. "Call me Sally and slap me silly. Who was that?"

I slapped the ten into the drawer and pushed it shut. "That is one of the four pains in my ass."

Bess hummed her approval as she watched Dante 'til he disappeared from view. "That is one pain in my ass I wouldn't mind."

"TMI, Bess."

Bess hushed me. "Oh, hon, you don't even know the half of it. That man that just walked out deserves his own book written."

I rolled my eyes. "Well, I'm sure he'd be more than willing to go on, and on, about how amazing he is. Damn, I'm sure any of them will." I had only met two of them, but I'm sure they were all arrogant asses. Dante had been nicer to me this time, but I assumed that was only because I was his hook up to get more cookies. Kellan still seemed like a huge ass. I growled as I remembered him holding the door open for me, treating me like a nuisance.

"So, did he ask you out?"

My jaw dropped. "Excuse me?" Bess must have smoked the good stuff today.

"I saw him eyeing you while you finished up with Frank. By the way, please tell me you didn't agree to go out with his son. I've seen him, you can do so much better."

I shook my head, trying to figure out when I stepped into the twilight zone. Dante asking me out? "No, he wasn't asking me out, and no, I'm not going out with Frank's son."

"Well, one of those answers I like, but the first one makes me believe that I need to slap some sense into that hunk of man, or one of the other ones are meant for you."

I grabbed the cup she was clutching in her hand. "None of them are meant for me. Shit, I'm starting to believe that the only man meant for me is Mr. Mittens."

"Hogwash. I know that there is a man out there for you. Sage found hers." We both turned to look at Sage who was chatting with Frank. "It's a shame they weren't meant to be together forever."

Sage had married her high school sweetheart. They had a wonderful marriage, and she had gotten pregnant, then Chad was deployed. He had only been gone for two months before Sage received word he wouldn't be coming home. "She's strong, though," I mumbled.

"That she is." Bess sighed and pointed to the cup in my hand. "Fill me up. I've got a new box set that released today that's calling me on my Kindle. It's gonna be an all-nighter."

I shook my head and got to work making her latte. "So, everything okay in the corner?"

Bess tilted her head. "What do you mean? You change the chairs or something, and we didn't notice?"

I laughed and grabbed the milk. "No. I just mean has it been noisy back there."

"Oh, you mean the manly grunting and the kids yelling."

"Yup, that would be what I'm talking about." I put the pitcher of milk under the steamer and smiled at Bess. It wasn't easy to have a conversation when I was making drinks. "Sorry, Bess." I grabbed the double shot of espresso and poured in the milk.

"Oh, hon. No need to apologize. You are a goddess when it comes to coffee. You do your thang, and I'll drink the deliciousness."

I snapped the lid onto her cup. "Back to the noise, is it every day?"

Bess grabbed the cup. "No, although we're not here every day. Mondays are the manly grunting, and on Saturday is the littles screaming."

"Bad?" I cringed, worried.

"Oh no, it's no big deal. Laura complained about it to Sage, but Laura complains about everything. She's the one who throws a fit with cliffhangers. She's a hard one to please." Bess took a sip, and a huge grin spread across her lips. "Heaven in a cup."

Sage came over and slammed the coffee pot on the counter. "Who was that manly hunk?"

Bess laughed. "I knew you noticed him."

"Pfft, he was hard to miss. Even Frank checked him out." Sage pointed at me. "He was one of them, wasn't he? Was he an ass to you?"

I shook my head. "He wasn't as bad as Kellan."

"Oh, so that was Dante. Definitely silver fox all the way." Sage bumped Bess, and they broke out into giggles.

"And this is why I have to deal with them. You two would be fawning all over them, and telling them there isn't a problem at all."

Bess batted her hand at me. "You need to loosen up, hon. They may be loud, but it's no big deal. It could be a lot worse."

Sage snorted. "Yeah, they couldn't be as hot, and then instead of hot assholes, they're just assholes."

"True that, honey." Bess waved to Sage and me then headed back to her book group.

Sage rinsed out the empty coffee pot. "So, what did the silver fox have to say?"

I shrugged. "Not much. He just came for cookies."

"Did he mention the meeting at all?"

I dumped coffee beans into the grinder. "Yeah. He just asked if I was really going to go through with it."

"I bet he was surprised when you said yes, huh?"

I flipped on the grinder and shook my head. Sage put a new filter into the coffeemaker and held out the basket to me. I dumped the grounds into it, and she shoved it back into the machine. "He didn't seem too surprised. I'm sure they think that I'm joking."

Sage crossed her arms over her chest and leaned against the counter. "And are you?"

I wiped my hands on my apron and looked at the wall. "Do I want them to shut down? No. Do I want them to just keep it down? Yes. I'm not asking a lot."

Sage pointed at the wall. "Well, I'm sure it'll all get figured out in the end. I think you guys just need to sit down and talk with your heads, and not pissed off."

That would be awesome, but I didn't know if that was possible with Kellan. When we had first met, he seemed decent, but as soon as I mentioned I had a problem with him, he flipped the asshole switch on. "Well, I have just under four weeks until the meeting. I guess we'll have to see what, if anything, they do."

Sage shook her head. "I think you better prepare, Molly, because from what I've seen and what you've told me, Powerhouse isn't going to take this lying down." Sage grabbed the pot of decaf and headed over to Bess' group in the corner.

I crossed my arms over my chest and closed my eyes. Sage was right, but I had no idea how to prepare for whatever Powerhouse was going to throw at me.

All I could do was pray I hadn't started a war.

****

Kellan

"Holy crap, man. How many cookies did you get?"

Tate grabbed the box out of Dante's hands and dumped it out on the desk in front of him.

It was Monday early afternoon, and we were all gathered going over the plans for the week.

Dante grabbed a chair, spun it around, and straddled it backward. "A dozen. I knew with you assholes here, I was going to need a lot."

Roman grabbed a cookie and pointed at Dante. "I still can't believe you went behind enemy lines."

Dante rolled his eyes. "Call it recon. I was getting a lay of the land."

Tate tossed Dante a cookie. "That's bullshit. What kind of recon can you do while ordering cookies?"

"I found out Molly is single, and that they have six different kinds of cookie." Dante ripped off half of the cookie and popped it into his mouth. "And, they don't have protein shakes."

I leaned against the wall. "Are you really surprised by that? It's a coffee shop, bro, not a juice bar."

Dante shrugged. "No, but I still asked."

"I don't know what you think we can do with that recon. What does the fact that she's single have to do with anything?"

I pushed off the wall and walked into the office. "I think I know exactly how we can use that to our advantage."

Roman followed me into the office and collapsed on the loveseat in the corner. "What are you thinking?"

"I think it's time Molly met someone." I turned on the computer and opened the internet.

"This is your plan? Find her a boyfriend?"

"I think you're losing your edge," Tate called.

"Just trust me. I know what I'm doing. I'll take care of Molly, and you guys need to make friends with all the other businesses." I typed in the website I needed to get the ball rolling on my plan and smirked as I entered Molly's name.

Dante walked in and watched over my shoulder. "Dude, you are fucking evil."

I grinned and sat back, waiting for the account to set up.

It was evil, but it was pure genius too. The first hit against Molly was in full swing, and I couldn't wait to sit back and watch her freak out.

Shit was about to go down.

****

Molly

"Mol, what is going on?"

I peeked my head out of the storage room. "I have no idea, but if anyone asks, my name is Harriet today."

Sage stood in front of the storeroom door. "I'm afraid you aren't even going to get away with that. These guys know who you are. Molly, did you get drunk and sign up for some shady dating site?"

"No!" I hissed. "You think I asked for this? Have you seen the guy in the corner? His hair is longer than mine, and *he's brushing it!*"

Sage shuddered. "Yeah, well, he's gone because I told him he was breaking the health code, but there's still seven guys out there who are wanting to see you."

It was Friday morning, and I was hiding out in the storage room because somehow, these guys were all here to date me, except I had no idea who they were. "Do you think it was Bess? She's always telling me I need to meet someone. Is this her weird way of bringing the guys to me?"

Sage shook her head. "That was my first idea too. I asked her, and she swears up and down that she didn't have anything to do with this. Although, she said the guy in the flannel isn't bad if you're seriously trying to find a guy."

I rolled my eyes and sighed. "Bess would think that."

Sage shrugged. "I don't know what you want to do. I need seven lattes, three Americanos, and four frappuccinos made, though. You can't hide in here all day."

The bell above the door chimed, and Sage turned to see who had walked in. "Please tell me it's not another one."

Sage's jaw dropped, and her eyes bugged out. "If these guys are here to date you, your ass better say yes."

Huh? There were actually good looking guys looking for me?

"Oh shit," Sage whispered. "I'll be right with you," she called to whoever had walked in.

"What's going on? You know I can't go out there."

Sage threw her head back and laughed. "You're going to have to come out because your kung fu men just walked through the door."

I rolled my eyes. "They're not mine."

"Well, I know they're not here to see me, although I will take the one in the blue shirt."

I peeked around the door again. They were all wearing blue shirts. "Sage, they're all in blue."

Sage patted her hair and winked. "I know."

I pushed past her and scurried to the front counter where they were waiting. "Hi."

"Hi, I'm Roman."

"Hi, I'm Tate."

"Hi, I'm Dan—"

I held out my hand and cut him off. "I got it." One time I make a complete fool of myself, and these guys just can't let it go. It was nice to put a face to the other two's names, though. "What can I get for you?"

Kellan smirked. "We were just going around and meeting all of our neighbors, and thought we would stop by here too, Cookie."

I growled at the name he called me. "How nice of you to stop."

Dante leaned against the pastry case. "And, we need a dozen more cookies."

Sage scurried to grab a box and whipped it open. "I can help you with that." Sage batted her eyelashes at Dante, and I couldn't help but roll my eyes. Dante quietly pointed out the cookies he wanted, and Sage filled the box.

"Is that all?" I asked Kellan.

"Give me one of your drinks too." He pulled out his wallet. "Try not to make it too frou-frou."

I pointed at the menu hanging on the wall. "I have over thirty drinks on the board. You wanna try to narrow that down a bit? Hot, cold, vanilla, butterscotch, hazelnut, or the other twenty flavors I have?"

"Hot, butterscotch, and big. Can you work with that?"

I gulped. "Coming right up." Big, and hot. My mind traveled to other things that were big and hot that had to do with Kellan as my eyes roamed over his broad shoulders.

Oh hell, what in the fuck was I doing? I grabbed a large cup and moved over to the espresso machine. Thinking of Kellan in any other way than as the enemy was not good. I grabbed the butterscotch flavor and the milk from out of the mini fridge. I had been playing with a new flavor the past week, and it was time to try it out.

"It sure is busy in here today." I glanced over at Kellan, who had turned around and was looking at all of the full tables.

Hmph, we normally weren't this busy on Friday. The seven mystery men who were all eyeing me up and taking up residence at tables scattered around the cafe made it seem much more hectic. "Yeah."

Bachelor #3 who had shown up half an hour ago stood up and gradually made his way over to the counter. He stood next to Kellan and cleared his throat. "Are you Molly?"

Oh, sweet Jesus. Here we go. Did this really have to happen right now with Kellan standing right there? "Yup, that's me." Too chipper Molly, reel it in. I dumped some milk into the small silver pitcher and turned on the steamer. "Can I get you something to drink?" That was another thing about these guys who were looking for me—only two of them had actually ordered something to drink. The rest had just stared at me creepily and looked around nervously trying to get the courage to come talk to me. All of them had asked Sage about me, but this was the first one of them who had talked directly to me.

"I saw your profile, and thought I would come down."

I crinkled my nose. "Profile?" Was this guy talking in code?

"Yeah, coffeebitchhot4you88. That's you, right?" He pulled out his phone and held it up to me.

I slammed down the pitcher of milk and grabbed his phone out of his hand. "Coffee bitch?" Right there on his phone was a picture of me pretty much standing right where I was, and I was smiling like an idiot at something in the direction of Bess' table. But who took this picture? I scrolled down and read my "profile" that was a load of shit. "This isn't me. Sailing?" I scoffed.

"Where do you keep your boat?" Bachelor #3 asked.

Kellan busted out laughing and grabbed onto the counter, so he didn't fall over. "Boat," he wheezed. Tate, Roman, and Dante had their hands over their mouths and had partially turned away. They knew. They fucking knew what was going on.

I handed him back his phone. "I'm sorry, but I think you have the wrong person."

He held the phone in my face, the horrible picture staring back at me. "But that's you," he insisted.

I pushed his hand away. "It is, but I didn't put that picture there. Although, I do have an idea who might have." I glared at Kellan who was now bent over, trying to catch his breath.

Bachelor #3 looked at the phone, disappointed. "So, you don't have a boat?" That sent Kellan into another round of laughter.

I shook my head. "No, I don't have a boat. I've never been on a sailboat in my life. I'm sorry to disappoint you, but I'm not the girl you're looking for." I hated to pop the guy's bubble. "I'm sure there is a girl out there with her own boat that would love to go out with you. Unfortunately, that girl is not me."

He shoved his phone into his pocket and stormed out the door.

I grabbed a cup and clanked a spoon against it. "Attention, any man here thinking they are going to meet a Molly who loves to sail, has her own boat, and has three gerbils." Yes, that was in the profile. "I'm afraid that girl doesn't exist, and you've all been duped by these four asses."

A round of moans went up, and I rolled my eyes. Did they really think there was a girl like that out there? Hell, was a woman like that really attractive to eight guys? I was still counting the long haired one who Sage asked to leave.

The remaining six guys stood up and ambled out the door.

"I cannot believe you did that!" I hissed at Kellan. I knew they were all responsible for this, but I knew Kellan was the ringleader of the group. "How did you get that picture of me?"

Dante was the only one who had managed to get a hold of themselves enough to talk. "We sent Tate in here yesterday to get the picture. You didn't even notice him."

Well, that explained the picture, but why would they even do this to me? "Are you four on drugs?" That was the only logical explanation for why they would set up a fake dating profile for me.

"No drugs, Cookie." Kellan gasped.

"Then, why would you do this?"

Kellan stood up straight. "To show you what you're messing with."

I growled. "This is about the business owners meeting, isn't it?"

"Ding, ding."

I glared at him and moved back to the coffee machine. I finished mixing up his drink and set it in front of him. "Thirteen ninety-five." I held out my hand, and he slapped a twenty in it. "I'm keeping the change."

Kellan shook his head and grabbed his drink. "Cancel the meeting, and you won't find out what else I have up my sleeve."

I shook my head. "Not happening."

"You're just doing this to yourself, then. I can do this every day, Cookie. It's entertainment for me and the guys."

"Then, I guess I'll just have to play along then."

Sage handed Dante the box of cookies. Dante grabbed the box and looked at me. "What does that mean? You're gonna date one of those guys?" Dante and the guys busted out laughing again.

"No, you idiots. If you want to act like a bunch of teenagers, I guess two can play that game." I tapped my chin and started thinking of revenge.

"Hit me with your best shot, Cookie." Kellan took a drink of his coffee, and his eyes bugged out. "What is this?"

I shrugged. "Just a drink I've been working on."

Kellan took another sip. "Well, whatever it is, it's fucking delicious."

Sage stood next to me. "Everything Molly makes is delicious." She glared at the guys. At least she wasn't drooling over them like she was before.

"I'll give ya that." Kellan held up his cup. "We'll see ya around, Cookie. We have more neighbors to visit this morning. Maybe we'll give them a couple of your cookies."

I growled and watched them walk out the door. "That ass is going to use my own cookies against me."

Sage put her arm around my shoulder. "He is, but I wouldn't worry about it. What I would worry about is what his next move is going to be."

I pressed my lips together. I was going to have to think of something quick to get back at Kellan. "Give me your phone."

Sage pulled her cell out and put it in my hand. "Um, and why can't we use yours?"

I cleared my throat and shrugged. "I may have forgotten mine at home today." I unlocked her phone and hopped on the internet. I was constantly forgetting my phone at home. Sage had threatened to sew the damn thing to my hand so I would start remembering it. Apparently, her threat hadn't worked.

Sage looked over my shoulder. "And just what exactly do you plan on doing by going on their website?"

"I have no idea what they do over there, and when they are actually there. We need to do some research on our enemy." I tapped on the schedule tab, and a grin spread across my lips. "I think I have the most brilliant idea."

"As long as your idea doesn't involve us taking karate lessons, I'm in."

I handed Sage back her phone. "Nope, we won't even have to go over there. All we need is a bunch of paper and a printer."

"I don't mean to doubt you, Mol, but this really doesn't sound like it can go up against what they just did."

I raised my eyebrows and tapped my fingertips together. "Oh, ye of little faith. This is going to blow their little dating scheme out of the water."

"Well, then, in that case, let the fun begin."

I rubbed my hands together, my idea taking shape in my head. Kellan and Powerhouse weren't going to know what hit them come Saturday morning.

Game on.

****

Kellan

"You think we hit up enough places?"

Dante held the empty box of cookies upside down. "I'd say we're good."

I clapped him on the back. "You can get more cookies tomorrow, man."

"That's if she even lets you in the place tomorrow." Tate laughed and opened the door to Powerhouse. "She was pretty pissed when we left."

I grabbed the empty box from Dante and tossed it in the garbage. "If she won't let you in there for cookies, we'll just send one of the kids over there to get them for you." Molly was definitely pissed when she had figured out I made her a dating profile. I couldn't blame her for being pissed, but she had to know who she was messing with. I collapsed into the chair behind the front desk. "I have to say, I'm feeling pretty good about the meeting."

Tate nodded. "Yeah, everyone seemed to be friendly enough."

Roman leaned against the front desk. "Although, that guy at the laundromat was giving me the eye."

We busted out laughing. "He did like what he saw in you, Ro. You might have to go over there and make sure we get his vote our way." Tate pointed at Roman.

Dante smirked. "I'm sure that's not the only thing he'd like to throw Roman's way."

Roman flipped Dante off. "Yeah, laugh it up, fuckers. I also had the yoga chick checking me out, too."

Tate waved him off. "You have a better chance with the laundromat guy."

I grabbed my car keys and stood. "As much as I'd love to spend the rest of the day with you fuckers, I'm gonna head home and do absolutely nothing until class on Saturday." Friday was usually a slow day at the studio, and I had made sure there weren't any lessons, so I didn't have to come in at all. I had plans to work on the front yard and wait for the delivery guy to come and deliver my new furniture.

I headed out the door, and Tate hollered after me. "You wanna get something to eat tomorrow night?"

"Text me. We'll figure something out." I slid into my car and drove around the building. My eyes traveled along the length of Java Spot and the corners of my mouth ticked up. I hadn't planned on going over there today with all of the guys, but Dante had been jonesing for cookies, and we were going to all of the other businesses, so it only made sense to stop there.

I had spotted the guys as soon as I walked in, and I knew my plan of attack had been perfect. The fact she hadn't put two and two together before we walked in gave me hope that the rest of my plan was going to be a surprise she wouldn't see coming.

The only thing I needed to figure out was how to get into the cafe without Molly knowing I was there. The chick who had helped Dante was just the person I needed. I just need to make sure she would help me, and not run back to Molly.

I flipped my visor down, grabbed my sunglasses, and slipped them onto my face. I was going to have her running with her tail between her legs in no time. Between getting friendly with other committee members, and all the tricks I had up my sleeve, she was going to cancel that meeting in no time.

This was war, and I had every intention of being the victor.

****

Molly

I poured the steamed milk into the espresso and snapped the lid onto the cup. "I'll be right back."

Sage shook her head. "And just where do you think you are going with that?"

It was Saturday morning, and I was eager to go check on my surprise for Kellan. Yesterday, I had put everything into motion, and now it was time to watch my handy work fall into place. I grabbed the two boxes of cookies I had packed up earlier and grinned from ear to ear. "I thought the boys over at Powerhouse could use a little pick-me-up this morning."

Sage rolled her eyes and laughed. "I wonder why they would need a pick-me-up?"

I shrugged. Sage was an important part in making my plan go off without a hitch, and she knew exactly why I needed to get over to Powerhouse.

"Make sure to take pictures."

I pursed my lips.

"You forgot your phone again, didn't you?" Sage grabbed her phone and tucked it into my pocket. "I don't even know why you have the damn thing. You never have it on you."

The walk to Powerhouse took a whole minute, and I was standing at the front door, trying to juggle the boxes and the coffee in my hand.

"Let me get that for you."

I looked up and saw an attractive man looking down at me. "Um, thanks." He opened the door, and I stepped in.

"First day?" he asked while he took his coat off.

"Um, no. I'm just dropping this off for Kellan. Your first day?" I had no idea why this man was making small talk with me. Did I actually look like someone who was about to do karate? I was still in my coffee-stained apron, and I'm pretty sure I looked like I had just rolled out of bed.

"Oh, too bad. It would have been nice to have some more people out on the mat."

I laughed. "I'm the last person you want to see out there. Two left feet."

Handsome smiled. "Well, I'll see ya around, and I'm Gavin by the way." The man made his way further into the studio before I could tell him my name, and I finally took the time to look around.

It was twenty to nine, and if the schedule I had seen online was correct, the adult cardio class was about to begin. I giggled to myself and set the boxes on the counter.

"But I have a flyer."

"You have to do it."

"I want my money back."

A huge grin spread across my lips, and I knew my surprise for Kellan was in full swing.

I moved closer to the mat and saw Kellan surrounded by six of my regular customers from the cafe—Bess and Frank included. "I've never seen that flyer in my life before."

Bess held the flyer in his face. "But it says right here you have senior citizen cardio at eight forty-five."

Kellan grabbed it and balled it up. "I know it says that, but I didn't make the damn thing."

"You have to do what the flyer says." Frank was dressed in clothes that I wished I could unsee. He had on shorts that barely came to his knees, a baggy white tank top, and to top it all off, he had sweatbands on his wrists, and one on his head. He looked like eighties aerobics come back to like.

I grabbed Sage's phone out of my pocket and quickly snapped a picture.

"You!" Kellan boomed.

Everyone turned to look at me, and I slid the phone back in my pocket. I pointed to my chest. "Me?"

Kellan stalked over to me and grabbed my arm. "Yes, you. In my office, now," he ordered.

Kellan towed me to the office and slammed the door shut. "Undo this."

I slowly blinked. "Undo what?" I wasn't going to cop to anything.

"I know you did this, Molly."

I peered out the large window that overlooked the mats. "I'm still not sure what 'this' is."

"You think you're funny, don't you? Fucking cute just standing here in your damn apron acting like you have no clue that fucking flyers are going around with the Powerhouse logo on them advertising one free senior cardio class."

"Wow. That's awfully sweet of you, Kellan. Now that you do mention it, I did see the flyer and showed Bess yesterday."

Kellan growled. "I didn't make the fucking flyer."

"Oh really? Then, I wonder who could have done it." I tapped my finger on my chin and tried desperately not to smile. "Did you ask Dante?"

"This is really how you are going to play this?" A vein in his neck throbbed, and he took a step closer to me. "This wasn't Dante, and I know for damn sure it wasn't Tate or Roman before you suggest them."

I held my hands up. "Then, I'm at a loss. You must have really pissed someone off for them to do this to you."

Kellan looked me up and down. "If you didn't come over to see your handiwork, then why are you here? You didn't step foot into Powerhouse until you had a problem with us. I find it hard to believe that you just came over for a friendly visit."

I beamed and clasped my hands in front of me. "I brought cookies, and coffee for you."

Kellan took another step towards me, and I scurried backward, slamming into the door. He caged me in with his arms and looked down at me. Kellan was only a couple inches taller than me, but he was rather imposing when he was this close. "Molly."

"Kellan," I gasped. My body betrayed me, heating at the one word that escaped his lips.

"Admit it."

I cleared my throat and looked him in the eye. "Admit what?" There were quite a few things I could accept at that moment, one of them being I was thinking things about Kellan that should not be crossing my mind.

"You made the flyers."

"No, I didn't." I really hadn't. Sage was a computer guru and had made them. I just told her what I wanted them to say, and she had done the rest.

Kellan growled.

"Is growling really necessary?"

"It seems to be my natural reaction when I come in contact with you."

I looked to the left. "Odd."

Kellan leaned in closer. "What's strange is you think it's okay to mess with my business and life."

I scoffed. "Me? You're the one who sent eight guys to the cafe yesterday!" He had a lot of nerve to think what I did was worse than the stunt he played yesterday. "You could have been sending psychopaths to kidnap me. All I did was show Bess, Frank, and a couple of their friends a flyer. It's not my fault they thought it was a good idea." I might have pushed them into coming today, but that was another thing Kellan didn't need to know.

"I'm running a business here, I can't afford to be giving free lessons to every Tom, Dick, or Harry who walks in the door."

"It's one lesson."

"One lesson for eight people I didn't agree to. Hell, Molly, I don't even offer a senior citizen class. I'm liable to break one of their hips."

I rolled my eyes. "Please, Bess is in better shape than I am." Kellan didn't say anything, just stared me down. "And Frank ran a half marathon last month."

"I can't believe I'm about to do a cardio class for senior citizens." Kellan pushed off the wall and ran his fingers through his hair. "You do know I'm going to have to get you back for this."

I put my hand on the door handle. "You don't have to. Just stop being so damn loud."

Kellan threw his head back and laughed. "Oh no, you're not going to win that easily."

I struggled to swallow. I had been hoping this would be the end of whatever was going on between Kellan and me. I hitched my thumb over my shoulder. "You think you have something better up your sleeve than eight old people wanting to aerobicize?"

Kellan sprung towards me and caged me in again. I cowered, and it only made Kellan even more imposing. "Last chance to back out, Cookie. You take your customers with you, cancel the meeting, and we'll call this even."

I narrowed my eyes, pursed my lips, and tipped my chin up. "Why am I the one who has to back down? All that really needs to happen is you just keep it down. I'm not asking for a lot."

Kellan leaned in close, his nose almost touching mine. "Do I walk into your coffee shop, and tell you how to make coffee?"

"No, that would be a ridiculous. You know nothing about coffee, let alone making it."

A sly smile spread across his lips. "And you know absolutely nothing about karate, so why do you get to come in here and tell me how to run my classes?"

"I'm not telling you how to do karate. I'm saying you need to be courteous to my needs."

Kellan licked his lips. "I need to be courteous to your needs, Cookie?"

"Y…y…yes," I stammered.

He stepped in closer, his chest rubbing against my breasts, and whispered in my ear. "But who's going to take care of my needs?"

I closed my eyes. "Stop playing games, Kellan."

"I think we're on a two-way street here, Cookie. I stop; you stop."

My eyes opened, and I looked into his green ones. "I don't need to stop anything."

"Then, I guess I don't need to either." He pushed off the wall and out of my space.

I yanked on my apron, pulling it down. "So, that's it? What are you going to do now?"

Kellan tilted his head toward the group of people out in the studio. "Looks like I need to figure out how to teach a bunch of seventy-year-olds."

I cleared my throat. "What about after that?"

"After that, I have three more classes, sparring, another class, and then about three private lessons." A smirk spread across his lips. "But you shouldn't worry about any of that. It's what comes after all of that you should worry about." He put his hands on my shoulders, moved me to the side, and opened the door.

"Kellan," I called before he stepped out of the office.

He looked over his shoulder. "Yeah, Cookie?"

I took a deep breath and pointed to the desk. "I brought you a coffee and some cookies. Sounds like you're going to have a long day." I patted him on the shoulder as I skirted around him.

He grabbed my hand and pulled me into him. "I mean it, this isn't over, Molly."

I nodded. "If that's what you want to think." I stood on my tip toes and leaned into him. "Hit me with your best shot, Mr. Karate." I pulled out of his grasp, waved to Bess and Frank who were waiting on the mat for Kellan, and ducked out the front door.

I sprinted back to the cafe and barreled through the door.

Sage's eyes bugged out when she spotted me and scurried over to me. "Well, how'd it go? How ticked off was he?"

I swallowed and leaned against the door. "I think I just started World War III."

Sage patted me on the shoulder and pressed her cup of coffee into my hand. "I believe that you're going to need this more than me." She sauntered over to the counter, and I closed my eyes.

My head was all over the place right now. Kellan had been close. I'm talking the close where my body noticed and thought how nice it would be to be that close with no clothes on.

There were rules to this kind of thing, and I'm sure I had just broken one picturing the enemy naked. I shook my head and took a sip of Sage's coffee. It was the blah black coffee she liked to drink, and I cringed. I needed flavor in my coffee, preferably hazelnut, but her black coffee was going to have to do.

Kellan was going to retaliate, and I needed to be prepared. How? I had no freakin' clue, but I needed to figure it out, and quick.

****

Kellan

"She did what?"

I grabbed the flyer off the desk and thrust it into Dante's face. "The little shit did that." He grabbed the flyer out of my hand, and his eyes scanned it.

"Holy fuck, this is fucking brilliant."

I yanked the flyer out of his hand and tossed it in the garbage. It was fucking brilliant, and that was what had pissed me off the most. Who would have thought she had it in her? "We need to figure out what we're going to do next."

"Hold on." Dante grabbed a cookie out of the box she had brought over and moaned. "Jesus Christ."

I snatched the cookie out of his hand and tossed it back in the box. "Do you think you could focus for five minutes? That is from the enemy, and we can't be moaning about it like it's the best thing since sliced bread."

"Well, they're pretty fucking close to being better." Dante wiped his hands on his pants. "Well, let's hear it. I'm sure you've already thought of what you're going to do next."

I grabbed my sparring gloves out of my bag and pulled them on. "That's the fucking thing, I don't know what I'm going to do next." I bowed onto the mat and squared up in front of the punching bag. All morning, I was distracted thinking of

Molly. I had managed to make it through the disastrous senior citizen class and was on autopilot through my other classes and lessons. Thankfully, Tate and Roman had shown up halfway through the day and helped out.

"So, what did you do with all of the old people?" Dante slipped off his shoes, bowed onto the mat, and stood behind the punching bag I was about to beat the shit out of.

"We basically stretched the whole time. One of the ladies, I think her name was Bess, insisted on hitting one of the bags." I shook my head, and side-kicked the punching bag.

"How'd she do?"

I shook my head and jabbed left, then right at the bag. "She actually did pretty well. Once she hit it, everyone else wanted to. Gavin was here today, so I had him work off to the side while I dealt with everyone else."

"Well, you were saying last week that we needed to get more adults into class. Maybe this is what we need."

I bounced on the balls of my feet, ducked, then jabbed with my left hand followed by another sidekick. "This wasn't exactly what I had in mind when I said that." Dante hadn't even heard the worst part yet. "They paid me, Dante."

"What?"

I stood still, and my shoulders dropped. "They insisted on paying me for today, and said that they'll be back next Saturday."

Dante put his arm around the bag and laughed. "You're shitting me. They actually liked class?"

They did, and I had no idea why. When I say all we did was stretch, I wasn't joking. The last ten minutes is when Bess had insisted on hitting the bag, and that might have been what convinced them to come back for more. Taking your frustrations out on a punching bag was therapeutic, no matter what your age. "I couldn't tell them no."

"So, now you added a whole other class to our already insane schedule."

I rolled my shoulders and put my hands up. "Move your head before I kick it." Dante took a step back, and I landed a dropkick right where his head had been. "You tell these people next Saturday when they come in that they can't take classes."

"But what are you going to teach them?"

I ran through the delta combo, landing each punch precisely. "Same thing we teach the kids."

"You're telling me we're going to give them white belts and make them go through belt promotions?"

I shook my head and bounced from foot to foot. "No. They all said they weren't in it to be black belts." Dante busted out laughing, and I had to admit when they had stated that, it was hard for me not to laugh. No one knew what it was like to become a black belt until they actually went through it. "I'm not sure what to call it. Kind of like a self-defense class mixed with a little karate."

"So, you're basically going to fly by the seat of your pants."

Yeah, that was pretty much what I was going to do. I had so much going on planning lessons for all of the other classes, I wasn't going to have much time for another one.

"So, while she messed with you, you still managed to turn it around and use it to your advantage."

I threw a punch at the bag. "Yeah, but she still needs to get payback."

"Well, when you figure out what you want to do, let me know. You know Tate, Roman, and I got your back."

"Yeah, give me a couple of days."

Dante walked over to the speaker and turned it on. "Until you figure it out, you wanna bug the shit out her by cranking the music?"

I chuckled and landed another dropkick. "Crank that shit up, and get out here with me. Roman was thinking of entering the sparring in that tournament coming up, and he wants me to train with him."

"So, that means I need to whip your ass into shape so then you can whip his into shape."

I wiped the sweat off my brow. "Yeah, since you two can't seem to train together without one of you trying to kill the other, I'm stuck with him."

Dante grabbed his bag and headed to the bathroom. "Let me change, and I'll show you how it's done." The door shut behind him.

I grabbed my phone and turned on some music. I glanced at the clock and saw it was already after four. Molly had closed the cafe by now and probably wasn't even there. I put on some Metallica and tossed my phone onto the small podium in the corner.

I glanced out the back door, and suddenly I knew just what my next move was going to be with Molly. I knocked my hands together and bounced around.

Molly was going down, literally.

****

Molly

"Can you help me bring these boxes to my car? I need to pick Sam up in five minutes, and I know I'm going to be late."

I hung my clipboard up next to the storeroom door and grabbed the boxes next to Sage's feet. "Sure. What are you taking these home for anyway?"

Sage grabbed the rest of the boxes and headed out the front door. "Sam has been bugging me to make a dog bed for Felly."

"His stuffed dog?"

Sage popped the trunk and dumped in the boxes. "Yes."

"He's one stuffed dog, why do you need six boxes?"

Sage grabbed the boxes from me and tossed them on top. "Because once he sat down and thought about it, he needs houses for all of his stuffed animals, not just Felly."

I patted her on the shoulder. "You need to write down all this good mom shit for me, so I have a handbook when I have a kid."

Sage laughed and slammed the trunk shut. "I'm flying by the seat of my pants here, Molly."

"Well, Sam is a pretty awesome kid. You're doing damn good." I honestly didn't know how Sage did it. Taking care of a little human being by herself was one of the bravest things someone could do. To go from having a loving husband, and a little family, to doing it all on your own was something only seriously strong people could do.

"I'll call you to remind me of that when he refuses to take a bath without his stuffed animals tonight." Sage slide into her car and pulled out of the parking lot.

It was half-past three, and I still had all of the dishes and a load of dirty aprons to take care of. I had been debating taking them home or running them down to the laundromat while I did the dishes. My laziness won out, and I decided I would just take them home instead of walking to the laundromat.

I plunged my hands into the soapy water and hummed along to P!nk playing over the speakers. It had been slow today, and I had been able to do my inventory during the day, so I could cut out a bit early. The new flavor I perfected last week was on the order board, and I already knew what next week's were going to be. I was, for once, ahead of the game and looked forward to an easy and peaceful week.

Well, as peaceful as it could be. I was on edge wondering Kellan's next move was going to be.

Dante had come in for a couple of cookies and asked for whatever drink I made for Kellan. He was in and out within five minutes, and I made sure he didn't take any pictures. They were up to something. They had to be.

I pulled the drain on the sink and started taking apart the espresso machine. This thing was my money maker, but damn if it wasn't a pain in the ass to clean and take care off.

My head popped up as I heard a chair scrape across the floor. "What in the world?" I whispered. I was the only one here. I had done a walk-through before helping Sage carry her boxes out to her car.

I looked around and held my breath. The noise sounded like it had come from the corner Bess always sat in. Unfortunately, from the counter, I couldn't see all the way back there. I patted my pocket for my phone and realized I had again left the damn thing at home. "When are you going to start remembering your damn phone, Mol?"

Another chair rattled, and I clutched my hand to my chest. What was going on? I edged over to the cordless phone next to the cash register, and slowly grabbed it from the base. My finger was poised over the nine button when the lights flickered, and I hightailed it out of there.

I quickly dialed nine-one-one, slammed the front door shut behind, and peered into the coffee shop.

What in the ever-loving hell was going on?

****

Kellan

I peered over the table and saw Molly with her face pressed against the front door, her hand cupped around her face, and her phone pressed to her ear.

"Shit." I sat back on my knees and sighed. Fuck, all I wanted to do was scare the living shit out of Molly, and then get the hell out of dodge.

Somehow, Molly had left, and now I was stuck in her god damn cafe while she called Lord knows who.

I fired off an SOS text to Roman and prayed to God he came to save me before the cavalry came to rescue Molly.

Five minutes went by, and there was no reply from Roman. I checked my phone one last time and shoved the damn thing back in my pocket when I saw he hadn't texted back. I looked over the table again and saw flashing red and blue lights. "Mother fucker." She had called the damn cops.

Decision time: wait her out or come clean.

I watched Molly frantically motion her arms as she talked to the cop and pointed into the cafe. The cop put his hand on his gun and cautiously moved to the front door.

I bowed my head. I didn't want to end up with a bullet in my ass, so I slowly stood up and held my hands over my head. Molly screamed when she saw me and flung her hand over her mouth. The cop drew his gun, and I knew I was close to being fucked.

"Stay where you are," the cop yelled. "Put your hands over your head."

I rolled my eyes and stuck my arms straight up. Did he not see I already had them over my head? "Molly, it's me, Kellan!"

Molly smashed her face into the glass of the door. "Kellan?" she mumbled through the glass. She fumbled with the lock on the door, and the cop followed her inside.

"Keep your hands up!"

"Molly, can you please call off the cops?" I was annoyed and pissed off that my stupid idea backfired in such a spectacular way.

Molly stopped and put her hands on her hips. "What are you doing in here?"

I looked at the cop. "Can I put my hands down now?"

"Ma'am, do you know this man?"

Molly pursed her lips. "Define *know*."

"Molly, for Christ's sake!"

Molly stomped her foot. "Fine, yes, I know him. He's not trying to kill me and steal all of the coffee."

The cop nodded and tucked his gun back into his holster.

I lowered my arms. "Really, steal all of the coffee? You really think someone would do that?"

"Well, what was I supposed to think when shit starts moving, and I'm the only one here?"

Honestly, I hadn't really thought that far ahead. "Um...I guess squeal like a little girl, and then I'd jump out, say gotcha and fucking leave."

"Ma'am, would you like to press charges?"

My eyes moved to the cop. "Seriously?"

He held up his hands. "You say you know her, but she doesn't seem too happy to see you here."

"Molly, come on."

She sighed and waved off the cop. "I know him."

"Then, why didn't you know that he was in your coffee shop?"

"Because I put out flyers to all my older customers to go to his karate studio for free classes, but not before he made a fake dating profile sending all these weirdos here for dates."

The cop scratched his head. "Are you serious right now?"

Molly and I both shrugged. "It sounds a lot crazier when you say it like that."

"But," I added. "The whole reason I did that was because Molly is trying to get my karate studio shut down."

Molly pointed her finger at me and shouted, "Because he's loud!"

"We're breathing!"

The cop shook his head and held up his hands. "I'm just going to write this off as a misunderstanding and call it a day. You two obviously have issues, but not any that the police department can help with." He shook his head again and walked out the front door.

I ran my fingers through my hair. "Boo."

Molly stalked over to me and stuck a finger in my chest. "You son of a bitch! What were you thinking? You scared the living shit out of me. I thought I was about to die."

"I know, and then I was supposed to steal all of your coffee."

"You hide in my cafe, make me call the police, and then you act like an ass."

I widened my stance and looked down at her. "I didn't make you call the cops. How was I supposed to know that you would freak out?"

"I'm pretty sure my reaction was typical for a single female all alone who hears shit moving around."

"It was a chair."

She pointed her finger in my face. "A chair that should not have been moving."

"Move your finger out of my face."

She clenched her teeth together. "Why should I?"

"Because I asked you to."

His eyes flashed. "You didn't ask, you told me."

"Molly. Last chance," I growled.

She shook her head and kept her finger in my face. "You can't tell me what to do."

I grabbed her shoulders, spun her around, and pinned her against the wall. I pressed my body fully against her and grabbed her arm that was smashed in between us. I reached for her other wrist and held her arms over her head. "No, but I can make you do what I want you to do."

She twisted against my hold, but couldn't budge. "You don't play fair." Her eyes flared with anger, and she shuffled her feet, trying to get her leg wedged between mine.

"And neither do you." Her body moved against me, and I couldn't fight the fact that she felt damn good.

"How is that so? I didn't do a damn thing to you."

I tightened the grip on her hands and leaned down. "Keep moving like that, and you'll see real quick what you're doing to me." She bucked her hips into me, and all thought of being pissed off at her fled.

"Does everything have to be a game and go your way?" she hissed.

I ran a hand down her arm and along her side. Her breathing hitched. "It's always nice when it does," I whispered in her ear.

Her head tilted to me, my lips brushing against her skin. "Wow," she muttered.

"I think you and I can come to a truce, Molly."

She hummed absently and squirmed against me. "Truce?"

Molly was just as affected as I was being this close to her. I never noticed the swell of her breasts—which were pressed against me—or how she had curves under that damn apron she wore all of the time. Her dark brown hair was pulled back like it always was, but small pieces had escaped her ponytail, framing her face. She smelled like coffee and tropical fruit. How that was possible, I didn't know, but I knew every time I smelled coffee from now on, I was going to think of her. "I'm good with a truce. You call off the meeting, and I'll stop with all the bullshit."

Her body stiffened against me, and I could feel her mood change. She bucked her hips against me, and I knew she was pissed. I released her arms and stepped back. Her skin was flushed, and her breathing was heavy. "So, that's what you're going to do now?"

What was she talking about? This was far from a plan. This was me feeling her against me and wanting to know what she would really feel like under me. "Molly, I don—"

She swiped her hand in the air. "No. Don't you 'Molly' me in that sexy voice." She tried running her fingers through her hair but ran into the ponytail. "I can't believe I didn't see this coming. I should have known that this was coming."

"What was coming?"

She frantically motioned back and forth between us. "You thinking that you could *seduce* me into giving you whatever you wanted."

That wasn't even what I had been thinking. My only plan was to scare her and then get ready for class. "You're wrong."

She shook her head. "I'm not wrong, and I can't believe I was that stupid. You had me for like ten seconds, Kellan. Totally had me." She pushed me out of the way and stomped over to the counter. She reached under it, grabbed a huge sleeve of cups, and started slamming them onto the counter.

"Molly, you're not stupid." Shit, she was probably one of the smartest chicks I knew. Molly could run circles around the girls I usually hooked up with. Wait, why was I comparing Molly to the girls I hooked up with? Molly wasn't in that category. She was just the annoying coffee chick next door. I watched as she finished stacking the cups next to the coffee machine. Well, she was now the pissed off and annoying coffee chick next door.

"I'm onto you, Kellan."

I walked to the opposite side of the counter from her. I decided it was probably for the best not to be so close to her for the time being. Before I could open my mouth, she was laying into me.

"This is war now, Kellan. To think that you could use your smoking hot looks and charm to get me to just roll over for you was low, but I should have seen it coming." She shook her head. "So, now you get war. Java Spot and Powerhouse at war, and there can be only one winner."

Now she was just talking crazy. Her ponytail was slowly falling down as she grabbed another stack of cups and angrily set them on the counter. I didn't have a clue what to say.

I caught a glimpse of the clock she had sitting next to the cash register and knew I wasn't going to be able to stay. Class started in half an hour, and Dante and I were the only ones there today. "I think you need to calm down, Molly. Whatever you are thinking is wrong. Way wrong."

She shook her head. "Don't you patronize me, Kellan. Run back over to your little karate studio and yuck it up with your friends on how you almost got the poor, pathetic barista to fall for you." She threw an empty paper cup at me and stomped over to the sink. She turned the water on high and glared at me.

"That isn't what I'm going to do, Molly. Although, I do need to leave, but that's because I have a class to teach."

Molly grabbed a remote from next to the phone and held it up to the ceiling. The radio she had quietly playing became a loud commercial as she turned it up. "Have a nice class, Kellan," she shouted, dismissing me. She turned her back to me and watched the water pour into the sink.

I tried one last time to talk to her but the commercial had ended, and a loud, indie rock song had started playing. I threw my hands up in the air and knew talking to her right now was pointless. She wasn't going to believe me no matter what I tried to say. "I'll talk to you later, Molly," I yelled.

She didn't turn around but flipped me off.

I walked out and sighed. What in the actual fuck just happened?

One minute, I was scaring the shit out of Molly, then I was ready to kiss her, and now she's pissed off at me, and I had no idea what to do.

I headed back to the studio, and Dante was sitting behind the front desk waiting for me. "You bring back some cookies?"

I rolled my eyes and headed to the bathroom. "No. Get your own damn cookies." I slammed the bathroom door shut and leaned against the sink. I hung my head and tried to get a grip on what I was going to do.

Molly had looked hurt when she thought I wanted to seduce her and that fucking stung. I knew I wasn't the greatest human being on Earth, but I wasn't a scumbag.

Had I seduced girls before? Oh yeah. Had I seduced them to get something I wanted before? No. The fact that she thought I was capable of being that big of a douchebag sucked.

When she had put her finger in my face and given me attitude, something had changed. I noticed her body, the way her nose crinkled when she was pissed, and how her fingers looked like just the right size to curl around my dick and make me cum all over her hand. "Jesus Christ," I cursed.

When had Molly turned into someone I wanted in my bed?

I looked in the mirror, trying to find the guy I had been before I went over to the cafe, because the guy staring back at me right now was completely different.

I wanted her to cancel the meeting, but now I also wanted her. I couldn't have the two at the same time.

I was royally fucked.

****

Molly

"Are you sure this is a good idea?"

It had been a week since I had called the cops on Kellan, and I hadn't seen him since. That was about to change. "Yes." It was the only idea I had at the moment. Well, that wasn't exactly correct. I had thought of water balloon bombing him, but that was my repressed thirteen-year-old coming out.

I packed the last of the cookies into the box and closed the lid. Sage took the box and loaded it onto our cart. "I don't know if they can handle twenty-five kids hopped up on cookies for their lessons."

They probably couldn't. That was why it was a brilliant idea. "It's customer appreciation day, Sage. He can't blame me for giving away free cookies to everyone to celebrate my anniversary."

Sage laughed. "And what anniversary was this again?"

I counted in my head. "My five year and ten month anniversary." Give or take a few days.

"You have officially lost it. I knew it was only a matter of time all of those sleepless nights thinking up new coffee drinks were going to catch up with you."

I glanced around the cafe and put my hands on the cart. Bess had agreed to man the counter for me while Sage and I handed out the cookies in front of the karate studio. I was hoping this was going to take fifteen minutes tops, and I would be safely tucked back in the cafe away from Kellan. "I haven't lost it. I just declared war, and now, I need to follow through." I had been on edge all week waiting for Kellan to do something, but all has been quiet. Now, I was going to make the next move before he did.

I wheeled the cart behind me, around the building, and parked it directly in front of Kellan's door. "Did you see them?" I asked.

"No, I was afraid to look in the windows. Did you see them ?"

I shook my head and tugged my apron down. "No. I didn't want to chicken out."

"Then why are we doing this, Molly?"

"Because you weren't there, Sage. You didn't see what he tried to do to get his way."

Sage bumped me with her shoulder. "Molly, you need to calm down. I know what he did sucked, but you need to get over it."

I couldn't get over the fact he thought he could just pin me against the wall, make me think he actually wanted me, and then have me agree to call off the meeting. No way, no how. I was not going to be duped like that. "It's war, Sage."

She sighed and crossed her arms over her chest. "You do know they are going to come out here as soon as they figure out what we're doing, right?"

They could come out here. I didn't care.

Cars started pulling up to the front of the building, and I knew it was go time. "All right, it's show time, Sage. Big smiles, and hand out these cookies."

Kids came running up to us, and I happily gave them two cookies each, explaining that they had two hands, and they might as well have a cookie for each. We explained to the parents about the customer appreciation day, and Sage gave them each a small vanilla latte. "Holy crap, there are a ton of kids," Sage mumbled as I grabbed the last tray of cookies.

There were a ton of kids, and that just made me even happier. A room full of kids all hopped up on sugar was the perfect revenge Kellan deserved.

"Hey, what are you doing?"

My back straightened at Kellan's voice, but I didn't turn around. Another wave of kids came towards us, and I loudly explained my theory of two hands deserved two cookies.

"Have a good day," I called as the last kids scurried by with their parents following behind.

"Molly," Kellan called.

I set the empty tray on the bottom of my cart and turned around.

My eyes raked over his body and took in his baggy white pants, black belt, black, fancy karate top, and the scowl on his face.

Kellan was hot.

Kellan was pissed.

Mission accomplished.

"Yes?" I said sweetly. I clasped my hands in front of me and smiled up at Kellan.

"What do you think you're doing?"

I motioned to my cart. "Oh, this?" I asked. "I was just showing some good ol' appreciation to some of your students."

"Why?" he growled.

"Because they come into the shop sometimes, and since today is customer appreciation day, I figured I would sneak over here quick and let them know how much I appreciated them."

He crossed his arms over his chest, and I swear I could see smoke rolling out of his ears. "Molly."

One word. That was all he had but that one word made me waver.

"Kellan."

"Can't we figure something out other than whatever it is we are doing?"

"Oh, you mean like have a conversation like adults?" I folded my arms over my chest and tapped my foot. "I tried that. You didn't respond well to it. Remember all of those lovely men you sent over to my cafe?"

"You just sent thirty kids into my studio with cookies smeared all over their faces and hands. I'm going to be scrubbing mats all night."

A smile spread across my lips. I hadn't thought of that when I had planned this. "Oh, I'm so sorry, Kellan. I guess I hadn't thought about that."

"You know an apology is only sincere if you mean it, right?"

I shrugged. "Then, I guess I don't mean it." I put my hands on the cart and turned it around.

"We need to talk, Molly."

I shook my head and pushed the cart. "That ship sailed when you decided to seduce me to get what you want. I told you this was war, Kellan. Gather your troops, or you're going to lose."

We headed back to the cafe, Sage hot on my heels. "Holy shit," she wheezed. "You were amazing!"

My hands were clammy, and my heart was beating a mile a minute. I had never talked to someone like that before. It was a rush. "Thanks," I mumbled. I wasn't sure if it was a rush I wanted to experience again, though.

"Damn, he was mad. Although, I do have to say that I was surprised he didn't yell or anything."

Me, too. I had fully expected Kellan to hit the ceiling, but he hadn't. I could tell he was upset, but he had managed to keep his cool for the most part. I wheeled the cart to the door and pushed it behind the counter.

"So, how did it go?" Bess asked.

Sage laughed. "We are out of cookies, and we pissed off Powerhouse. Mission accomplished."

I grabbed the empty cookie trays and dropped them into the sink. "Except now we have to prepare for retaliation." I realized we were going to be stuck in a never-ending loop of me going after him and then waiting to see what he did next. I was already racking my brain for my next move.

"We only have two weeks until the meeting, right? How bad can it get before then? We totally have this in the bag." Sage and Bess high-fived. Sage gave Bess the rundown of what happened.

Bess threw her head back and laughed. "I would definitely say you are giving them a run for their money."

I left Sage and Bess and headed into the storeroom. I closed the door and listened. I pressed my ear to the wall next to the racking and heard kids screaming and someone telling them to quiet down.

I turned around and leaned against the wall. It sounded like Kellan had his hands full, and I couldn't stop the smile that spread across my lips. Hopefully, Kellan realized I wasn't someone to mess with.

Kellan said he always won; well, he had never played against me.

He was going down.

****

Kellan

"How? How do they get chocolate smeared all over the bathroom mirror?"

Tate was in the bathroom cleaning up the chocolate disaster that had exploded in there, and I was picking up all the empty coffee cups. "Because they're five years old. Whatever they touch gets dirty."

Molly had definitely won this round. I was sure we would be finding cookie crumbs and chocolate around the studio for the next month.

"So, what are we going to do next?" Tate walked out of the bathroom and collapsed onto the mat. "We can't let her get away with this."

We couldn't, but I really had no clue what to do. I was still bothered by the fact that she thought I was a douchebag, and I didn't want to do anything else that would help to solidify that theory. "What do you have in mind?"

Tate shook his head. "Dante and I got this one. We've been cooking something up."

"Like what?" I really didn't like the sound of that. Tate and Dante coming up with a plan was never a good thing.

"You can just take a back seat on this one, man. It's time we pulled our weight a little bit."

Now was the time that Tate decides to help out? I didn't need help with Molly, I needed help running the damn studio. "Just tell me what you two are planning?" I had been party to some of the pranks Tate and Dante had pulled. I was more than worried about Molly.

"Nope, not happening."

I bowed onto the mat and looked down at him. "At least tell me when you are doing it, so I know when to take cover."

Tate shook his head. "I'll let you know when it's done."

"Are you trying to sound like Al Pacino right now?"

Tate grimaced and held his hand out. "I plan to make her an offer she can't refuse."

I grabbed his hand and hauled him up. "As long as she doesn't end up sleeping with the fishes, I really can't say anything."

Tate clapped me on the back. "I promise not to throw her in the Mississippi River."

"The fact that you had to make that promise to me actually scares me."

Tate bowed off the mat and grabbed his socks and shoes. "Have no fear, Kellan. You just take the night off, and don't even think about Molly."

I crossed my arms over my chest and watched Tate tie his shoes. There used to be a time not very long ago where that would have been a possibility. Now, after I felt Molly in my arms, I couldn't help but think about how I was going to get her close to me again.

I was trying to take Molly down, and now, all I wanted to do was go down on her.

Fuck me.

****

Molly

I opened my car door and stepped one foot out. I was dog tired and really didn't feel like working today. Thankfully, we were only open until one on Sunday, but that meant I still had eight hours left. My fingers felt around on the key fob, popped the trunk, and I slowly got out of the car.

My seven days a week were starting to catch up to me. I was going to have to take a day off before I fell over. Sage normally had off Sunday and half of Saturday so she'd have time with Sam. So, that meant I was here all of the time.

"This is what you wanted, Molly," I mumbled as I grabbed the clean laundry basket out of the trunk and slammed the lid shut. No life, but a successful cafe was what I had.

"Molly!"

I dropped the basket full of clean aprons and towels and spun around. I clutched my chest and winced, thinking for sure this was the way I was going to die. All alone in a parking lot with a laundry basket, barely awake, "Please don't kill me!" I squealed.

"Molly, it's me, Kellan." I peeked open one eye and saw Kellan walk around the back end of a Challenger

I opened both eyes and looked around. "What are you doing here? Do you know what time it is? Is this your next plot of revenge? Because if it is, I'm way too tired for this. Can we reschedule for tomorrow?" Apparently, when I thought I was about to die, I became chatty.

"You haven't gone in yet, right?"

I tilted my head. "Um, no. I just got here."

Kellan walked over to the basket that had dumped at my feet. "I'll walk you in."

He kneeled down, gathering all the towels, and I looked down at him. I should have helped put them back in the basket, but he was the reason I had dropped them in the first place. "Um, you still haven't told me why you're here. I've never seen you here at the butt crack of dawn."

Kellan chuckled. "Butt crack of dawn?"

It was an accurate description of the time of day. "Yes."

"I'm always up at this time, Cookie."

"But not here."

Kellan finished shoving everything back in the basket and stood up. "No, not here." He grabbed the basket off the ground and looked at the cafe. "You wanna open the door, and I'll bring this in?"

"Only if you tell me why you are here." I wasn't going to budge until he told me his motive.

"Tate called me late last night."

"That's nice. I hope you two had a great conversation."

Kellan tucked the basket under his arm. "He told me yesterday that he was going to take over the next maneuver in the war."

I narrowed my eyes and glared at him. "Go on."

"He wouldn't tell me what he did. Just said he would let me know when he was done."

"So, he called you last night to tell you he was done." He nodded and glanced at the cafe. "Something is going to happen when I walk through that door, isn't it?"

"Honestly, I have no idea. He called me for two seconds. Said 'The crow flies at midnight. It is done,' then he hung up. I didn't even get a word in."

I closed my eyes and tilted my head back. "You gotta be kidding me."

"That's why I'm here. I have no idea what they did, and I just want to make sure it wasn't something ridiculous."

"They? You said it was Tate. Now it's they?" I could be walking to the world's biggest boobie trap right now.

"Uh, yeah. It was Tate and Dante."

I opened my eyes and looked at Kellan. "Dante is the silver fox, right?" I slapped my hand over my mouth. Shit, that was not what I wanted to say out loud

Kellan smirked and shook his head. "You know I'm going to have to tell him that now, right, Cookie?"

I curled my lip and growled. "You better not."

"We'll see. Right now, I'm more concerned with what's going on in your cafe."

I looked over my shoulder at the cafe. "You think they let a wild animal out in there?"

Kellan busted out laughing. "An animal?" he wheezed.

"I have an active imagination."

"Cookie, you are giving those two way more credit than they deserve. I'm assuming they rigged a bucket of water over your door or something juvenile like that."

Oh, well. I could handle something like that. "Just for that, you're going to be the first one walking in." I held out my keys. "Give me the basket, and I'll follow you."

Kellan grabbed the keys and shook his head. "See, now you don't mind me being here, do you?"

I rolled my eyes and nudged him towards the door. "Hurry up, I have cookies to pull out and coffee to start brewing."

"If you had any cookies in there, I'm sure they are all gone. Dante sniffs your cookies out no matter where he is."

I snorted.

Kellan turned around and shook his head. "Wrong cookie, Molly."

I shrugged. "Don't tell me you didn't think the same thing," I mumbled.

He stuck they key into the door and cautiously opened it and stood off to the side. "I did, I just didn't think you would think the same thing."

I cautiously peered over Kellan's shoulder and didn't see anything unusual. "It looks exactly how I left it."

"That's what they want you to think. I know they did something."

We walked in, and I set the basket next to the door. I twisted the lock on the door and turned on the lights. "So, what do we do now?"

"Now, I walk around and try to figure out what Dumb and Dumber did."

I grabbed Kellan's arm. "Wait, how did they get in here?"

Kellan ran his fingers through his hair and looked down. "Uh, well. I have a key."

"How did you have a key to *my* cafe?"

"I think her name is Sage? She knew who I was."

"Sage? Sage gave you the keys to the cafe?" That traitor! Whose side was she on?

"Yeah."

"Why would she give you the keys to the cafe?"

Kellan shrugged. "I don't know. I told her I wanted to sneak in here and scare you, and she got this kind of dreamy look in her eyes and gave me the keys."

That bitch. She was dead to me. Well, at least for a couple of days. "Give me back the keys, right now." I held out my hand.

"I can't. Tate has them right now."

I growled. "Then, give me your keys."

"What, why?" Kellan scoffed.

"Because until I get my keys back, I'm going to have yours."

"Hell no. I don't know what you would do to the studio. I'm not an idiot."

I lunged at his pocket and managed to get my fingers inside. He clamped down on my wrist and held onto my arm. "Get out of my pocket, Cookie."

"Never," I said through clenched teeth. My fingers were wrapped around his keys, and I wasn't about to give up.

"Molly, I don't want to hurt you." Kellan's voice was low and rough next to my ear. He had pulled me close and wrapped one arm around my waist while the other held my hand in his pocket.

"So, then don't."

"Let go," he insisted.

"Not happening. You broke into my cafe."

"It's not breaking in when I have a key."

I growled and tried to yank my hand out. "A key that you aren't supposed to have!"

"But it was given to me."

He moved backward and pinned me against the door. "Molly. Let. Go."

"No. This isn't going to work, I'm onto you."

Kellan sighed and pressed his hips into me. "What are you yammering about now?"

I shook my head and tsked. "You tried to seduce me into giving what you wanted before. I'm not going to be that stupid twice."

Kellan pulled my hand out of his pocket, twisted my arms over my head, and pinned them against the door. "You are far from stupid, Cookie. I was the stupid one."

Well, that was the last thing I expected him to say. I struggled against the hold he had on my arms, but I couldn't move. How did I always seem to get myself in these situations with Kellan? Pushed up against a wall twice in a week weren't good odds. "Please let me go."

"Drop the keys."

"Never."

"Then, I guess we're at a standstill until one of us let's go."

I assessed the situation and knew I was on the losing end. Having Kellan this close made me realize the man was built like a brick house. His arms were not only holding my wrists, but they were caging me in. He shifted his weight, and his biceps flexed, making me appreciate the fact he worked out.

He pressed his hips into me, and his chest was crushed against mine. He was all hard muscles and warm heat seeping through my clothes. If he kept this up, I couldn't be held accountable for my actions. I was only human, and I couldn't ignore the fact Kellan fit perfectly against me. I licked my lips, and his eyes heated with desire. "Kellan," I breathed out.

"Let go, Molly."

His words could mean two things. Let go of the keys, or let go and just kiss him already. "I can't."

He leaned in, his lips only a breath away from mine. "Molly, please." His plea was low and rough, and I felt it straight to my core.

"I don't know what you want."

"I don't know what I want any more either."

I bit my bottom lip and tried to get a grip. It was Kellan. The asshole from next door who had been making my life hell. But now, he was also Kellan, whose body fit against mine perfectly, and whose lips I wanted to taste. "What's happening?" I whispered.

"I think I'm going to kiss you."

My breath hitched, and I gasped.

"Tell me to stop, Molly."

The one word to make him stop was stuck in my throat, and I didn't try very hard to get it out.

"Fuck it." His mouth was on mine, and every coherent thought I had flew out the window. His lips were demanding and unyielding, taking what they wanted. He released my wrists and trailed his hands down my arms and into my hair. "What are you doing to me?" he mumbled against my lips.

The same could be said of him. This wasn't what I should be doing, but it felt so right that I didn't care if it was wrong. I draped my arms over his shoulders and hummed as his lips traveled across my jaw and kissed their way up my neck.

"Tell me to stop," he growled.

I shook my head and leaned into his touch.

He pressed a kiss below my ear. "Tell me to go to hell."

My fingers delved into his hair, and a moan ripped from my lips. I didn't want to talk right now, all I wanted to do was feel.

"Tell me I'm an ass." His tongue licked the shell of my ear, and a tremor rocked my body.

"You're an ass, but don't stop."

His body shook with laughter.

He still was an ass, but I couldn't help the way he made me feel. His lips were electric on my skin, and I craved his touch like my next breath.

Kellan buried his face in my neck, and my body relaxed into him. "This just made everything a whole lot more complicated."

Kellan sighed. "Sure fucking did, but it felt damn good."

"I need to make coffee."

Kellan pulled away, and I felt beyond awkward. My arms dropped to my sides, and I realized I had dropped the keys when Kellan and I had been all hands and arms. I spotted them on the floor next to my feet and looked up at Kellan. He was too busy looking anywhere but at me and had moved back two more steps.

I could tell he regretted kissing me, and while that sucked giant donkey balls, I was still pissed off at him for getting the keys to the cafe. I crouched down, grabbed the keys, and side-stepped around him.

"Hey," he protested. "Give me back my keys."

I darted behind the cash register and held my hand up to stop him. "No. As soon as you give me my keys back, you'll get yours."

"Molly."

I shook my head. "You're giving me a severe case of déjà vu, Kellan." If we kept arguing over the keys, we were either going to end up sprawled out on one of the tables together doing something we might seriously regret, or I was going to beam him upside the head with the damn keys. As much as I'd like to feel Kellan pressed against me again, I was leaning towards hitting him. "I need to make coffee, and you need to figure out what stupid thing your friends did."

"How am I supposed to get home if you have my keys?"

"I guess you're going to have to call Tate and tell him to bring back my keys."

"He's not going to be awake for hours."

I shoved them into my pocket. "Not my problem."

"You're not playing fair, Cookie."

I grabbed the basket for the coffee grounds and a filter from under the counter. "I have twenty minutes until customers start showing up. Find what they did, and quick."

Kellan flexed his fingers but didn't say anything. He turned and looked around. "What time does Sage get here?" He started searching under tables and moving chairs around. I don't think he had a clue what he was looking for.

I poured some beans into the grinder. "She's not. She only works half a day on Saturday, and then has off Sunday and Wednesday."

"So, who's helping you today?"

"Um, me, myself, and I?"

Kellan turned around. "You're going to run this shit by yourself today? Why does Sage need so much time off?"

"Because her son likes to spend time with her, too."

Understanding dawned in Kellan's eyes. "Ah, I didn't know she had a kid. Or a husband."

I quickly ground the beans and dumped them into the filter. "Had."

He quirked an eyebrow at me. "What does *had* mean? She leave him?"

I shook my head and flipped on the coffee machine. "No, she loved him, still does. He was overseas when his platoon got hit by a roadside bomb. He was the only one who didn't make."

"Son of a bitch," Kellan whispered. "That fucking sucks, Cookie."

I swallowed around the tightness in my throat I always got when I thought of Sage losing her husband. They were great together, and I knew Sage still missed him like crazy. "Yeah, it really does."

Kellan went through all the tables, then he headed into the bathroom. I prayed to God he didn't find anything in there. I finished up a pot of decaf, then headed to the small freezer in the back to pull out cookies. Every Monday or Tuesday, I made four huge batches of cookie dough, froze it, then just pulled out little pucks of dough every day to make fresh cookies.

I was bent over the freezer, a bowl in my hand when I heard Kellan yell. "Mother fucker!" I assumed he had found whatever trap Tate and Dante had set. I finished filling up my bowl with cookie dough, set it on the counter, then cautiously headed down the short hallway to the bathroom. The door was closed, but I could see the light under the door, and heard Kellan mumbling under his breath.

"Um, everything okay in there?"

"Depends on your definition of okay."

Well, that didn't sound good. I put my hand on the door handle and tried to open it. "Can I come in?"

Kellan opened the door, and I looked around. Everything looked normal. Everything except for the toilet paper on the floor. "You wanna tell me where your cleaning stuff is?"

I hitched my thumb over my shoulder. "Under the sink." Kellan tried to walk past me, but I grabbed his arm. "What happened?"

Kellan growled. "Shrink wrap on the toilet."

I tilted my head and squinted. "Why would they...Oh," I mumbled, realizing what happened.

"Yeah, I'll clean it up."

I followed him back to the kitchen sink and opened the cupboard underneath. Three bottles of laundry detergent fell out and spilled all over the floor. I screamed and held onto the sink as the floor instantly became slippery. Kellan grabbed me around the waist, pulled me to his body, and held onto the sink with the other hand. "Holy fuck, Molly."

"Me? I didn't do anything." I tried to bend over to grab the bottles, but could barely stay on my feet.

"Why didn't you have the covers on them?" Kellan managed to bend over, hold onto me, and grab one of the bottles and drop it into the sink.

"I didn't do this. This isn't my soap!"

I watched over my shoulder as Kellan moved his arm down my body, stretched, and tried to reach for another bottle. His feet slipped, and his ass ended up in the huge blue puddle of soap. "Fucking Tate," he swore.

I giggled as he slammed his hand on the floor, splashing soap in his face.

Kellan looked up and shook his head. "And what are you laughing at?"

I bit my lip and struggled not to laugh at the small drop of soap on his cheek. "Not a thing. I was just wondering if this was how those bubble parties start." I snorted and put my hand over my mouth.

"Yuck it up, Cookie. We gotta figure out how we're going to clean this up without sliding all over the place."

I nodded to the basket that was over by the front door. "I'll try to make it over to the door. I just need to make it there."

Kellan grabbed the two now empty bottles of soap, and I dropped them into the sink. The whole floor behind the register was now covered in blue soap, and it was slowly starting to seep past the register. "Easy, Cookie."

I made it two steps when I felt my right foot slip, and I ended up ass over tea kettle on top of Kellan. "Shit, sorry," I mumbled as I struggled to sit up.

Kellan was now completely laying down in the soap, and my body was sprawled out on top of him. He wound his arms around my waist and splayed his hands on my ass. "You really can't stay away from me, can you, Cookie?"

I smacked his shoulder and rolled my eyes. "I see your assyness is showing again."

"Come on, I know deep down you really like my assyness."

I was going to see the back of my head if I kept rolling my eyes every time he spoke. "Just help me up so we can clean this up." I glanced at the clock and winced. "Crap. Think we can get this cleaned up in three minutes."

Kellan smacked my ass and sat up, lifting me with him. "I'm going to say that there is no way you are going to get this cleaned up. I'll be amazed if you get to the door in three minutes."

He was right, but I was searching for a bit of positivity. I looked down at the blue soap all over the floor and realized there wasn't any positivity in this. "Right, well. Help me up."

Kellan's hands circled my waist, and he lifted me to my feet. I hunched over and held onto his shoulders. "How did you just lift me up?"

"I own a karate studio and was on the competitive circuit for six years, Cookie. Sitting up with you in my lap doesn't take much."

I thought this over. If we would have been reversed, I would still be laying on the floor slipping around in the soap. "Maybe you should be the one to make it to the door. I'm not the most graceful person even on solid, non-slippery ground."

"The only way out of this is to crawl, Molly. Get the towels, throw them on the ground to scoop everything up, then grab the mop."

My head snapped up, and I twisted around to see who was knocking at the front door. "Damn, Frank is knocking at the door. That man is always here every morning at six on the dot."

"Did you lock the door?"

I slid off Kellan's comfy lap, and into the cold, wet soap. "Yes, it's habit."

"Damn, I thought maybe the old man could be our savior."

Not today. Frank cupped his hands around his eyes and peeked into the cafe. I needed to get to the door before he called the cops. "No, that would definitely not be Frank. He's here for the coffee and brownies."

"Brownies? You make brownies too?"

I got on my hands and knees, and slowly pulled myself across the floor. "Yes. Double chocolate and mint."

Kellan's hand wrapped around my foot. "You mean to tell me you've made brownies this whole time and you didn't tell me?"

I looked over my shoulder at him. "What is with you karate guys being obsessed with sweets? Dante buys all of my cookies, and now you sound like you're about to drool just over the word brownies."

"We work hard."

I continued my snail's pace crawl. "And what does that have to do with brownies and cookies."

I heard a huge splat behind me and then Kellan came sliding past me on his stomach. He made it to the edge of the slippery floor and managed to pull himself up. "It means we work hard, so we can eat all of the junk we want." He patted his stomach and winked.

I sat back on my butt with my legs tucked under me. "Well, I guess that makes sense. Although, I don't think I could do it. I'd eat all of the cookies and then be too full to work them off." Frank banged on the door again. "You better let him in before he breaks the glass. That man takes his morning coffee very seriously."

Kellan managed to make it to the door without falling on his ass, and let Frank in. He grabbed the basket and threw a towel at me as he dropped the basket next to the counter.

"What in the world went on here? Is this one of those bubble parties I saw on TV? Should I have worn my swimming suit today? You should really put a notice up on these things, so we know ahead of time, Molly."

Kellan snickered and started laying towels out on the floor.

"No, it's not a party, Frank." I grabbed two towels and started pushing the soap to the drain in the floor.

"Then, what went on?" Frank looked from me to Kellan and turned bright red. "Oh damn, please tell me I didn't walk in on some crazy shit from the seventies."

"Seventies?" Kellan asked.

"Hippies." Frank rubbed his chin and stared off into space. "So many hippies."

Kellan shuffled over to me with towels under his feet. "Um, is he okay?"

I glanced over at Frank and shook my head. "He's okay. I'm not sure what happened in the seventies, but it obviously scarred him."

After fifteen minutes of corralling the soap over to the drain, the floor was semi-clear of the slippery substance, although the same couldn't be said for Kellan and me.

Kellan pulled his shirt away from his chest and looked down his body. "I'm going to kill Tate."

I dropped the last of the dirty towels in the basket and sighed. "Not if I kill him first. I have soap in places that there shouldn't be when I have clothes on."

Frank had managed to grab the pot of regular coffee and was now sitting at his table by the window with two of his buddies who had arrived. Sunday mornings were a bit slow until the church crowd started rolling in. I had a solid two hours before the rush would come.

Kellan took his shirt off and tossed it on top of the dirty towels. "I'll run this over to the laundromat, and then I'm going to grab a shower at the studio."

I mentally picked my jaw up off the floor and tried to focus on what Kellan had just said. His perfectly sculpted chest was right in front of me, and I couldn't form a coherent thought. I licked my lips and wondered if he would let me lick his nipples. Just one, well, both would be better.

Kellan snapped his fingers, and I gently shook my head. "Huh?"

"You know it's usually the girl who has to remind the guy where her eyes are," Kellan smirked and shook his head. He took advantage of my stupor and reached into my pocket. He snagged his keys and tucked them in his pocket.

Damn him. Not only was I totally busted for checking him out, but he had also gotten his keys back. Shit. "Sorry, I'm just distracted by, you know, um… getting everything done." I waved my hand behind me. "You know, coffee." I clamped my lips closed and pasted a cheesy smile on my face. Shut up, Molly.

Kellan picked up the basket and put it under his arm. "Give me fifteen minutes, and then you can take a shower."

As much as a shower sounded fantastic, I didn't have any clothes to change into. "I'll just try to wash off as much as I can in the bathroom. I'll be fine."

"Cookie, your ass looks like you sat on a smurf."

I twisted around to look at my butt, and I had to admit that was a pretty accurate description. "I don't have anything to change into, and I don't have the time to go home. I'll just slap on an apron."

Kellan shook his head. "Not happening. I have clothes over at the studio you can change into."

I sputtered trying to tell him I was fine, but he walked out the door and headed down to the laundromat.

"Running out of coffee, Molly. I didn't want to interrupt you and your man, but a man needs coffee." Frank raised his cup and the coffee pot over his head.

I rolled my eyes and grabbed an apron from under the counter. I strapped it on, hoping it covered most of the blue on my shirt, but I knew nothing could hide the blue all over my khaki pants.

The only good that had happened out of this was the floor looked clean, and you could eat off it. I just wished it hadn't taken three bottles of detergent for it to get that way.

Ten minutes later, Frank had his coffee pot refilled, and three more customers wandered in looking for an early morning caffeine fix. They all gave me strange looks when they saw the blue all over me, and I tried not to let my backside face them, but that was near to impossible.

Once they all had their coffee, I turned around, leaned against the counter and closed my eyes.

I was going to kill Tate and Dante, and I wanted to kiss Kellan.

If that wasn't a huge plot twist, I didn't know what the hell was.

****

Kellan

I pulled a new Powerhouse shirt over my head and tugged a pair of worn track pants on. Thankfully, I always had a change of clothes at the studio, and even if I didn't, I always had the stock of Powerhouse apparel to steal from. I left the clothes I had grabbed for Molly on the toilet seat and shoved my feet into a pair of sandals.

She may hate Powerhouse, but she was going to be sporting our blue and gray logo all day. There was no way she was going to be able to stay in her wet and sticky clothes for her whole shift.

My soapy clothes were in a pile next to the shower, and I was half-tempted just to throw them away. Tate and Dante had done a hell of a job pranking Molly. They had terrorized the bathroom and the whole kitchen area.

Brilliant, but not. If I hadn't been a victim of their pranks, I would have been laughing right alongside them.

I slipped out the back door that was right next to the back door of the cafe and tapped on the window. Molly was leaning against the counter, her head tilted back, and her eyes closed.

She jumped when she heard my knock and shuffled over to the door to let me in. "I always forget about this door," she mumbled while she opened it.

"Really? I use ours all of the time." Lately, I had been parking on the side of the building and leaving the parking spots by the front door for parents and students. I slipped in through the door, and she locked it behind me. "I don't know why you are locking it, Cookie. You need to go get showered."

"Kellan, I'll be—"

"Molly, I'm not taking no for an answer. Go shower, and I'll take care of everything over here."

She propped her hands on her hips. "Just what do you know about making coffee?"

"About as much as you know about karate."

She laughed and rolled her eyes. "That would be nothing, Kellan."

I flipped the lock, opened the door, and motioned for her to go. "Then, you better hurry back before I burn the place down, or serve everyone protein shakes."

I pushed her out the door and locked it behind her. "No protein shakes, Kellan," she shouted at me.

I shrugged. If she didn't hurry back, I couldn't promise what would happen. "Your clothes are in the bathroom."

Her arms were folded over her chest, and I swear I heard her growl. She stomped into the studio, and a grin spread across my lips. She may not like to admit it, but I knew she was going to thank me for insisting she go shower. She was going to feel a hundred times better, and look sexy in Powerhouse colors from head to toe.

"Hey, Muscle! You think you can get me a cookie?" I turned around and saw Frank standing at the counter.

"You talking to me?"

"You're the only one who's got more muscle than anyone else here. I'd say it's a good bet I'm talking to you."

I walked up to the counter and rested my hands on it. "I don't think Molly has any cookies ready right now."

Frank pointed over my shoulder. "That time says one minute. Bring me a chocolate chip when they come out." He moseyed back over to his table and gave me the stink eye when he sat down. I didn't know what his problem was with me, but ever since he thought Molly and I were getting it on, he had been acting like he wished I would drop dead.

I walked over to the timer she had sitting next to the oven, and it rattled on the counter. I peeked into the oven and saw two trays of cookies and a small pan of brownies. When did she have time to bake? I hadn't been gone that long, had I?

By the time I heard the back door open, I had the cookies off the trays and was loading them into the display case. "Feel better?" I asked as I turned around. My eyes did a full body scan, and I had to say that Powerhouse blue looked damn good on her.

Her wet, long brown hair was pulled up on top of her head, looking like she had just gone three rounds in bed, and her face was washed free of the regular makeup she wore.

Molly, the feisty barista, was hot as sin.

"Yeah, much. Thank you for letting me use your shower. I'm surprised you have one."

When we had decided to rent out the space, we negotiated with the landlord that we needed to have a shower. It was nice after a hard work out to be able to clean up without having to go home all sweaty as hell. "It's definitely nice to have. Although, I never thought this would be a reason we would need it."

"Did you get the cookies and brownies out of the oven?"

I nodded. "Yeah. I was surprised you were able to bake that quickly."

"I didn't. Well, I did bake, but just not today. I have pucks of cookie dough and pans of brownies in the freezer. I just pull out what I need at the beginning of the day."

"Good thinking."

She shyly looked down at the floor. "I, um, better get back to work. My morning rush will be coming in soon."

I hitched my thumb over my shoulder. "Yeah, I'll head back to the laundromat and throw the towels in the dryer."

"Okay," she mumbled. She side-stepped around me and busied herself by wiping down the counter.

And now we were going to be awkward around each other. I couldn't blame her. It was fucking weird that one minute we were ready to rip each other's clothes off, and the next, I was trying not to rip her clothes off.

I headed over to the laundromat, waited for the towels to dry, then headed back over to the cafe with the basket under my arm.

The parking lot was full of cars now, and there was a long line in front of the cash register. Molly was frantically making drinks, taking orders, and calling out people's names when their drinks were ready.

I set the basket next to the counter and bumped Molly out of the way. "Scoot over. I can take orders."

"I highly doubt it. You don't even know the names of the drinks."

"How hard can it be? They're all mocha-latte-whip-a-bullshits." Molly's jaw dropped. "Just need to ask them what size they want."

The next lady in line thrust a twenty at me. "I'll take three of what he just said. All large."

"But...you can't. How am I..." Molly sputtered as I stuck the twenty in the drawer.

"How much is that exactly, Cookie?" I hadn't thought someone would actually want whatever shit I had just spewed.

Molly pressed a few buttons on the register, and the drawer popped out. "She gets six eleven back."

Luckily, the next four people just wanted black coffee, and I was easily able to ring that up.

"Excuse me, can you tell me what this is?" The lady who had ordered my made up drink walked up to the counter and pointed to her cup.

"I'm sorry. I just made you a double shot triple chocolate mocha. We don't make whatever it was that he said." Molly wiped her hands on her apron. "I can refund you your money."

"What? No! I loved this. It's the best coffee I've ever had here, and it's hard to beat your smoked vanilla latte. You should totally add this to your menu." The woman gave Molly a thumbs up and headed out the door.

I leaned against the counter. "You can say thank you now."

"What? You made me make up a drink on the spot!"

"Yeah, but it was a fucking phenomenal drink according to that lady." I grabbed a five out of my wallet and stuck it in the register. "And now, you need to make me one." Waking up early, and then having a soap wrestling contest on the floor with Molly had taken it out of me.

Molly growled. "I'm back to hating you."

"You're *back* to hating me? So, what were you at before?"

She grabbed the little thing she dumped grounds into then shoved it into the machine. I had no clue what she was doing, but it looked confusing as fuck. While the machine made strange noises, she pumped something that resembled chocolate syrup into a cup, dumped some milk into a different cup and shoved it under a spigot that I think blew air into it. "I was tolerating you."

"You kiss all the people you tolerate? I can only imagine what you would do to me if you liked me."

Molly glared at me. Her hands were all over the place, dumping this in there. Sprinkling something on top of the drink, then dumping the frothy milk on top. She gave me the cup and crossed her arms over her chest. "Drink. Leave."

I shook my head and grabbed the cup. "I do have to get going, but not because you want me to leave. I need to head over to Tate's and kick the shit out of him." I took a sip and closed my eyes. Holy shit that was fucking good.

"You approve the mocha-latte-whip-a-bullshit?"

I took another drink and set it down. "More than approve, Cookie. You need to add that to the board and call it the Kellan mocha-latte-whip-a-bullshit special."

"Or I could just call it the Triple Mocha."

"I guess that works too, but mine is catchier."

Molly grabbed a paper cup, dumped my coffee in it, and snapped on a lid. She thrust it at me and pointed to the door. "Thank you for helping me today. Kick Tate in the balls for me and make sure you get my keys back from him."

I shook my head and grabbed the cup. "Should I be expecting retaliation?"

"The meeting is in a week. I guess you'll just have to wait and see."

"You're still going to go through with the meeting?"

She tilted her head. "Are you going to stop screaming like a bunch of banshees?"

"It's not screaming, Cookie. I think you need to come over and see what we do at Powerhouse. I believe that it's only fair since I just worked over here."

Molly rolled her eyes. "And what exactly is that going to prove?"

"It's not going to prove anything. I just think you should come over." She shook her head. "One class. That's all. They are only half an hour long. Come this Wednesday. That will give you enough time to talk yourself into it."

"Or give me time to chicken out."

I pushed off the counter. "You won't. Six o'clock. Be there, Cookie, or I'll come and get you." I didn't give her a chance to argue. I sauntered out, waving to Frank as I opened the door and headed around the building to lock up Powerhouse.

I was going to show Molly just what Powerhouse was, and what it meant to me. This was my last chance before the meeting. I was going to make it a good one.

****

Molly

"Stop. It's not funny."

Sage wheezed and waved her hand at me as she tried to catch her breath. "How…did you…oh, my God."

It was Wednesday afternoon, and Sage was still laughing about the soap incident. "I don't even know why you started laughing about it."

She opened the cupboard under the sink and pointed to the edge of the door. It was smeared with blue soap. "I saw it, and then all I pictured was you on the floor, slipping around, and I just couldn't hold it in anymore."

I never should have told Sage what happened, but it had just poured out when she had walked through the door Monday morning. She had barely listened when I laid into her for giving her keys to Kellan. Thankfully, I hadn't told her Kellan and I had kissed. She would have had a field day with that.

I hadn't seen Kellan all week, but Dante had been in every day getting cookies and brownies. I had to refrain from kneeing him in the nuts the first time I saw him, and he handed me a plastic bag. After I had peeked inside and saw it was the panties I had accidently left at Powerhouse after my shower, all I wanted to do was melt into a puddle of embarrassment.

"So, tonight's the big night, huh?" Sage wiggled her eyebrows.

It was, and I was racking my brain trying to figure out how I was going to get out of it. Kellan didn't know where I lived, and I could just go home, but then it felt like I was letting him win. "Yup. Are you sure you can't go with me?"

"And just what do you think I will do with Sam? That's right before his bedtime."

"Tomorrow's Thursday. Let him skip a day of school. They never teach anything on Thursday."

Sage slowly blinked. "Did you just hear what you said? You really are desperate not to go by yourself, aren't you?"

I clasped my hands under my chin and dropped to my knees. "Sage, I need you. I can't do this by myself. I'm weak and uncoordinated. I. Will. Die."

"What is going on here?" Bess was standing at the counter, her coffee cup in her hand.

"Molly has a date with Mr. Kung Fu."

I smacked Sage's leg. "It's not a date," I hissed.

"Well, where is he taking you? That will help me decide if it's an actual date." Bess set her cup down and leaned on the counter.

"He invited me to come to class tonight." I stood up and brushed my knees off. I had been on the floor too often lately.

Bess nodded. "Okay. What for?"

"He said I need to see what he does so I can better understand the whole yelling thing."

"It's not a bad idea. I think you should go."

I grabbed Bess' cup and shook my finger at her. "No more coffee for you. You're supposed to be on my side. I'm your caffeine dealer. You don't turn on your dealer."

Bess put her hand on my forehead and looked at Sage. "I think she must have hit her head on Sunday when she was rolling around with Mr. Hot and Sexy."

I pushed away her hand and growled. Why, oh why had I told Bess about the soap too? "I'm never telling either of you another thing again."

Bess put her hands on her hips. "Hogwash. If you hadn't of told me, you know damn well Frank would have."

"What's that?" Frank hollered.

"You and your big mouth," Bess shouted back.

Frank gingerly stood up and ambled over to the counter. "Woman, I think that's the pot calling the kettle black."

"I don't believe we asked you to come over here, did we?" Bess said, rolling her eyes.

Oh Lord. It looked like it was going to be one of those days where Bess and Frank were at each other's necks.

"What are we discussing over here? The fact that Molly missed her chance with my son? He met someone, and I don't like her one bit." Frank slammed his hand down on the counter. "I told him he's got the wrong one, but he just won't listen."

Sage hopped up on the counter next to the sink and swung her legs back and forth. "What makes you think she's the wrong one?"

"Because she ain't Molly, and she's got a damn ring in her nose," Frank growled. "I don't know what is going through the kid's head, other than she's got a nice body."

Frank checking out his son's girlfriend gave me the creeps. "I don't know if you should be checking out your son's girlfriend."

"Nonsense. She flaunts it; it's hard not to look." Again, creepy. Frank pointed his finger at me. "That's why you would have been perfect for him. You don't flaunt a damn thing."

I wasn't sure if I should be offended or not. I think he meant it as a compliment, but it sure didn't feel like one. "Thank you, I think."

"You'd be thanking me even more if you were going out with him."

"Frank," Sage called. "You just said that he had a girlfriend. Why are you still trying to set him up with Molly?"

"Damn kid doesn't know what he's doing, that's why."

Bess asked me to make her another coffee and turned to Frank. "Well, you're going to have to find another girl for your boy, because Molly has a date tonight. Hang it up, Frank. The Molly being your daughter in law ship has sailed."

I shook my head. I didn't know that boat was even floating, let alone had the possibility of sailing.

"It's him, isn't it?" Frank grumbled.

"You mean the guy Molly was wrestling with Sunday? It sure is," Sage said smugly.

"Is that what they call it these days, wrestling? It sure as hell was kissing, though." Frank shook his head and ambled back over to his table.

"Kiss!" Sage shouted. She jumped down from the counter and pressed me back against it. "You didn't mention anything about a kiss. You're holding out on me. Dear old Frank knows more than I do."

Bess snickered. "If there's been a kiss, then you are aware that this is more than a date."

I finished Bess' drink and ignored their stares.

"Is she just going to ignore us now?" Bess asked as she grabbed the drink I set down in front of her.

"She better not be. All she has to do is tell us what, when, where, and how they kissed."

I rolled my eyes. "It really has been too long for you, Sage, if you don't remember how to kiss."

She grabbed a wad of napkins and tossed them at me. "You damn well know what I mean. I want to know how you and Kellan got to doing more than argue and pulling pranks on each other."

I shrugged. "It just happened."

"Well," Bess said. "Do you want it to happen again? Is he a good kisser? Did he grab a little T&A?"

Sage's eyes bugged out, and I sputtered. "What do you mean T&A?" Sage asked.

"Come on, girls. You know what T&A is." Bess waved her hand at us. She put a hand on her boob and grabbed it. "Tits," she said before grabbing her butt. "And ass. T&A."

"I think we were just schooled by a sixty-year-old," Sage mumbled as we watched Bess saunter back over to her table. It was Wednesday afternoon, and although it wasn't an official Moaner meeting day, they were still all sitting in the back corner cackling like a bunch of hens.

"Maybe we need to read more books," I mumbled.

"At least the books Bess is reading. How crazy is it that I think she has a better sex life than I've ever had?"

"Both of us," I agreed. I closed my eyes and hung my head. "He kissed me, Sage, and I liked it," I whispered.

Sage rested her arm on my shoulder and leaned into me. "I think if you didn't like it, we would have to take you to the doctor to have you checked out."

"But I shouldn't have liked it. The man has been torturing me, and honestly, he's an ass."

Sage laughed. "Most men are, Molly."

I hung my head. "I just need to stay away from him. Once the meeting is over, there won't be a reason for him to talk to me anymore. Right now, I'm just thrown in his face, and I'm just something to entertain him."

"You really think that you're just entertainment to him?"

I sighed. "That's the only thing that makes sense, Sage. I'm a nuisance, and soon, I won't be. There's no point in me going over there tonight."

"And now you're trying to talk yourself out of it, aren't you?" Sage grabbed me by the shoulders and stood in front of me. "Molly, there's something you need to know."

"What's that?" I asked, defeated.

"You are fucking amazing. So fucking amazing. If Kellan is too big of an ass to see that, then you don't need the Kung Fu Ass. I don't know what would have happened to me if I never would have met you. You are selfless, loving, kind, smart, successful, and let's not forget, hot as hell."

A tear streaked down my cheek, and I wiped it away. "You have to say that. You're my best friend. Well, all of it except for the hot as hell. That's a bit weird."

Sage's eyes watered, and she leaned her forehead against mine. "Go to the class tonight, be the amazing Molly that you are, and don't worry about anything. You know you are amazing, and it's up to Kellan to see that."

"I don't even know what I want. Part of me wants to kiss Kellan again, and the other half of me wants to never see him again."

Sage sighed. "You'll figure it out. You always do." She patted me on the shoulder, wiped her eyes and grabbed the pot of Columbian roast. "I'm gonna go do refills."

I wiped my eyes and headed into the storeroom. I shut the door and stared at the wall that was connected to Powerhouse.

"What are you going to do, Molly?"
I had five hours to figure it out.

****

Kellan

"Tate told me about a girl."

My head popped up, and I looked at Tate's mom, Sue. "Tate has a girlfriend?" How did I not know that?

"No, not Tate. You."

I scoffed and shook my head. "I don't have a girlfriend, either, Ma."

"Then who is Molly?"

I stretched my legs out, and leaned back in the kitchen chair I was sitting in. It was half past three, and I was over at Tate's mom's house. She had called me earlier to come before classes to mow her lawn. I had just finished up, and we were sitting at the kitchen table. "Molly is the woman who owns the coffee shop by Powerhouse." I wasn't going to tell Ma anything more than she needed to know.

"He said you've been seeing her."

"If by seeing her you mean pulling pranks on each other and in a war, then yeah, we've seen each other."

She sighed and took a sip of her coffee. "When are you boys going to fall in love?"

"I can barely fall asleep at night, Ma; I think falling in love isn't in the cards for me."

"Then you need to get a new deck, Kellan, and deal the cards in your favor."

I laughed and drained my glass of tea. "So, you're saying you want me to cheat love?"

Sue waved her hand at me. "You know what I mean. Now, tell me why Molly isn't someone you want to spend time with."

"I never said she wasn't. I just said I'm not dating her." Just kissing her when the time feels right.

"So, when are you going to start dating her?"

"Can't predict the future, Ma." I grabbed my glass and walked to the sink. "I need to get to the studio for classes tonight. Call if you need anything else, yeah?"

"I'll have to come by some day. I haven't been to the studio in a while. Maybe I can grab a cup of coffee when I'm there, too."

I sighed and knew there wasn't going to be anything to keep Sue from moseying on over to the cafe. "Let me know when you're coming over, and we can grab a cup of coffee together." There was no point in trying to keep her away. That would just encourage her to come more.

Sue waved goodbye, and I headed out to my car.

Molly was supposed to come to class tonight, and I was nervous as fuck. I didn't even know if she was going to show.

I hadn't been to the cafe since I invited her.

The meeting was Friday night, and I knew I needed to make her see things my way, or I didn't know what was going to happen. I didn't think she could get me shut down, but she could make my life hell.

Now, I just needed to get through three classes, and a stunt work class before I could sway her.

Here we go.

****

Molly

Why did leggings have to be so tight? They left absolutely nothing to the imagination, and right now, a little imagination would do me some good. Cramming my thick thighs, and bubble ass into something the likes of meat casing was not pretty. Not. At. All.

"Did you have to get me ones with such a bright pattern on them?" I swear Sage had found the most outrageous and annoying leggings, and decided my legs not only need to be lumpy and bumpy, they needed to be so bright you would see me from across the room. The neon green and light blue swirling pattern was ridiculous, and I seriously questioned Sage's sanity.

"I didn't pick them out, Sam did. Those are his favorite colors." Sam was sitting on the couch playing with Mr. Mittens.

My anger deflated, and I knew I couldn't be mad at the kid. I turned around and looked at my butt in the mirror. "Please tell me you at least bought me a black shirt." Hopefully, I could pull the shirt down far enough to cover my butt. Damn, hopefully, it was long enough it touched the floor. I could start a new craze by working out in a dress.

Sage pulled out a black shirt, and I thanked the clothing gods. "Sam was over shopping by the time it came to get a shirt.

You lucked out. I'm sure he would have insisted on the matching skin-tight shirt."

I grabbed the shirt out of her hand and shut the bathroom door. "He's still my favorite five year old," I mumbled.

"He damn well better be," Sage called.

I rolled my eyes, tugged my shirt off, and pulled on the new one. I had called Sage panicked an hour ago, telling her I had nothing to wear to class tonight. I had ripped apart my closet and had a breakdown thinking I was going to have to go to class in khaki capris and a Java Spot shirt.

Thank God for small miracles that Sage hadn't bought a shirt that was as tight as the leggings. "What do you think?" I opened the door and stood there waiting for the verdict. If you only looked at me from the waist up, I didn't look half bad.

"Hot. Totally hot."

I looked down at my legs and stuck one out. "I think we need to talk about what you think is hot." My legs encased in stretchy color vomit was not hot.

Sage grabbed my arm and pulled me into the kitchen. She thrust a water bottle into my hand. "Take this, it helps you look the part."

"What part?" I mumbled.

"You know. The athletic type."

I shook the bottle and gave it a squeeze. "Well, then I better just stand there with the bottle in my hand all night, because as soon as I try to kick or punch, the jig will be up." Athletic was the one word that I would never use to describe me.

Sage giggled and handed me my keys. "Go, or you're going to be late because I know you are going to sit in your car for fifteen minutes to talk yourself into actually getting out."

I sighed. "You know me so well, Sage." I glanced at the clock and saw it was already twenty to six. If I didn't get my ass in gear, I wouldn't have time for my mental pep talk. "Lock up when you leave?"

"We are right behind you. I promised Sam we would go to Pizza Ranch tonight."

"Pizza!" Sam yelled as he sprung from the couch, and Mr. Mittens jumped down. "Let's go, Mom!" Sam tugged on his mom's arm and pushed us all to the door.

I grabbed my wallet and managed to get out before Sam slammed the door shut. The kid really had a thing for pizza.

"Have fun, and be yourself!" Sage called as she drove away.

That was easy for her to say. Besides, if I were truly myself, I wouldn't be anywhere near a karate studio.

I slid into the car and cranked the engine.

Before I knew it, I was sitting in front of the karate studio, ready to start hyperventilating.

"You can do this, Molly. Just go in there, kick some ass, and leave. Totally easy. Just go…ACK!" I jumped as someone pounded on my window and scared the living shit out of me. Gavin was standing beside my car looking down at me. What did he want?

I hit the button to roll down the window and realized I didn't have the car started for it actually roll down. "Dammit," I mumbled as I opened my door and grabbed the water bottle Sage had given me.

"You doing a class tonight?" Gavin asked.

I slammed my door and pushed my glasses up my nose. Did people do karate with their glasses on? If I had to take them off, I was going to be blind as a bat and liable to punch Kellan right in the balls. Gavin cleared his throat, and I spun around.

"Hey! Fancy meeting you here?" I was losing it. Absolutely losing it.

Gavin chuckled and pointed to the building. "I'm here every Wednesday. Adult class at six. Are you here to see Kellan?"

I scoffed and screwed up my face. "Kellan, phfft. Never. I'm here to get my kick ass on?" I cringed, unsure if that even made sense.

"Get your kick ass on, huh? I guess I can get behind that?" Gavin opened the door and motioned for me to go in first.

"Oh hell," I mumbled as I pushed off the car and shuffled through the door. I scanned the large space and saw it was crowded with parents and a shit ton of kids. There was no way I was going to do this with all of these people watching.

Gavin put his hand on the small of my back. "No need to look like you're ready to run. They just finished up the kid's classes. Everyone is leaving."

I breathed a sigh of relief and stood off to the side of the door, waiting for everyone to get out so I could make a right and proper fool of myself.

"Well, well, well. If it isn't Molly." Dante stood in front of me and crossed his arms over his chest. "Bring me any cookies?"

I rolled my eyes. "Sorry, no. I guess you're just gonna have to break into the cafe and steal them again," I growled. I was still a bit salty about the fact they had the key to the cafe.

A smirk spread across his lips. "I think that's doable."

"You made it!" Bess came breezing through the front door, and not only did my jaw drop, but so did Gavin's and Dante's.

She was dressed head-to-toe in a bright-ass, blinding pink leotard, and had a lime green swimsuit over the top. She had pink wrist and headbands on, and to top it all off, leg warmers. Bess had time-traveled back to the eighties, and decided the fashion needed to come back to twenty seventeen. "Holy shit," Dante whispered under his breath.

I tried to pick my jaw off the floor. "Ah, um, Bess. What are you doing here?"

"Thought I'd get some kick ass in tonight. I signed up for adult classes after Kellan gave us the free class. He sure is a sweetheart." Bess winked at me and fluffed her hair. "Although, Tate is what keeps bringing me back."

Dante choked and sputtered. Gavin clapped him on the back, and they both tried not to laugh. "Unfortunately, Tate isn't here yet."

Bess' shoulders sagged. "Well, I guess I'll have to get my gawk on with you two hunks." Bess hooked her arms through Dante and Gavin and pulled them towards the mat. "I need help getting my shoes off, you two fine strapping men can give me a hand, right?"

Dante looked over his shoulder at me, his eyes begging for help. There wasn't much you could do to get out of Bess' grasp.

"Hey, you made it." Kellan walked out of the office and leaned against the front desk.

I rocked back on my heels. "Yup, totally made it. Ready to kick some ass." I pumped my fist in the air and gave a battle cry.

Kellan smirked. "You might want to reel it in a bit Xena, Warrior Princess. There won't be an unnecessary ass kicking tonight."

I really needed to tone it down on the ass kicking. I swallowed the lump in my throat. "No ass kicking, got it." I mentally cringed, wondering if I was ever going to say something that made sense around Kellan.

"Take off your socks and shoes, Cookie, and meet me out on the mat." Kellan pushed off the counter and sauntered over to the mat, bowed, and started talking.

I hastily kicked off my shoes and stuffed my socks in them. Tate hastily ducked through the front door, and kicked his shoes off next to me. A smile lit his face when he looked at me. "Glad to see you made it, Molly." He patted me on the shoulder, and slipped into the office. Great, now I could make a fool of myself in front of Tate, too.

Dante was standing at the side of the mat waiting for me. "Bow," he instructed me. "Shows respect."

I bowed, feeling awkward, but I didn't want to offend the karate gods.

Kellan stood in the front of a wall of mirrors and clapped his hands. "We got a pretty big class tonight. Let's bow, and get things going." Kellan bowed, and I watched as everyone bowed back to him. I half-assed bowed back because I was only thirty seconds in, and already confused. Didn't I just bow to the karate gods?

"Okay, everyone spread out on two lines. Make sure your arm's length apart." Kellan stretched out his arms, and I looked around trying to find the nearest corner I could hide in.

"Molly."

I looked over my shoulder and saw Gavin standing behind me. He motioned to the spot next to him, and I scurried over there, thankful someone had taken pity on me. I gave him a small smile and pulled off the hair tie I had on my wrist. I piled my hair on top of my head and rolled my shoulders back and forth. I could do this. I hope.

Kellan turned around, faced the mirror, and his eyes connected with mine. A smirk spread across his lips, and I couldn't decide if I wanted to kiss him or punch him. It was a toss-up ninety percent of the time. "Fifty jumping jacks total. Ten to the mirror, turn to the window, ten, and so on. Everyone ready?"

I panicked, trying to remember the last time I had done jumping jacks. It had to have been sophomore year in high school. Well, this was going to be interesting. At least I had worn a sports bra and strapped the girls in.

The first ten jumping jacks weren't bad. I managed to stay with the rest of the class, even through the twenties. It was when we approached thirty when I started to struggle.

"You okay?" Gavin huffed out as he continued to jump up and down.

"Yeah, totally," I wheezed. This was when my jumping jacks became just jumping in the air with the occasional arm flail. Graceful, I was not. The huge mirrors put that on display for everyone to see. Even Bess wasn't having a problem.

"Forty-seven, forty-eight, forty-nine, fifty!" How were these people able to talk while they jumped all over? I was out of breath and wondering if this was the way I was going to die.

I bent over and braced my hands on my knees. "Damn," I gasped.

"Ten burpees, and then we can get to kicking ass," Kellan called.

I couldn't see him since I was bent over trying not to die, but I was sure the damn man had a huge smile on his face.

"What is a burpee?" I whispered. Kellan was speaking a whole new language that I had no idea how to translate. I raised my hand and looked toward Kellan.

He made his way over to me and crossed his arms over his chest. "What's up, Cookie?"

"What is that?"

"What?"

"A burpee. What is it?" I finally stood up straight and didn't feel like I was going to keel over.

"It's that." Kellan pointed to Gavin who was throwing his arms in the air, then threw himself on the ground, did a push-up and jumped up to do it all over again.

I turned back to Kellan and crossed my arms over my chest. "I thought this was a class to kick ass, not *my* ass."

"Gotta warm up. Just try to do a couple of burpees. I'm sure you'll have no problem doing them."

I rolled my eyes. "You apparently missed my transition into the thirties with the jumping jacks."

Kellan shook his head. "No, I saw it, Cookie. You can't get much by me with these mirrors." He winked at me, sauntered to the front of the class and watched everyone finish up their burpees.

I watched Bess do two burpees and knew I had to at least try one. I couldn't be outdone by a woman who was almost in her seventies.

My eyes watched Kellan, waiting for him to look away. As soon as his eyes traveled to the other side of the class, I tossed my arms in the air and dropped to the mats. Hard. Like a ton of bricks.

Gavin squatted next to me. "Try putting your arms down to catch you next time."

I groaned and closed my eyes. "That advice would have been much better thirty seconds ago before I threw myself down like a rag doll."

Gavin held out his hand to help me up. "I'm going to guess this is your first time trying to kick ass, huh, Molly?"

Gavin hoisted me off the mat, and I resumed my position of being hunched over with my hands on my knees. "What was your first clue, Gavin?"

"Don't worry, babe, you'll get it eventually."

Babe? Huh? Where had that come from? What was it with people giving me nicknames all of the time? I was Cookie to Kellan, and now I was babe. Just great. I had to say I liked Cookie better. It was much more original than babe.

"How are ya doing, hon?" Bess hollered from the other side of the room.

Everyone turned to look at me, and I was back to wanting to find the nearest corner to disappear into. "Peachy," I gasped. I rubbed my chest, and silently apologized to my boobs for the body slam they had just endured.

"Okay," Kellan called. "I want everyone to form two lines behind the punching bags. We're going to work on our combos tonight."

I moved to the back of a line and propped my hands on my hips. The only thing I thought of when he said combos was the delicious little pretzels filled with cheese. I definitely should have eaten before I came to class.

"Let's start with left, right, dropkick." Kellan punched the bag with each hand, then landed a kick that rocked the bag back and forth.

"Holy crap," I mumbled.

Gavin looked over his shoulder and smirked at me. "Pretty impressive, huh, babe? It's amazing what these guys can do."

"These guys?"

"Kellan, Tate, Dante, and Roman. I haven't really been to many classes with Roman, but the other three are amazing. Dante kicks my ass every time in sparring." Gavin smiled like getting his ass kicked was one of the best things that have ever happened to him.

"You're really into this, huh?" Here I thought Gavin was going to kind of be a helping hand to me.

Gavin bounced back and forth and threw a punch in the air. "It's a great workout."

I pasted a fake ass smile on my face and tried to calm my breathing. I was definitely on my own.

The line slowly progressed, and I was finally standing behind Gavin, watching him kick the shit out the punching bag. He was impressive, but he didn't have the same smoothness as when Kellan had done it. When Kellan did anything karate-ish, he looked like he was doing it effortlessly.

Gavin strutted to the back of the line, and I eyed up the punching bag. What were the odds I was going to break my hand or foot?

"Hands up. Protect your face." Kellan put his hands up and spread his legs apart. I tried to mimic his stance and felt like a fool.

"Now, just jab left, put your hand back in front of your face, and then jab right." Kellan deftly punched the bag, sending it rocking. "Your turn, Cookie."

Oh damn, here we go. I clenched my fists and said a prayer to the karate gods. I needed all the help I could get.

I swung my left arm and missed the bag. "Shit."

Kellan shook his head and smirked. "Step a little closer to the bag, Molly."

I scooted a half a foot forward, afraid I would be too close now.

"Just hold your arm out," he instructed.

I stuck out my left arm and was five inches away from the bag. "How the heck am I supposed to hit the bag?"

Kellan moved behind me and put his hands on my hips. "Move forward more," he whispered in my ear.

A sweet chill ran down my spine. "Um…okay." I clumsily shuffled forward 'til my fist touched the bag. "This okay?"

Kellan tapped my arm. "This one first." He stepped back, but I could still feel him behind me.

I punched my left fist, ignoring the sting, put it back up by my face, and then swung my right.

"Now dropkick."

I had no idea what a dropkick was. My leg connected with the bag as I kicked and it hurt like a son of a bitch. "Holy mother of God." I grabbed my foot and hopped up and down. "You could have warned me that it was going to hurt." I hobbled off to the side and leaned against the barrier they had between the mats and the chairs.

"It shouldn't hurt, at least not as much as it does now." Kellan grabbed my foot, and I braced my arms on the half wall. "You should have hit with the bottom of your foot and heel. That's what a dropkick is."

"That wasn't explained to me. I thought a kick was a kick."

Kellan rubbed my foot. "My bad, Cookie. Next time, just hit with the bottom of your foot."

"This kicking ass is much more complicated than I imagined."

Kellan gently set my foot down and looked up at me. "You're doing good. Just try not to hurt yourself anymore."

I scoffed. "That might be easier said than done. As I like to tell people, I have the grace of a newborn giraffe."

Kellan chuckled and stood up. "Hop back in line, and I promise to explain stuff better."

I gave him a mock salute and managed to make it back in line without falling on my ass.

Gavin fell back in line next to me. "Doing okay?"

"Never better. Just figuring out the bag isn't as cushy as it looks."

Gavin made small talk, mostly of which I listened to half-heartedly, because my eyes kept finding Kellan, and my brain refused to think of anything except what he looked like with his shirt off.

I needed to focus, or I was going to make an even bigger fool of myself.

****

Kellan

I tried to focus on Bess working on the combo, but my eyes kept straying to Molly at the back of the line talking to Gavin. I noticed when she had gotten back in line that he had purposely sought her out.

"Can I try it one more time?" Bess asked.

I nodded my head and forced myself to watch her. "That was good. Next time, try to land your punches at one target. Right in the center."

Bess trotted to the back of the line, and Cam stood in front of the bag, her legs braced. "You think about getting a drink with me tonight?" she asked.

I tried not to grimace and shook my head. Cam had been trying to get me to go out with her since she started class, and I had turned down all of her advances. She wasn't a bad looking woman by any means, but she gave off the vibe. You know, the one where you know she chews men up and spits them up. I wasn't interested in becoming her next prey.

"Got some plans after class tonight."

Cam landed her two punches and drop-kicked the bag, rocking it backward. She batted her eyes. "You say that every night. Why don't you just come out for one drink? I promise not to bite." A cheshire grin spread across her lips. "At least, not hard."

"I'll keep that in mind, although these are plans I can't cancel."

"Maybe next time." She sauntered to the back of the line, and I watched Molly size her up. She couldn't hide her look of disgust fast enough. Gavin noticed her look and glanced at what she was looking at.

Gavin's eyes traveled up and down Cam's body, and he licked his lips. Gavin was an ass, and if he thought Cam was something worth looking at, he needed to talk to her and not Molly.

We ran through the line one more time, and this time, Molly managed to hit the bag the first time, although her kick landed more south than it should have.

"All right, now for the next fifteen minutes, I want you all to pair up, and grab one focus paper each."

Molly looked around, and I knew she had no idea what I was talking about. It was hard for me to remember when teaching new students that everything was confusing the first couple of classes. "Dante." I held out my hand, and Dante gave me a focus paper. Focus papers were just laminated pieces of paper that, when kicked and punched, made a noise, so you knew you were hitting your target. They were used when working one on one with someone. I winked at Molly, letting her know I was trying to help her out.

Cam raised her hand and stepped right into my view of Molly. "Do we get to pick our partners?"

"Yeah, I think you guys can manage that." This chick was a piece of work. She popped out her hip, flipped her hair and licked her lips.

I looked anywhere but at her. "Grab a paper and a place on the mat."

Everyone dispersed and grabbed papers off the shelf on the wall.

Tate stood next to me and crossed his arms over his chest. "Man, she had a hard-on for you. When are you going to hit that?"

"Who are you talking about?"

Tate licked his lips and nodded at Cam.

"You're fucking kidding me, right? That chick is a straight-up psycho."

Tate wagged his eyebrows. "The feisty ones in bed normally are psycho."

"Well, I'll leave that one to you."

"Figured you would. I noticed you can't seem to keep your eyes off of Molly. Got plans for you two tonight?"

I hadn't. I didn't know what to do with her after class. Typically, I went home, ate some dinner, and then passed out. "Don't worry about Molly and me. We need to help Dante out." I nodded over to Dante who was helping everyone pair up.

Dante, Tate, and I roamed through the pairs, helping when needed and just watching to see how people were improving. Molly had paired up with Gavin, who was trying to showboat for her. Gavin was getting pretty good at karate, but his ego was too big for his head.

Molly held the paper out and slammed her eyes shut when Gavin started kicking and punching.

God damn, she even looked pretty when she was fearful of getting her hand kicked off.

"Oh, ah! Oh, my God!"

I spun around and saw Cam collapsed on the floor, clutching her foot. Fuck!

Dante and I made it to her at the same time, and we both kneeled next to her. "What happened?" I asked.

Cam whimpered and cried.

"She went to kick, and her leg came out from under her. I'm not sure what happened," her partner answered.

"Should we call an ambulance?" Dante asked.

Cam shook her head and grabbed my arm. "No, no," she gasped.

"Cam, you need to see a doctor. You might have pulled something or maybe even worse," I said as I looked at her leg and saw it was already turning purple around her ankle.

"You can drive me. I don't want an ambulance." She gasped when Dante touched her ankle, and I knew this was more than a sprain.

"I don't know."

Cam pouted out her bottom lip. "Please, I can't drive myself like this."

The class had gathered around, and I couldn't exactly be an asshole and tell her no. "Fine, I'll take you to the emergency room."

Tate was standing over us. "How are we going to get her to your car? Should we lift her?"

"Yeah, that's going to be our only option. She shouldn't put any weight on it."

Cam batted her eyes at me. "Oh, you can carry me, Kellan. You're more than strong enough." Un-fucking-believable This chick was laid out on the floor, her ankle turning fifty shades of purple, and she was still managing to flirt with me.

She threw her arms around my neck, and I had no choice but to wrap my arms around her. I lifted her up, trying to touch her the least possible, but she splayed her body against me like a sponge. "Grab the door, Dante," I muttered as I moved off the mat. I slipped on my shoes and headed towards the front door. Dante grabbed my keys off the counter and held the door open.

Molly's light laugh reached my ears, and I looked over my shoulder to see her with her hand on Gavin's arm, smiling. Well, shit.

Cam whimpered in my arms and rested her head on my shoulder. This was not how I had pictured my night going. I was going to spend it with the wrong woman, while Gavin swooped in on Molly.

Damn cocksucker.

****

Molly

I was done. Stick a fork in me, done.

After Kellan had left with Cam, Dante had taken over the class and worked the hell out of us. I had a newfound appreciation for what Kellan and the guys did here.

Plus, I totally understood what Kellan meant when he said they yelled and screamed to make sure they were breathing. By the end of the class, Dante had me grunting with the best of them.

I was leaning against the wall, looking down at my shoes, willing them to magically get on my feet. My psychic abilities were lacking.

Gavin walked up to me and put his hand on the wall next to my head. "Good job out there tonight."

I scoffed. "I think you mean good job on not dying. That's the only thing I accomplished tonight."

Dante, who was sitting at the desk, chuckled and shook his head. "You gotta start somewhere, Molly. I think avoiding death is a good start."

I rolled my eyes and turned my attention back to my shoes. I think my ability to bend over was gone. Driving home shoeless was my best option.

"You wanna get that drink we talked about earlier?" Gavin asked, turning his body into me.

"Ah...um...as much as I'd love to, I think I'm going to have to pass. I'm pretty sure I'm liable to pass out in the next fifteen minutes." Err, I really didn't want to go out with Gavin. He had been really kind to me all night, but he was also a type of cocky that I didn't like. Besides, I'm pretty sure any date we would go on would have some type of physical activity, and I had met my quota for physical exertion tonight. I was good for the next five years.

"How about another time?"

"I'm normally really busy with the cafe. I seem to spend all my waking hours there."

Gavin chuckled and leaned in even further. Can this man not catch a clue? "How about I come by the cafe tomorrow, and we can discuss this then."

I looked over Gavin's shoulder and saw Dante stand up. He crossed his arms over his chest, and I'm pretty sure if Gavin had been facing him, Dante would have killed him with the death glare he was giving him. "Well, I'm always there." Not exactly an invitation to come, but not exactly rejection either.

"I'll see ya around, babe." Gavin winked at me, giving me the creeps, and headed out the door.

"I never realized how big of an ass bag that guy is."

I couldn't help but snort. I was glad I wasn't the only one who thought that. "He's definitely something else."

"You did do good tonight, though."

I laughed and gingerly bent over. "It was touch-and-go for a minute there. Pretty sure my body is going to feel like I got ran over by an elephant tomorrow."

Dante chuckled and moved from behind the desk and crouched in front of me. "Stand up, Molly. You look like you're about to fall over."

A groan escaped my lips as I tried to stand up. "I'm just driving barefoot. This is hopeless. I'll never be able to touch my feet again."

Dante shook his head and grabbed my shoes. "Shut it, woman." He lifted my foot, and I grasped the wall, feeling my leg giving out. He quickly slid my socks and shoes on, and I barely had to move.

"You're my hero, Dante."

He stood up and looked down at me. "I'm far from anyone's hero, Molly. Get home, get some rest, and don't let that ass bag, Gavin, pressure you into going out with him."

I waved my hand at him and pushed off the wall. "Pfft, even if I did say yes to a date with him, it wouldn't last for long. Most guys run when they find out how boring I am."

Dante shook his head. "Crazy woman," he mumbled under his breath.

That wasn't the first time I had been called that. "All right, I'm gonna haul my dead ass home, and pass out for the night. Have a good evening, guys," I called as I shuffled toward the door.

"When's the meeting?" Tate asked as I put my hand on the door.

"Friday night. Six o'clock."

"Should we be worried?"

I shook my head and pushed the door open. "I'm sure we'll figure something out, Tate. I wouldn't lose any sleep over it." I gave them both a quick smile and headed over to my car.

I fell into my seat with my legs hanging out of the car. My body screamed at me, wanting to know what I was thinking putting it through that tonight. It was going to be an act of God if I would be able to get out of the car. Reclining with my seat back, and just vegging out in my car, was looking pretty damn appealing.

Headlights flashed across the parking lot. I held my breath, hoping that it would be Kellan getting out of the car. The door opened, and my hope was popped like a balloon when Bess' husband climbed out.

"Son of a bitch." I managed to lift my legs into the car and slammed the door.

Tonight had been good until Cam had managed to break her ankle and whisk Kellan off with her. I had seen the way she had been eyeing him up all night and knew she was after him. Kellan, thankfully, didn't seem too impressed with her, although he didn't appear to be put off when she basically draped herself over him when he lifted her up.

I had never felt my heart hurt the way it did when he walked out the door with her. Kellan and I weren't technically together, but I felt there was something there. I got that Cam had hurt herself and needed help, but why did it have to be Kellan to help her? Cam was the kind of woman who went after what she wanted relentlessly, and unfortunately, she was going after Kellan.

I sighed and cranked up the car. There was no point in sitting in the parking lot waiting for him to return. It wasn't like he was just going to drop her off and come back. I moved my arm back to grab the seat belt and cringed as I felt every muscle in my body scream in protest.

Who was I kidding? Cam was a much better fit for Kellan. I did forty-five minutes of karate, and I was ready to die. Before Cam had hurt herself, she wasn't even winded and looked like a runway model. Plus, Cam looked like she belonged with Kellan. I looked like I belonged with a big house full of cats.

I was foolish to even think I had a chance with Kellan.

I backed out of my parking spot and headed back to my house where I belonged. Spending the rest of my night soaking in the tub, with Mr. Mittens keeping me company.

After the meeting Friday, I would never see Kellan again, and everything will be over. I would go back to the boring barista, and Kellan can get back to kicking ass and collecting phone numbers.

Back to normal, and boring as hell.

****

Kellan

"Dude, you look like fucking shit. What time did you get home last night?"

I swung open the front door and flipped off Roman, Dante, and Tate. Not what I wanted to hear this morning. "Four."

Tate pushed into my house and plopped down on the couch. "How did it take that long?"

"Yeah, couldn't you have called someone for her? Why did you need to stay with her?" Dante rubbed his chin. "Seems pretty fishy to me."

I stepped back from the door and motioned for Roman and Dante to come in. They apparently had better manners than Tate.

"I did ask her if she had any family she wanted me to call, she said all she had was her mother in a nursing home. I couldn't exactly leave her there." I sat down next to Tate and kicked my feet up on the coffee table.

Roman wandered into the kitchen, and Dante sat down in the recliner. I heard Roman rummaging around, and knew he was going to find the half a pizza I had planned to have for lunch today. "Score!" he yelled. Dammit.

Tate grabbed the remote off the coffee table and flipped on the TV. "So what did she break?"

"How come all of the fun stuff happens when I finally take a night off? Nobody ever breaks shit when I'm there." Roman walked into the living room with the box of pizza and dropped it on the table. "I'm gonna order more pizza."

I flipped open the box and saw there was only one piece left. "You inhale that shit? There were four pieces in there."

Roman ripped off a huge bite from the piece he had in his hand. "I'm hungry," he mumbled.

I leaned back into the couch and laced my fingers behind my head. "She tore her Achilles. She's going to need surgery."

"No shit. That fucking blows." Dante flipped through the channels and landed on a cooking show. "You taking her to surgery and nursing her back to health?" he asked, smirking.

"No, you asswipe. Cam is not the type of chick that does it for me."

Tate laughed. "You mean the type that wants to get your balls in a vise and slowly twist the handle until you become her little puppy dog?"

"Good to know I'm not the only one who got that vibe from her." Cam was a man-eater, plain and simple.

Roman held his hand out to me. "Where's your phone? I wanna order some pizza."

"Where is your phone?" Dante asked.

Roman shrugged. "Not really sure. I had it at the bar last night, and then I woke up with it gone."

Tate shook his head. "Who'd you take home with you last night?"

"I don't think I did take anyone home, but I'm not one hundred percent sure."

I dug my phone out of my pocket and slapped it into his hand. "You're a piece of fucking work, Ro."

"I have fun, ain't nothing wrong with that. I don't have anyone tying me down, so I can do whatever I want."

"Yeah, until that whatever you want ends up pushing a baby out and starts calling you daddy," Dante jested.

Roman flipped Dante the bird and headed into the kitchen. "Fucking ass," he mumbled under his breath.

"How was class after I left?"

Tate laughed. "You mean how was Molly, right?"

Yeah, that was exactly what I meant, but I didn't want to act like some lovesick ass. "No, I mean, how was class? Finished up with no incidents?"

Dante hollered for Roman to bring him a beer, and popped up the footrest on the recliner. "Yeah, I took over and finished it out. Bess kicked ass like she normally does. I still can't believe that broad is over sixty. She does better than half of the class, and they're all under forty."

I couldn't help but laugh. Bess may dress like she just popped out of an eighties aerobics video, but she was in damn good shape. "Yeah, her kicks were pretty impressive from what I saw."

Dante snickered. "I wasn't sure you saw much last night other than Molly."

Tate nudged me with his foot. "Yeah, you two seemed pretty fucking cozy when you were showing her how to hit the bag."

"I was just showing her how to do it."

"I don't remember him putting his arms around Gavin when he first started, do you, Tate?" Dante asked as he tapped his finger on his chin.

"Yeah, now that you mention it, I've never seen Kellan teach that hands-on before." Tate propped his chin on his hand

and turned to examine me. "How come you never taught me like that?"

Dante busted out laughing, and even Roman laughed in the kitchen. "You need to get laid, Tate, if you're looking for Kellan to wrap his arms around you," Roman called.

Tate reached his arms out to me, and I pushed him away. "I never taught you, and keep your damn arms away from me."

"So, what's the deal with you and Molly?" Dante asked.

That was the question I had no answer to. We kissed. Twice. And it was fucking fantastic. "I don't know."

Dante chucked the remote at me. "Since when the fuck does Kellan Wright not know? You always got shit locked down, know what you're going to do next. Is this the chick that comes along and changes everything?"

"You know," Roman announced as he walked back into the living room and collapsed on the floor. "I don't fucking understand why you get a chick, and everything changes. Why can't shit stay the same, and she just comes along for the ride?"

Tate, Dante, and I all looked at each other, wondering where that had come from. That was the most Roman had ever said about dating in his life.

"Because if you get a girlfriend, you can't really have her tag along to the bar with you while you pick up random chicks and take them home to bang," Dante explained as if that wasn't common sense.

"Fuck off," Roman growled. "You know that's not what I fucking meant. I just wonder why chicks have to change everything. Kellan is going to start dating Molly, and then we're never going to see his ass except for when he's teaching. It's bullshit. I can guarantee you, if I were ever to get a chick, I wouldn't disappear off the face of the Earth."

"Dude, he just wants to go on a date with her, not marry her and have fifty kids," Tate laughed.

Roman pointed a finger at me. "And that is where it all begins. One date and she sucks you in."

Tate scooted forward on the couch and looked down at Roman. "How drunk did you get last night? Are you sure you still aren't buzzin'?"

"I'm hungover, not drunk. And Kellan has shit for food in the house, so I'm suffering for the next half an hour until the damn pizzas show up." Roman draped his arm over his eyes. "All I'm saying is, just don't turn into one of those pussy whipped douchenozzles that can't see ten feet past their woman."

Dante chuckled. "Tell us how you really feel, Ro."

I chuckled. These were my boys. The guys who, no matter what was going on, had always been there for me. It was me who had first talked about opening Powerhouse, building the dream up in their minds until they decided it was something they wanted too. I wasn't about to fall for some chick and leave them behind. "You guys have nothing to worry about. I don't plan on going anywhere."

"That mean you're not going to go after Molly?" Dante asked. "Her cookies are more than a good reason to date her."

I pointed my finger at Dante and leveled my gaze at him. "Stay away from Molly's cookies."

Dante held his hands up. "The only cookies of hers I want are in her bakery case, man. I'll leave the rest to you."

I stared at the TV. "Fucking better be."

"And so it begins," Roman mumbled.

He was wrong. It had started the instant I had kissed Molly and had been unable to forget the taste of her lips.

I needed to taste her again.

****

Molly

I was dying. Seriously.

Why do people do this to their bodies? It was Friday morning, more than a day since I had gone to karate class, and I was in more pain than I was yesterday.

I had barely made it through work Thursday, spending most of the day on a stool when I wasn't manning the espresso machine. Thankfully, Sage had helped and picked up the slack.

"Why don't you go lay down in the storeroom? Things have slowed down for a bit."

I rolled my eyes at Sage. "I'm not going to lay on the floor in there. It's clean, but it's hard ass tile. I really doubt that is going to help how I feel."

"At least take the stool back there and moan in peace. You're starting to scare the customers. Every time you move, I have no idea what sound is going to come out of your mouth. Frank asked me if you were dying or having sex this morning." Sage snapped a dish towel at me. "Get, I'm serious. I'll holler if I need anything."

I mumbled under my breath and shuffle/pushed the stool into the storeroom. Why I couldn't stay up front was ridiculous. I wasn't moaning and grunting that much.

"Ugg…" I moaned as I sat down. Okay, I take that back. Maybe I was groaning more than I realized.

I reached out, grabbing the shelf in front of me, and tried to stretch my arms. It wasn't right, me being this sore. Adding some more physical activity to my day probably wouldn't be a bad idea. I was twenty-nine years old, and I was moving like I was ninety.

"Hey."

Oh shit. I looked over and saw Kellan leaning against the door, with his arms crossed over his chest. "Hey. Did you come to watch me die?"

He shook his head. "Well, I came to see you. The whole dying thing I hope doesn't happen."

"Well, after Wednesday night, it's possible. I hurt in places that should be illegal."

Kellan pushed off the door. "I probably should have stretched you out more. Give me your hands and turn towards me."

I quirked an eyebrow. "Why?"

Kellan laughed and grabbed my hands. He twisted me on the stool, and my legs dropped open. He stepped in between my knees, and slowly raised my arms over my head. "Because you need to stretch out now. It'll help, I promise. Your muscles are contracting, and you need to keep moving. Have you been drinking enough?"

"Wine and coffee." Kellan laughed. Well, he asked. Coffee got me through the day, and the wine helped to numb me at night.

"You might want to add some water in there, too."

"Duly noted," I groaned. My arms were directly over my head, and while it hurt, it also felt damn good. "I didn't think I'd ever be able to raise my arms over my head again."

Kellan snickered and slowly lowered them. "You could always come to class once a week, and you could make me coffee in exchange."

"I highly doubt a cup of coffee equals the price of one of your classes, Kellan."

He smirked and dropped my arms to my sides. "You're right, but I'm willing to work something out." He put his hands on my thighs, and rubbed his way down my legs and cupped my calves. "Legs sore, too?"

I nodded and tried to swallow the knot that had formed in my throat. Kellan's hands on me were like magic, even if all they were doing was helping me stretch.

"Probably the side and dropkicks you were doing. When you're not used to doing something like that, you really feel it the next couple of days." His hands worked their way back up my legs, rubbing and kneading.

I licked my lips and closed my eyes. "Is this something you do for everyone in your classes?"

I heard Kellan laugh, and I opened my eyes. He was pressed close to me, and his hands were moving up my sides. "No. Only for people I make an exception for."

"Oh really," I whispered as I tilted my head back to look up at him. "So Bess and Cam didn't get the same service after their first class?"

He slightly shook his head. His hands delved into my hair, and he leaned down. "I'd have to say this is a first."

"Oh."

A smirk crossed his lips, and his eyes crinkled. "Oh is right, Molly. I'm going to kiss you."

"Oh." That was the extent of my vocabulary at the moment. Kellan touching me forced all thought from my head, and all I could do was focus on his touch.

"I'm gonna take that as an okay, Cookie."

I slightly nodded, and that was all he needed. His lips were on mine, and I moaned as his taste reached my tongue. Kellan was like no man I had ever kissed before. He took what he wanted, nipping and licking, but he also gave back. His hands roamed over my body, and I arched my back, yearning to be closer to him.

"Kellan," I gasped. His lips kissed their way across my jaw and down my neck.

"Put your arms around my neck," he whispered in my ear.

My arms had a mind of their own and instantly wound their way around his neck. His arms circled my waist, and he lifted me up, my feet leaving the ground. "Wrap your legs around me," he growled. His face was buried in my neck, his mouth sucking on my earlobe.

Holy fuck. Who would have thought a little ear play would have me in a puddle at this man's feet doing whatever he asked? My muscles protested as I lifted my legs, but there was no way in hell I wasn't gonna get my legs around him.

"Molly!"

I whimpered and locked my ankles behind Kellan. "Shh…maybe she'll go away." I tilted my head, giving Kellan more access to my neck.

His body shook against mine. "You're a nut, Cookie."

"Molly, there's someone here to see you," Sage called again.

"Son of a bitch," I mumbled.

Kellan patted my butt. "Go see who it is. I'll stay here."

I groaned and slowly dropped my feet to the floor. "It's probably the milk guy wanting to show me pictures of his grandkids," I complained. "They're adorable, but do I really need to see pictures of them every week?"

Kellan laughed and pressed one last kiss to my neck. "Go on." He patted me on the ass, and I slowly shuffled out to the front counter.

I was in a haze from Kellan's kisses, and I didn't even notice who was waiting for me until they said my name.

"Oh, Gavin. It's you." Not who I had been expecting at all. Gavin hadn't crossed my mind, well, ever. "I wasn't expecting you."

A sly smile crossed his lips, and it took everything in my not to wince. When I had first met him, I had thought he was good looking, but now, he didn't do anything for me. "Thought I would drop in to get a coffee and see you."

"Well, here I am," I said, laughing nervously. "What can I get you?"

"Do you have green tea?"

Huh, he was a tea drinker. Nothing wrong with that, just not what I had expected. "Yup, I sure do. Iced or hot?"

"Iced, no sugar."

I gagged a little and nodded. I wasn't a fan of tea to begin with, and then to not add sugar made it sound even more gross to me. "Coming right up." I could brew tea in my sleep, but I tried to look like I was concentrating really hard so Gavin wouldn't try to talk to me.

My plan didn't work.

"So, this is your place, huh?"

Don't roll your eyes, Molly. Don't do it. "Yup, she's all mine."

"Pretty impressive."

It was impressive. "Sure is." Talk about a strained conversation.

"So, do you have any plans tonight?"

Shit. Hell. Damn. Fuck. I snapped the lid on his tea and set it in front of him. "Not really sure yet."

Gavin nodded, and I realized I had just set myself up. Damn, I should have told him I have plans for the rest of my life, and none of them included him. "Maybe we can grab some dinner tonight?"

Shit! Abandon ship! "Oh…um…I'd love to…but…well. I'm just going to be straightforward, Gavin. I have to wash my hair tonight."

He laughed. "Then how about another night."

Gah, get a clue man. "I have to wash my hair every night, for the rest of my life. It's a disorder. You know." I caught a glimpse of Sage over Gavin's shoulder, and she had her hand over her mouth trying not to laugh.

Gavin shook his head. "All you had to do was tell me you don't wanna go out with me, Molly." He grabbed his cup and stormed out.

Sage rushed to the counter and burst out laughing. "You did not just tell that poor man you have a disorder where you have to wash your hair every night, did you?"

I shrugged. "I panicked. The guy couldn't take a hint. He asked me out after class, and I told him no. Then he comes here and asks me again. What the heck was I supposed to do? Go out with him?"

"He's not bad looking. Although, he is no Kellan."

And that was the damn truth. Gavin had nothing on Kellan. One look from Kellan had me begging for him to touch me. "Speaking of Kellan, I left him in the storeroom. Try not to bother me unless the cafe is burning down, okay?"

Sage saluted me. "Aye, aye captain. I'll let you get back to Kung Fu Hottie."

I basically skipped back to Kellan, hoping we could pick up where we left off. I know I had thought I just needed one more kiss from him, but I knew that one more kiss would never be enough.

Except when I walked through the door, he wasn't there. "What in the world," I mumbled. I plopped down on the stool and looked around.

What happened?

* * * * * * * * * *

Kellan

"Who pissed in your Cheerios?"

I growled and fell onto the couch in the office. "No one."

Dante leaned back in the chair behind the desk and steepled his fingers in front of him. "I think the punching bag you just beat the hell out of would disagree."

"I was working out, you got a problem with that?"

Dante raised his hands and shook his head. "Nope. I just don't want to be the next thing you hit."

I flexed my hands, knowing they were going to be bruised later. I had snuck out of the cafe after hearing Molly agreeing to go on a date with Gavin, and I had to hit something. As much as I would have liked that something to be Gavin's face, I settled for one of the punching bags.

"So, you gonna tell me what happened, or just sit there glaring at your hands?"

I balled up my fists and growled. "I went to the cafe this morning."

"I'm gonna assume that things did not go well."

"Oh, they were good. Fucking fantastic. Until fucking Gavin showed up, and Molly agreed to go on a date with him not even a minute after we made out in the storage room."

"Say what?"

I scoffed and hit the cushion next to me. "You heard that right, man. I thought I had her. She was all over me, moaning my name, and I was ready to take her right there if she would have let me."

"Hold on, hold on. So, where did Gavin come into this?"

"He fucking came to see her. I was standing in the storeroom, listening to them talk when he asked her out. She said she would love to, and then I booked it out the back door. I didn't need to hang around any more than that."

"I don't believe you."

I rolled my eyes and leaned back. "Well, you fucking better start. I know what I heard."

"And I know what I heard after class on Wednesday. He cornered her, and I could tell just by the way she looked at him that she wasn't interested."

"Well, something must have changed from then to now. She said yes, Dante."

Dante shook his head and stood up. "Then he pressured her into it, Kellan. She doesn't like the fucking guy."

I waved my hand at him, twisted around and laid down on the couch. "It doesn't matter. I'm over it."

"Yeah, real over it," Dante scoffed. "Why didn't you stay and ask her what was going on?"

I draped my arm over my eyes. "Cause I'm really not into torturing myself, Dante."

"So, you're just going to tap out?"

I gave him a thumbs up. "Yeah. I need to focus on the school right now anyway. Molly was just going to be a distraction I didn't need." Now that I knew she didn't want me, I wasn't about to fight for her. I wasn't into sharing either.

"Now you sound like fucking Roman."

"He had a point."

"Who had a point?"

I lifted my arm and saw Tate and Roman standing in the doorway. "Roman."

Roman puffed out his chest and patted himself on the back. "About time that happened."

Tate elbowed him in the side. "You're a douche."

"Oh well." Roman replied.

"What are you two doing here?" Dante asked.

Roman pushed off the door and walked over to the trophies in the corner of the room. "Wanted to see if you guys wanted to go to Palmer this weekend. Regionals are this weekend."

I sat up on the edge of the couch. "You competing?"

Roman shrugged. "I don't plan on it, although that could change when I see who's all there."

Dante pointed at me. "You have the meeting tonight, and we have classes tomorrow."

"I wasn't planning on leaving until after the meeting. I got the car packed already."

"I'm in." I stood up and clapped my hands. This was what I needed.

"Seriously?" Roman asked. "You were the last one I thought who would say yes."

"I need to get out of here." I would only have to see Molly at the meeting tonight, and then I could get the hell out of dodge.

"I still think you should talk to Molly," Dante replied.

I shook my head. I didn't want to fucking talk anymore. I wasn't interested in begging to be with her. "No. I'm done, Dante. You can handle class tomorrow. We'll be back Sunday."

Dante threw his hands up. "Fine, what the fuck ever. I guess I'll be the responsible one this time."

I grabbed my keys off the desk and tossed them in the air. "I'm gonna pack a bag, and then I'll meet you guys at the meeting."

"Wait, don't you think we should talk about what we're going to do tonight? At least have some type of plan?" Tate asked.

"She can't shut us down. We'll just have to figure out a way to work around each other." I didn't fucking care. Molly wasn't going to get her way.

****

Molly

"How do I look?"

"Like Molly!" Sam shouted. He was once again camped out on the couch with Mr. Mittens, feeding him kitty treats.

I tilted my head and squinted my eyes. "I guess you're right about that, buddy."

Sage laughed and crossed her legs. She was sitting on the toilet, lid down, and helping me figure out what to wear tonight. "Are you sure I shouldn't just stick with the clothes I usually wear? I think I look like I'm trying too hard."

"Nonsense. You look fine. So you're not in your regular apron and khakis. It's not like you are going there in a wedding dress."

I was wearing a pair of skinny jeans, black satin flats, and a white, stretchy top that seemed to accentuate every inch of me. I wasn't dressed up by normal standards, but compared to what I usually wear, I looked like I was going to a grand ball. "I'm just putting on what I normally wear."

Sage grabbed my hand and tugged me back in front of the mirror. "I don't think so. You're wearing this because you don't have time to change." She looked at her watch and shook her head. "You need to be there to open the shop up before anyone gets there, so you better get going."

She pushed me out of the bathroom, and I glanced at the clock on the microwave. Damn, I had five minutes to get to the cafe. "Lock up when you leave?" I grabbed my keys and slung my purse over my shoulder.

"We're right behind you again. Sam needs to get home and take a bath," Sage shouted so Sam would hear her.

"Oh, Mama. No bath."

Sage rolled her eyes. "Not talking me out of it, big man. Set down Mr. Mittens and let's go. You can use the bath chalk tonight, if you want."

"What?" Sam yelled. He pushed Mr. Mittens off his lap and jumped off the couch. "Out of the way, Molly. I've got some wall coloring to do."

I managed to brush Sam on the head as he sprinted by. "It was good seeing you too, buddy," I laughed.

Sage pulled the door shut behind us, and we headed down the stairs. "I forbid the use of the bath chalk after he thought he could use it on the couch and the TV."

I cringed. "Shit, I bet that didn't end very well."

Sage laughed. "It thankfully wiped off, but I can still see squiggles on the TV when the light hits it just right. Some days, I wish he would have been born a girl, but then I remember I don't have to deal with mood swings, tampons, and PMS. I'll take coloring on the walls over that any day."

Sam was standing next to Sage's car, jumping up and down. "Come on, Mama! I've got a bath to take."

Sage sighed and gave me a quick hug. "Stop worrying, you look gorgeous, and make sure to give me all of the details tomorrow."

I waved her off and slid into my car. Lord knew if there were going to be any details. I had no idea what was about to happen.

When Kellan had disappeared after I had helped Gavin, I was clueless. Here I thought we were getting somewhere, and then poof, gone.

I mindlessly drove to the cafe, not even remembering the ride there. Kennedy, the owner of Zen Spa and Relaxation, was waiting at the door when I pulled up. Kennedy came in every Tuesday and Thursday and got her usual order of a skinny vanilla latte, and an iced green tea to go.

"Hey, Kennedy," I said with a smile. "Sorry, I'm running a little behind." I unlocked the door and held it open for her.

"No problem. I had a late class and just headed over when it was over."

I flipped on the lights and moved to the bakery case to grab the tray of cookies Sage had put together earlier. "How are things going over at Zen?"

Kennedy sat down at the table closest to the front counter and leaned back. "Pretty good. Definitely, can't complain." She played with a dark red lock of hair and twirled it around her finger. "My parents still come by weekly to see if I'm failing yet."

I rolled my eyes and set the cookies down in front of her. "You would think after three years, they would figure out that you aren't going to fail." Kennedy was only twenty-five, looked like she was eighteen, and ran the most successful yoga studio in a hundred-mile radius. Her parents still treated her like she was ten even though she was more successful than most twenty-five-year-olds.

She was tall, lean, and drop dead gorgeous. I was envious of her clear, porcelain skin, dark cherry red hair, and legs that went on for days. The fact that she was so friendly on top of being a natural beauty intimidated most people, me included when I had first met her. "I'm sure one day they won't keep looking over my shoulder." She giggled and grabbed a cookie off the plate. "Maybe when I'm forty."

I grabbed a cookie and clinked it against hers. "Here's to hoping," I agreed.

"Oh, thank God there are cookies." Karl, the owner of the laundromat, walked through the door and grabbed two cookies, one for each hand. He plopped down next to Kennedy and leaned his head against her shoulder. "Who thought owning a laundromat would be so stressful."

"Bad day?" Kennedy asked.

Karl grumbled and ripped off a huge chunk of a cookie and shoved it in his mouth. "Bad doesn't even begin to describe it," he mumbled around the cookie. "When are the hotties showing up? They are the only thing that is going to make this day better."

"Anytime. We're just waiting for Gus, Mel, and the Powerhouse guys," I replied. I wiped my hands on my pants and wished I could be anywhere but here.

"Honey, I will take a piece of the silver fox, and break off a bit of the young one for later," Karl said, fanning himself. "I swear, when they all walked into the laundromat, I was going to fall over, and pray that one of them would give me mouth to mouth."

Kennedy bumped him with her shoulder and giggled. "You're shameless, Karl."

"Sweetheart, when you get to be fifty, there ain't nothing left to be ashamed of."

"Are we too late?" Bess and the Moaners walked through the door and took seats at the table next to Kennedy and Karl.

"I told you we shouldn't have stopped to get a Whopper. Now we missed the parade of hotties," Gretchen grumped.

"Nonsense, it's not even six. We haven't missed anything, right, Molly?"

"Uh…um…no, you haven't. The meeting hasn't started yet. But, I do have to ask why you guys are here?"

Bess shook her finger at me. "We have just as much of a right to be here as these guys do. Damn, we are in here almost every day. I can't say the same for Karlton here."

"It's Karl," he said, rolling his eyes and turning to look at Bess. "I'm sorry I have a business to run and don't have time to sit around at Molly's fabulous coffee shop all day." Karl winked at me, then went back to glaring at Bess.

"Thanks, Karl," I mumbled. Karl and Bess were always ripping into each other, and no one knew why. Sage and I joked that Karl had lost some of Bess' underwear over at the laundromat, and she never forgave him for it.

"Well, we're staying, and if you don't like it, you're going to have to drag us out of here." Bess leaned back in her chair, and I had to say, she looked intimidating. She must have put on her extra sassy pants tonight.

Karl waved his hand at her and grabbed the plate of cookies. "Whatever, but the cookies are only for people on the committee."

"Pish," Bess said, waving her hand at Karl. "We brought our own snacks." Bess nodded at the members of the Moaners, and they all grabbed their purses, plopping them down on the counter. "You don't get to be our age and not realize it's always good to be prepared."

Kennedy and Karl's jaws dropped as two-foot-long subs emerged, along with a jar of pickles, three bags of full-sized chips, and a six-pack of soda.

"Sure you ain't got the whole sub shop in there?" Karl asked.

Bess flipped him the bird and grabbed the jar of pickles. "You all can have some except for Karl. He has the tray of cookies that are going to go straight to his ass."

Kennedy grabbed Karl's arm and held him back as he tried to jump at Bess. "Why, you old bitty! Just see if I ever let you in my laundromat again!"

"You know what you can do with those cookies, Karl? Shove them right up you—"

"Okay! That's enough!" I yelled. World War III was about to start in the café if I didn't step in. "Both of you, chill out."

"I don't even know why she's here," Karl mumbled under his breath.

Bess grabbed a pickle out of the jar and waved it at Karl. "For Molly. That's why, you asshat. She and Kellan are like a damn romance novel come to life. I can't miss this stuff."

Karl turned to look at me, and his jaw had hit the floor again. "You and head Kung Fu Hottie are bumping uglies?"

Kennedy reached her fist out to me. "Get it, girl."

I rolled my eyes and bumped her fist. "We're not. We're…shit, I'm not sure what we are."

"But you're something, right?" Karl asked.

If you would have asked me earlier today, I would have said yes. Now, I wasn't so sure.

"Yes, they are," Bess said matter of factly.

Karl folded his arms over his chest. "I totally would have gone for the silver fox. They know things those young bucks haven't experienced yet."

Bess cringed and pursed her lips. "You talking about Frank?"

I snorted and covered my mouth with my hand. I guess to Bess, Dante probably wasn't a silver fox. "He's talking about Dante, Bess."

Bess rolled her eyes and ripped a large bite off her pickle. "Honey, if you're looking for experienced, I'll send my Joe your way. He can show you a few things you never would have found possible." She wagged her eyebrows and high-fived Gretchen.

"Preach it," Gretchen taunted.

Thankfully, Gus and Mel walked in, and the discussion of the talented Joe stopped.

Once everyone sat down, I made a quick pot of coffee, grabbed a few cups and sat next to Kennedy.

"Either these guys are late, or are going to be here at seven o'clock on the dot," Kennedy mumbled.

I glanced at the clock and saw that it was five to seven. Kellan wouldn't be late. But, from what I had seen of the other three, I wouldn't have put it past them. "I'm sure they'll be here."

"So, are you still wanting to shut them down?" she asked me quietly.

I shook my head. "No. I never wanted that. I just wanted them to keep it down and be courteous to me." I cleared my throat and leaned into Kennedy. "I took one of their classes. The grunting makes more sense to me now."

Kennedy's eyes bugged out. "You took one of their classes, but I've been bugging you for years to come over to Zen and you won't!"

I laughed and grabbed a coffee cup. "I almost died, Kennedy. Physical activity isn't my thing. I'm still sore as hell, and I took the class Wednesday."

She waved her hand at me. "You're always the sorest on the second day. Tomorrow, you should be on the other end of the pain. Whenever I try out some new poses, I feel it for days."

Well, that was good to know. Although, I'm sure Kennedy wasn't in as much pain as I was when she tried something new.

Everyone turned when they heard the door open, and my eyes instantly went to Kellan, who lead the guys into the café. They stayed at the door, spreading out into one line blocking the door, and crossed their arms over their chests. Talk about intimidating.

Kellan looked like he was ready to kill, and the rest followed suit.

"Yes to the hottie lineup," Karl mumbled. He stood up, his eyes traveling over them. "I'm still going to go with the silver fox."

Oh, for God's sake. Could Karl not control himself? I stood up and cleared my throat. "You guys can have a seat, if you want."

Kellan shook his head. "We're good. This isn't going to take long." His eyes were like stone, not giving anything away. When I had been in his arms, they had told me everything. Desire and need had burned in them. Now, he looked at like I was just another person walking down the street.

Kennedy grabbed my hand and pulled me down next to her. "Hang in there, hon," she whispered. I nodded my head and swallowed the knot that had formed in my throat.

Kennedy stood up. "I'm the president of the Falls River Business Committee I call this meeting into order. Karl, please sit down."

Thank God Kennedy oversaw this meeting. I would have been a blubbering fool if it had been me. Karl huffed at Kennedy, but he thankfully sat down.

"We're here to discuss the matter of Powerhouse being too loud and disturbing Java Spot Café." Everyone nodded their heads in agreement. "So, we'll start with Powerhouse explaining their side."

"Should someone be taking notes?" Mel asked.

"Notes won't be necessary," Kellan called. "When I said this won't take long, I meant it."

"Oh, um…" Kennedy stuttered. "Does that mean there won't be a problem anymore?"

Kellan shook his head. "Sunday through Friday, Powerhouse doesn't open until four pm. Java Spot is open from six in the morning until three pm. On those days, the yelling that Miss Rey hears will stop. What she was hearing was myself and the guys practicing. That won't happen anymore."

Kennedy looked down at me. "Does that work for you?"

I shrugged. He was giving me what I wanted, what wouldn't work for me? "Okay," I whispered.

Kellan continued. "The only problem we are going to run into is on Saturdays. I have morning classes, and private lessons all afternoon. The afternoon won't be an issue, but the mornings, I'm not going to be able to quiet down the yelling."

I raised my hand. Yes, *raised my hand.*

Karl snickered, and Bess threw a chip at me. "Put your damn hand down, girl."

I cleared my throat and slowly lowered my arm. "I can deal with Saturdays. I understand not being able to quiet a ton of kids."

Kellan dropped his hands to his sides and flexed his fists. "Good, we done here?"

Kennedy looked around and nodded. "Ah, well, I guess that's all we need you guys for. You're more than welcome to stay for the rest of the meeting, if you want."

I stood up and raised my hand again. "Can I just say that, um, even during the week, I'm okay with you guys grunting and stuff. I understand it better now."

Dante laughed. "Still sore for the class on Wednesday, darlin'?"

"Just a smidge," I replied.

"Don't worry about the week. We rearranged our schedule. We're good," Kellan cut in.

Kennedy cleared her throat, and you could feel the tension hanging in the air. Kellan was steaming, and it looked like he was about to blow.

"Then, we're all good." Kellan nodded at Kennedy, turned, and headed out the door.

Dante raised his hand in goodbye. "Glad we were able to figure this out, Molly." He gave me a small, sad smile, like he knew something I didn't. They all filed out the door behind Kellan, and the door slammed shut.

Gus stood up and looked at Kennedy and me. "We really got other shit to talk about, or can I get out of here? I left Jill with the kids, and she was about ready to pull her hair out."

"No, I was just trying to sound important," Kennedy snickered.

"I'm out too," Mel said. "I left the baby with my mom." Mel and Gus left as fast as they showed up, and the group was down to Kennedy, Karl, and the Moaners.

"I didn't even get to eat my sub," Gretchen complained as she started tossing food in her purse. "Can't find a good show these days. Damn kids rushing through a good argument, not letting me sit back and watch." She grabbed a pickle and shook it at me. "This is why I read. Give me a good Kristen Ashley book, and I'm entertained for hours." Gretchen and the two other Moaners cleared the table and stormed out the door.

"What was that?" Karl asked, looking at the door. "It's like I fell down the damn rabbit hole walking into here. I swore those boys were going to put up and fight, they agree with everything and leave. Then," he said, swinging his arm over to Bess. "I gotta deal with the Moaners and their old leader."

Bess rolled her eyes and pulled a soda out of her purse. "I think you mean *fearless* leader."

Kennedy sat down, and I wandered over to the fridge to see what food I had stashed in there. Not only did we sell cookies and muffins, but also a wide variety of soups and sandwiches.

Karl and Bess argued while I made some sandwiches and tried not to remember how Kellan had just looked through me like I was no one. I slathered mayo onto six slices of bread, piled ham, turkey, cheese, and lettuce on them, and cut them all in half. They were huge and would more than feed the four of us.

"I don't have any chips, but this should fill the hole," I mumbled. I plopped down in the chair next to Bess, who had moved to the same table as Kennedy and Karl.

Bess leaned over and grabbed her purse. "No worries, hon. I didn't let Gretchen take all of the food." She pulled out a bag of potato chips and ripped it open.

Karl grabbed a handful of chips. "This is the first good thing you've done all night, Bess."

I hopped up and grabbed a stack of plates and a pile of napkins. "Here ya go, Karl," I muttered.

Once we had our plates piled high, and my mouth was full of yummy turkey and ham, Bess started the twenty questions.

"Kellan sure was looking good tonight, wasn't he, Molly?"

I nodded. Yup, even looking like he was ready to beat the crap out of someone, Kellan still looked hot as sin.

"Definitely wouldn't turn that man away from my bed," Karl agreed.

"Doesn't seem to be anyone you'd turn away from your bed," Bess mumbled.

Here I thought these two had reached some type of truce, but that was short-lived.

Karl tsked, and shook his finger at Bess. "It's called appreciating the male form. I know you're a fan of it too."

Bess rolled her eyes. "Back to Kung Fu Hottie."

"Hey, that's what Sage calls him," I said, giggling.

Bess winked at me. "Who do you think I got it from? Now, you wanna tell us what happened from you and that boy looking at each other like you couldn't wait to undress each other to him acting like he couldn't get out of here fast enough?"

I picked at my sandwich and shrugged. "I honestly don't know."

"Sage said you two were going at it hot and heavy."

Karl sat up, his elbows on the table. "Oh, do tell Uncle Karl. I've hit a bit of a dry spell, and I'll take anything I can get. Even a little guy-on-girl action."

Kennedy's light giggle floated around us. "I think you might need to join the Moaners for one of their meetings, then."

"We're not taking new members," Bess replied, glaring at Karl.

Karl waved his hand at Bess. "Not interested anyway, honey. All I want to hear about is Kung Fu Hottie, and our girl, Molly."

I rolled my eyes. "We kissed. A lot."

Kennedy leaned over and bumped. "Did you like it a lot?"

Bess and Karl snickered. "Why does it suddenly feel like I'm back in high school," I mumbled.

"Just dish the dirty deeds, sweetheart," Karl ordered.

I sighed. "He kissed me. He kissed me like I've never been kissed before. If Sage hadn't called me to help a customer, I'm pretty sure we would have ended up shutting the door, and taking exactly what we both wanted. I like him, and now it seems that he can't stand to be around me."

Bess tapped her chin, then steepled her hands in front of her. "So, now we need to figure out what happened in the time you had seven minutes in heaven in the closet, to him leaving and acting like a typical grumpy man."

"But, why did you have to help the customer at the counter? Why couldn't Sage?" Kennedy asked.

I pursed my lips and cringed. "Because it was Gavin."

Karl sat on the edge of the seat and pushed his plate aside. "Now we're getting somewhere. Who's Gavin?"

"He's one of Kellan's students. I met him twice and did the class Wednesday night with him. He asked me out, twice."

Bess nodded her head. "It's about time these men start seeing our Molly for the scorching hot woman she is."

"So, he came in to ask you out while you were in the closet making out with Kellan?" Karl fanned himself. "Dear Lord, I think I'm going to have to hang out over here more often. All this time I've been hanging at the spa eyeing up the yoga hotties when I could have been over here with all of the karate hotties."

Bess perked up. "There's yoga hotties?"

Kennedy giggled. "There are three of them, although they're all gay."

Bess sat on the edge of her seat and clenched her hands. "Together? Like one of them books, where it's three friends who do freaky deeky shit with each other, but then they all agree that they need a woman to share their freaky deekyness with?"

Karl burst out laughing. "You really think that shit is real? Girl, I ain't never met a gay man who had two gay men at his beck and call, then decides he needs a woman to throw into the mix. You are crazy, child," Karl tsked. "If those three hotties are going to include anyone into their freakiness, it's damn well going to be me."

Bess shook her head. "Kennedy, you go on and tell this fool that he doesn't have a chance to be asked to take on the freakiness of three men. He'd probably up and have a heart attack."

"I think we'd all have a heart attack if that was really going on," I mused. "I can barely get one man to notice me, I couldn't imagine three."

Bess shoved the rest of her sandwich in her mouth. "It's out there. I swear on my life it is."

Karl rolled his eyes so hard, I was afraid he saw the back of his head. "Believe what you want, woman. I guess when you get to be your age, you need to live off fantasy." Karl grabbed his sandwich and stood up. "Now, if you'll excuse me, I have to refill the machines and head home."

Karl ambled out the door.

"I better be going too. I have an early class in the morning, and I still need to stop at the pharmacy." Kennedy grabbed some of the empty plates and dumped them in the sink.

"You think you can give me a ride home, Kennedy? Gretchen drove us all here, and now I don't have a way to get home." Bess folded over the bag of chips and dropped them in her purse.

Kennedy wiped her hands on her pants. "Shouldn't be a problem. Where do you live?"

Bess hitched her purse over her shoulder and beamed at Kennedy. "Over off of Anderson. Just a couple of miles from here."

"Sounds good." Kennedy leaned over and wrapped her arm around me. "I'll see ya later, hon. I'm glad we were able to work everything out. We should try to do a girl's night sometime."

I nodded, agreeing that it'd be good to spend the night out having fun for once. "I'll mention it to Sage. She needs to get out more."

Bess and Kennedy left, and I was once again alone.

I closed my eyes and leaned back in my chair. That sucked. Like, rip my heart out *suck.*

Kellan seemed to be the only one who was actually pissed off. Dante had talked to me, and the other two had never actually spoken to me before, so I couldn't really gauge if they were pissed, but it didn't seem like it.

Was Kellan upset that Gavin had come to see me at the cafe? But, why? I hadn't told Gavin to come see me. He had basically insisted on coming to the cafe, and he was a grown man. I couldn't tell him what to do. I wasn't interested in Gavin at all. When I had first met him, he had been handsome and nice to me, but after Wednesday night, I discovered we were not a good match. He was much too pushy, and to be honest, a bit full of himself.

Some would say Kellan was the same, full of himself, but that's not how he came across to me. He was confident and knew what he wanted out of life. Not to mention, sexy as sin.

Ugh, I needed to either figure what was going on between us or stop thinking about him. I was liable to go crazy if I kept going the way we were.

I needed to talk to him and just get things straightened out. Apparently, he must have thought that something was going on with Gavin and me. From the outside looking in, I'm sure that's what it looked like.

I stood up and headed to the kitchen and cranked on the oven. After I had the flour, sugar, and cocoa on the counter, I had a solid plan of what I was going to do.

Kellan was going to find out what exactly I wanted, and the way I was going to do it was through his stomach. Then, hopefully, he'd kiss me, and a whole lot more.

****

Kellan

"You gonna tell me why you were such a dick to Molly, or are we just going to act like that didn't happen?"

I fidgeted in my seat and leaned my head back. "I don't know what you are talking about."

Roman glanced at me then turned his eyes back to the road. He had insisted on driving, and I was more than okay with that. I was so much on edge that I'm pretty sure I would have driven the damn car off the road, and not even blinked.

I knew she was going to be there tonight, but seeing her after tasting her sweet lips again was more than I could take. Especially knowing Gavin was more than likely going to be tasting her too.

"I thought you liked her?"

I growled low. "And I thought you said relationships only make guys into pussies. The fact that you are questioning me why I'm not with Molly is fucking confusing to me right now. I figured you would be the one who would be happy that there is no Molly and me."

"Well, at the time, I didn't realize what *not* being with Molly would do to you. You're acting like a goddamn bear with a stick in his paw, and refusing to let anyone help you."

"I don't need fucking help. I wasn't looking for a damn relationship, so it's probably for the best that she found someone else."

Roman flipped on his blinker and exited the highway. "Well, from the way she was looking at you tonight, I think you're the only one thinking it's for the best."

"So, is this all you're going to talk about all weekend, or can we just move on?"

Roman shook his head. "Hey, if what you want is for me to move on, fine. Moving on."

I slouched down in my seat and watched the trees whirl by. We were half an hour away from the tournament, and I was ready to get out of the car. Roman was in an exceptionally good mood, and it was clashing with my shitty one.

"You think Jim is going to be here?" Roman asked,

"I would expect so. He's always lurking around at the tournaments." Jim always seemed to be around.

"You ever miss it?"

I looked at Roman. "The endless practices, never knowing where you were going to be sleeping, or Jim always yelling at us. Which one of those do you think I would miss?"

"It wasn't all that bad. When we first started out, it was fucking awesome."

I scoffed and turned back to the window. "That's because we didn't know any better." The first couple of years were pretty awesome. We were treated like rock stars, and we even had the occasional groupie who wanted to show us her appreciation behind closed doors. But then it had all changed when the competition started getting tougher. Jim telling us if we weren't competing, then we better be in the dojo practicing our asses off. I loved karate, but Jim made me hate it for a while.

"It was, Roman, but that was because we were young, and didn't know how we should be treated."

Roman tapped his fingers on the steering wheel. "I can't wait for the day that we get kids from the school competing in tournaments. Kicking ass and taking names, hopefully."

I nodded. "We'll get there someday. Right now, we've got a good three years before we have any original black belts come up in the school."

"Are we transferring over the red and blue belts that applied?"

"Yeah. I was planning on letting them know on Monday. They are going to have to go through each belt level to prove they know everything, but I don't see that as being a problem." Malaki and Titus were going to fit in just right with Powerhouse. We had given them one month of classes free to see if they were going to make it at Powerhouse, and after the first two classes, Dante and I decided that they were perfect. Titus was one hell of a sparrer, and Malaki's forms were solid. We would be going to under-belt tournaments in no time.

"You need to talk to Molly."

I slammed my hand on the dash. "Mother fucker. I thought we had moved on from this!"

"We did. I just needed to get that in there."

I pulled my hood over my eyes and leaned back into the seat. Molly was the one thing I didn't want to think or talk about. There was no way what I had heard was wrong. Who tells someone they would love to go out with them and then not go out with them? Did she look upset when we had walked into the cafe tonight? Yes. But she also had looked hot as fuck. Probably dressed up for her date with Gavin. I had never seen her out of her normal work attire, and it had been a kick to the gut when she had stood up.

Her curves were perfectly outlined in her tight jeans and white shirt that begged for me to touch and taste. I could tell she had been nervous and scared when we had walked in, but I had tried to keep my eyes off her. When she had stood, I had nowhere to look but at her.

Roman turned into the hotel where the tournament was being held, and drove up and down the aisles looking for a parking spot. "Jesus, was it always this packed when we competed?" I asked.

"Yeah, but we didn't notice, because we were always the first ones here, and the last ones to leave." Roman found a spot in the way back and shifted the car into park. "And Jim barely ever let us out of the hotel."

I opened my door and headed around to the trunk. "How did we have him as our coach for over six years?"

"We liked the fame, man. And the chicks." Roman winked and opened the trunk.

We grabbed our bags, and I was thankful I had packed light. The trek to the front desk was going to be a hike.

Roman shut the trunk, and we swung our bags onto our backs. "If you had the chance, and Jim wasn't there, would you go back?" I pondered.

"Yes, in a fucking heartbeat." Roman instantly replied. "Jim was the reason I quit. I love this shit, man. The fucking rush you get when you make it to grands, and step out on that big stage with the lights pounding down on you? Fucking amazing."

Roman always had been the show boat out of all of us. Not that any of us were shy, but it had always been Roman who had shown the brightest and excelled under pressure. "You could go back now. Use Powerhouse as your sponsor. You know we've got your back."

We were halfway to the front door before he answered. "It's not the same. I mean," he looked around and shook his head, "I am pumped to be here tonight, but it doesn't feel the same without Dante and Tate here. We were a fucking team that dominated. I come back, and I'll be known as the washed up kid that couldn't seem to cut it in the real world."

I laughed. "Washed up? You are fucking far from that. You're twenty-seven years old, not ninety. And, you can still spin that bo faster than a fucking airplane propeller, man. You know you still fucking got it."

"I talked to Sue about it."

"Damn, you must really be serious if you spoke to Sue about." Roman's parents weren't alive, and Sue had stepped in to fill the void his parents dying left.

"Just thinking," Roman mumbled.

We made it to the front doors, and the lobby was crowded with people milling around. "Shit man, are you sure we're going to be able to get a room?"

He smirked. "I booked a suite three months ago."

I grabbed his shoulder. "Hold on. Are you admitting to the fact that you actually planned something?"

Roman laughed and shrugged off my hand. "Yeah, but don't get used to it." He sauntered off to the front desk, and I wandered into the small cafe next to the gift shop.

The intoxicating smell of fresh roasted coffee hit my nose, and I looked behind the counter, expecting to see Molly standing there.

"What can I get you?"

I looked at the barely out of high school teenage boy in a dark green apron and shook my head. The Java Spot is not where I was. "Um, a latte?" I had no idea what the drink was called that Molly made me. Normally, when I ordered coffee, it was black.

The kid rolled his eyes. "What flavor? Regular or Skinny?"

I scratched my head and looked at the board behind him. "How about you just make me something that tastes good?"

He huffed and pressed a couple of buttons on the register. "I at least need to know what size you want."

It was after eight, but I knew the tournament would still be going on until well after ten. "Give me the biggest you got."

The kid took my money, acting like I was a complete bother, then turned around to make my coffee.

Roman sauntered into the coffee shop and leaned against the counter. "Should have known that you were in here."

"I need something to keep me awake."

Roman shook his head and laughed. "You don't find it ironic that you never would have stepped foot in this coffee shop before you met Molly? Now I leave you alone for five minutes, and this is where you go? I thought for sure you would have wandered over to the tournament."

"I didn't come in here because of Molly." I grabbed my cup from the barista and walked into the hotel. "I went in there because I wanted a coffee."

Roman punched the button for the elevator. "Keep telling yourself that, man. But the sooner you realize that Molly is affecting you even when she isn't here, the better off you'll be."

I flipped him off, took a drink of my coffee, and abruptly spat it out on the wall of the elevator. "What the fuck is this shit?" I sputtered, trying to get the awful taste out of my mouth.

Roman was bent over laughing, holding onto the wall. "Holy fuck…your face…" he gasped as he continued to laugh like a jackass.

"Is it too much to ask for a guy to get a decent cup of coffee?" I wiped off my mouth and set the rancid coffee on the floor.

Roman stood up and put a hand on his stomach. "I do know of a place where you can get a good one."

The elevator dinged, and the doors slid open. I grabbed the cup of coffee, flipped off Roman, and stepped onto our floor. I dropped the cup into the trash can by the elevator and waited for Roman to pull it together and haul his ass off the elevator.

All I wanted to do was drop my bag in the room, figure out where the tournament was, and not think of Molly anymore. The first two weren't going to be a problem. The forgetting Molly was going to be a lot harder than I thought.

****

Molly

I was having a major case of déjà vu.

It was Saturday morning, and I was standing at the door of Powerhouse with a box full of brownies, and a large cup of coffee. The lights were on inside, but I couldn't see anyone moving around.

I had left Bess manning the counter at the cafe, so I could come over here and beg Kellan to tell me what I did to upset him. Then, I planned to fix it and hoped he'd kissed me. A lot. I was especially looking forward to the kissing part.

With the cup in the crook of my arm, I managed to pull the door open and stumble in. I always seemed to stumble into Powerhouse. One day, I'd like to not make a fool of myself here. That day was obviously not today.

"Molly!" Tate walked out of the back office and leaned against the front desk. "You taking class again today?"

I set the coffee down and wiped my hand on my pants. I hadn't calculated Tate being here. "Oh, um, no."

"She brought me cookies, didn't she?" Dante called. I peeked around Tate and saw Dante sitting behind the desk in the office. "Molly has the best cookies."

"Cookies?" Tate asked.

I clenched the box to my chest and shook my head. These guys were savages when it came to sweets of any kind. "No cookies today. I was actually hoping to talk to Kellan for a second."

Tate turned around and looked at Dante. Dante pushed back from the desk. "He's not here right now, Molly."

Well, that blew my plan out of the water. I had thought for sure that Powerhouse opened at nine on Saturdays. "Oh, well I guess I can wait for him to come in."

Tate shook his head. "He's not going to be in today, Molly."

Dante stood next to Tate and look down at me. "He went to a tournament with Roman. They left after the meeting last night."

My shoulders sagged. Of course. I had finally gotten the courage up to talk to Kellan, and he had left. "Oh, well, then I guess I'll just leave these for you guys. I'm sure Kellan would have shared them with you anyway." I thrust the box into Tate's hands.

Tate opened the box and licked his lips. "Holy fuck, brownies."

Dante grabbed one, took a huge bite, and moaned. "There's no way Kellan would have shared these with us. Every time Ma makes brownies, he gets the whole pan, and we get shit. Serves him right not to be here."

Tate took a brownie out and shut the box. "Yeah, he definitely isn't getting any of these. We will tell him you stopped by, though."

I nodded my head. "Thanks," I whispered. There were four different kinds of brownies in the box, and I had slaved over them all night. Now, Dante and Tate were going to eat them all, and I had no chance of talking to Kellan. Mission: fail. "I'll see you guys around."

They both waved, their mouths full of brownies, and I headed back to the cafe. At least they seemed to be enjoying them.

"You're back already? I knew it wouldn't take much to get that boy to see he was an ass."

I plastered a smile on my face and grabbed my apron off the hook. "Yup, I'm back."

Bess crossed her arms over her chest and tapped her foot. "Well, spill, chick. I need to know what that hunk of man did when you gave him the brownies."

"Well, Tate and Dante ate them."

Bess held up her hand. "Hold on, did we switch teams here? Are you trying to see if my ménage books are real? Trying to get some two-way kung fu action?"

A laugh escaped my lips, even though I was feeling anything but happy. "No. Kellan wasn't there, so I gave them to the guys."

"Well, you should have waited for him to show up."

I shook my head. "I think I would have been waiting until Monday night. He's out of town at some karate thing. He went with Roman."

Bess scowled. "Oh damn, I liked my story better. Maybe you should go after Tate and Dante. You've already got them hooked with the cookies and brownies."

"I can barely get one man, Bess. I think I'll leave the ménage to your romance books."

She tsked and started wiping down the counter. "Ain't nothing wrong with bringing a little romance novel to real life. We all need to find our Prince Charming who can fuck us all night then go out to get donuts in the morning."

I sighed and grabbed an empty cup. "I'd settle for just finding a guy that wants to be near me."

Bess tossed the rag into the sink and patted my shoulder. "It'll come, hon. If all else fails, there is always Frank's son. I heard he broke up with his internet girlfriend." Bess snickered and moved toward the door. "Love always wins, Molly. Even in real life." She raised her hand, waved to me, and disappeared out the door.

Love always win? Phfft. Love was taunting me right now, and I was getting ready to throw in the towel.

All I was winning was a load full of confusion, and a one-way ticket to heartache. Kellan had dropkicked my heart, and I had no way to get back up.

I was down for the count.

****
Kellan

"He made it to the grands. If he doesn't, he was robbed."

Roman and I were sitting at ring fourteen, watching the fourteen to seventeen-year-old black belts compete in creative weapons. This was the age where you could see who was going to be great. Some of these kids had been black belts for close to ten years, and they were only sixteen or seventeen. "I don't know, man. I think the judges might be leaning towards the first chick that went."

Roman shook his head and crossed his arms over his chest. "If they do, they're ridiculous. She bobbled."

She had, but she had gone on, and to the untrained eye, you didn't see it. Now, the judges should be the ones to see it, but if they were looking down at their notepads, they missed the half-second slip. "I agree that he was better, but you know how this shit goes, man. It's not always about who does it best." I couldn't tell you how many times I had put my heart and soul out there, giving it everything I had, and then had the trophy given to a kid who knew the right people. But each time that happened, it made me strive to work even harder so that the next time I went up against them, they wouldn't have a choice but to give me the trophy.

The seven competitors stood in front of the three judges, waiting for their scores.

The first kid stepped forward. "Third," Roman mumbled.

With each one who stepped forward, Roman mumbled the place he thought they should get. While he was doing that, I was mentally adding up the scores. "He got it," I whispered to Roman.

"He damn well better have."

The judges stood and bowed to the competitors. They started with seventh place, working their way up. The last two standing were the guy and girl who were the best who had competed.

"Takes you back to when you were as good as they were."

I knew that voice, and I didn't want to turn around. We both had seen Jim wandering the past day, but we had been able to avoid him. Until now.

Roman and I turned around in our seats to see Jim had sat in the row behind us. "Jim," I mumbled.

Jim crossed his arms over his chest and propped his feet on the back of my chair. "I have to say, I was rather surprised to see you two here. When you guys left me high and dry, I figured you knew not to show your faces around here anymore."

"Last I checked, this wasn't a Cornerstone tournament," Roman replied. Jim ran three tournaments throughout the year, but regionals weren't part of them. We knew that a Cornerstone tournament was not a place for Powerhouse to be unless we wanted to be treated like shit. But it looked like Jim didn't care that this wasn't his tournament.

Jim shrugged. "I'm just here to help keep the integrity of all of the tournaments up. I sure hope you're not here trying to find sponsors. I've let everyone know what kind of people you two are."

I was sure Jim had gone out of his way to tell anyone who would listen to his side of the story. Which was all bullshit. "I didn't think the word integrity was in your vocabulary."

Jim glared at me. He knew not to mess with me. While Roman was the hot headed one who spoke before thinking, he was aware I could destroy him if I wanted to. Jim had royally fucked the four of us over the past years, but we had never publicly said anything. A few perfectly placed words in the right ears could send Jim's notoriety on the circuit down in flames. "What are you two doing here? Everyone knows you think you're too good to be here."

I shook my head and rested my arm on the back of my chair. "And I wonder where they could have gotten that idea from? Plenty of people have walked away from the circuit before, Jim. I don't know why you took our leaving so hard. Look around, there are hundreds of kids around here who would love to be able to have you as their coach and sponsor." There were. You couldn't walk ten feet around here without running into someone who didn't know who Jim or Cornerstone M.A. were. What they didn't know was how big of an asshole Jim was to work for. Don't even get me started on the cut and missing wages all of the time.

Jim's eyes narrowed. He knew he was reaching the end of his leash before I would rip into him. The difference between Jim and me was, I didn't give a fuck what people thought about me. I wasn't here to impress anyone or find some unsuspecting kid to steal money from and pay pennies to win the tournaments. "I don't need to be looking. I've already found what I was looking for." He leaned forward and rested his forearms on the back of our chairs. "You just watched her win."

Of course. I should have known Jim would have his teeth sunk into one of those kids. I was more surprised he hadn't signed the boy. "She was all right," Roman agreed. "Although, the boy was flawless. Much better than she was."

"Yeah," I agreed. "Couldn't find a number significant enough that he would bite on?" Odds are, Jim probably low-balled the kid too much, and the kid went elsewhere. Jim always was a cheap bastard who only cared about lining his own pockets.

When you got on the circuit, you needed a sponsor. There was no other way to afford all of the travel and expenses. That was where Jim came in, throwing around money, and then he thought he owned you. Jim had pushed us to win, and when we brought home the big cash prize, he would take his more than generous cut, claiming he had made us.

"Gotta look for the diamond in the rough, boys. Girls kicking ass are all the rage right now. I'm already in talks to have her in a movie."

And this was the reason why people gravitated to Jim. He had so many connections to movies and stunt work that it was understandable people would be blinded when they first met him. It was after all the new and shiny wore off that you realize he's screwing you over. Roman and Dante had done stunt work a handful of times, but barely made pennies when everything was said and done. "And I bet you're taking care of all of the contracts for her too, aren't ya, Jimmy?" Roman sneered.

Jim's face turned red, and he grunted. He hated when he was called anything but Jim. It used to be Roman's game to call him anything else to rile him up. "I don't think that's any of your business."

I shook my head and turned back around. Jim was still a piece of work. I felt sorry for whoever fell for his line of bullshit.

"But it looks like you put your money on the wrong horse, Jimbo," Roman said, laughing. "Looks like your girl didn't take first."

The girl looked crestfallen, and her arms hung heavily at her side. She wasn't bad at all; she just wasn't up to par with the boy. She had definite potential, but she had the wrong coach on her side. Jim was going to sell her being a girl, more than the fact she was a kick-ass martial artist. "Pfft," Jim scoffed. "This tournament ain't nothing. Besides, she still gets a hefty amount of points in the rankings. I'm not worried one bit."

Jim was right, to a point. You didn't need to always get first to take home first overall, but it sure boosted one's confidence if they did. Jim stood up, his massive girth and staggering height looming over us. "You might want to take some notes on how to make a superstar, boys, if you plan on bringing your rinky-dink Powerhouse to play at the tournaments anytime soon." A smirk touched his lips. "Cornerstone always comes to win." He lumbered over to the girl and put his arm around her shoulder. Her mother was there and instantly started talking off Jim's ear. They disappeared into the crowd leaving the ring.

"You as surprised as I am that she lost with Jim being her coach?" Roman asked.

I shrugged and crossed my ankles. "Yes and no. I think Jim has some pull, but when they are that far apart in skill, there is no way they could give her first without people wondering what in the hell is going on." Jim rigged shit. It was always rumored on the circuit but never verified.

I stood up and moved to the ring. "Hey, where you going?" Roman called as he followed me.

"Someone needs to congratulate the kid," I replied over my shoulder.

He was looking down at the card with a big one on it that the judges had given him.

"Good job, man," I boomed as I clapped him on the shoulder. "That was pretty fucking tight out there."

The boy tipped his face up, and his eyes went wide as he realized who I was. "Holy crap," he proclaimed. "You're Kellan Wright." He turned to Roman, and his jaw dropped. "And you're Roman Yeck."

Roman held his hand out. "I sure am," he smirked. "And what's your name, kid?"

The kid dropped his card and grabbed Roman's hand. "I'm Ryker. I used to watch you compete all of the time. I still watch all of your videos on YouTube. You handle a bo staff like no one I've ever seen before."

Roman brushed off the compliment. As much as he liked being the center of attention, he never let it go to his head. "I don't know about that. The way I saw you spinning the shit out of that bo puts you in equal competition with me. How old are you?"

I bent over to pick up the kid's card. He may be star struck now meeting Roman and me, but he was going to want this card if he wanted to claim his big ass trophy.

"I just turned sixteen."

"Right on. What dojo do you practice under?"

"Uh, right now, I don't have one. I just moved here a couple of months ago."

Roman looked over at me. He was thinking the same exact thing I was. This kid needed to be part of Powerhouse. "You ever heard of Powerhouse? We're a new dojo, but we've hit the ground running. We're always looking for new students."

Ryker's eyes darted to the floor, and he shook his head. "Um, yeah, I've heard of it."

"Why don't you come in and see if you like it?" I suggested.

He shook his head and grabbed the card out of my hand. "As much as I'd like to, I can't."

"Why not?" Roman demanded. He wanted this kid at Powerhouse as much as I did.

"I moved here to live with my aunt. She doesn't have the money for me to continue doing karate. Thanks anyway," he mumbled.

Right there was the reason why a lot of kids stopped lessons. They weren't cheap. "Don't worry about that right now. Just come in, and we'll see where it goes." If anything, we could always have Ryker help out with classes, and in return, he could practice under Powerhouse.

His head snapped up, and his eyes darted between Roman and me. "Are you serious? I really mean it when I say I can't afford it. I asked my aunt if I got a job and paid for half if I could still do lessons, and she said she couldn't afford that."

Roman put his hand on his shoulder. "Don't worry about it, kid. Just come in when you can, and we'll talk."

"I can't believe this is happening," he mumbled.

"Believe it, kid," I said, assuring him.

"Go get your trophy, and we'll see you around," Roman added.

Ryker stumbled away, a huge grin on his face. "Thank you so much, Mr. Wright and Mr. Yeck," he yelled. "Um, I'll have to talk to my aunt. It'll probably take a week to convince her."

"No worries, just come when you can," I replied. He waved and turned around.

"Oh shit," I mumbled. "Hey, kid! Where do you live?" People came from all over to compete in tournaments. The kid could live on the other side of the state.

"Falls City! I walk by Powerhouse every day on my way to school," Ryker shouted over his shoulder. Well, if that wasn't a small world.

I lost sight of Ryker in the crowd, and when Roman turned his head, a huge grin spread across his lips. "Tell me you didn't plan that shit."

It wasn't exactly my intention to invite him to Powerhouse, but I wasn't opposed to it. "Hey, I can't help it that we were more impressive to him than Jim was."

Roman scoffed. "Jim probably wanted him to pay a shit ton just to step into Cornerstone."

We weaved through the crowd, stopping here and there to watch the competitors. I grabbed a chair in the back row by the main stage and pulled my phone out.

"Checking in with Tate and Dante?" Roman asked. He grabbed the chair next to me, flipped it around, and straddled it.

There weren't any messages from them, and I was actually surprised. I expected at least one phone call and a couple of text messages. I swiped across Dante's name and put the phone to my ear. It went directly to voicemail. "Hey, it's Kellan. I was just checking in to see how classes went today. Hit me back when you get the chance."

I called Tate with the same result.

"Neither of them answered?" Roman asked.

I shoved my phone in my pocket and looked at the stage. Twenty-five and up black belt traditional forms were running, and I knew each and every guy up there on stage. They had all been my competition before. "I'm sure they're busy doing private lessons. They had a full afternoon of them."

"I'm sure that's what's going on."

I twisted my head around to look at him. "What does that mean?"

"It could mean they're over at the cafe eating Molly's cookies."

I growled and elbowed him in the side. "Shut the fuck up."

"Not much you can do about it, man. You walked away from Molly. Can't really blame Tate or Dante if they go after her now. You know how Dante is about her cookies."

I leaned back in my chair. "Talk about Molly's fucking cookies one more time, and I'll beat the shit out of you right here."

Roman chuckled and crossed his arms over her chest. "As much as I'd like to see you try, I think you need to think about what you just said." He stood up and looked down at me. "You don't say that shit about a chick you don't care about." Roman wandered over to the next ring, and I turned back to the main stage.

So what if I didn't want Dante or Tate dating Molly. Or even Gavin. That didn't mean a damn thing.

Molly could date whoever she wanted.

I just didn't want to know about it, and if she dated any of my friends or Gavin, I was going to beat the shit out of them.

Easy as that. Didn't mean a damn thing.

I took a deep breath and tried to push her out of my mind. I had gone most of the morning not thinking about her. But now that Roman had mentioned Dante and Tate being only a short walk away from her, it was bugging the fucking shit out of me.

I called Dante one more time and waited for the beep of his voicemail. "Listen, fucker. You better stay far away from Molly. No one gets her cookies but me." I punched the end button and clutched the phone in my hand.

There, that solved that.

Now I just looked like a possessive asshole to a chick I had no right to feel that way about.

"Smooth, Kellan," I mumbled.

I was so fucked.

****

Molly

"Go."

"No."

"Yes."

"No."

"Now."

"No."

Sage slammed the tray of cookies on the counter and propped her hands on her hips. "Get your ass moving, before I drag you by your ponytail over there."

"This isn't really a side of you I like," I muttered.

"Well, it's a good thing we're not talking about me right now. We are talking about you and Kung Fu Hottie. I'm still hurt that you didn't call and tell me how the meeting went."

I rolled my eyes. "Reliving that night was not something I wanted to do."

"Or, how you went over there Saturday."

I was going to kill Bess. As soon as Sage walked in the door, Bess had been right behind her, ready to tell her about my crash and burn weekend. "You're not allowed to talk to Bess anymore."

Bess cackled from the corner. "Good luck with that one, sweetheart," she called.

"Take off the apron, fluff up your hair, and get your ass over there."

I giggled and touched my head. "What? Fluff up my hair? Do you know who you are talking to, Sage? I don't fluff." Ponytail matted to my head, that was what I did. Everyday.

She threw her hands up in the air. "Then just take off the damn apron, and go get your man." She thrust a box full of cookies at me and pointed to the door. "You have five seconds. Five…four…three…"

"All right, all right," I caved. "I'll freakin' go. It's not like he's going to want to see me." I reached around and untied my apron. "If he wanted to talk to me, he wouldn't have left me with an empty storeroom and complete and utter confusion."

"No, he wouldn't have," Sage agreed. "But we're talking about a man here, and half the time, they don't even know what they are doing."

"Amen, sista!" The Moaners yelled.

"When did my cafe become the Jerry Springer show with me being the main attraction and the Moaners the rowdy crowd? Huh, Sage?" I pulled my apron over my head and tossed it on the counter. "I'll be back in five minutes. Have a huge pot of coffee and a tray of cookies ready for me to drown my confirmed heartache in when Kellan tells me to get lost."

Sage shoved the box of cookies she had packed up into my hands. "I doubt I'll see you the rest of the day. Kellan isn't stupid."

"Get your man, hon!"

"Give the ol' pow pow!"

"Show him what you're working with!" Each Moaner shouted.

I made it halfway to the door and stopped. "What if he's not there, and what is pow pow?"

The Moaners cackled. Bess stood up moved her hips side to side. "That is pow pow, honey." They all erupted into laughter, and I knew any advice from them was sketchy, at best.

"Don't make me have to count to five," Sage shouted. She held up one finger, "One."

"Oh, for Pete's sake. You are all crazy." I flounced out the door and headed around the building. Once I made it around the corner, I pressed my back to the building and looked up.

"What am I doing?" It was Wednesday afternoon, and somehow Sage and the Moaners had worn me down, convincing me I needed to go and talk to Kellan. I hadn't seen him since the meeting, and I wasn't sure he was going to want to see me now.

I had tried to act like nothing was wrong, and I was okay with Kellan and me not talking anymore, but it was killing me. I had no idea what I had done.

"Molly?"

Oh crap. I dropped my head and saw Roman standing in front of me. "You're like a ninja."

Roman ran his hand through his hair and chuckled. "Um, thanks?"

I shook my head, trying to get words to form that made sense. "I mean, I didn't even hear you walk over, like a silent ninja." Silent ninja? Sweet Jesus.

"Oh, yeah." He shoved his hands in his pockets and looked at the box in my hands. "You heading over to Powerhouse?"

My eyes dropped to the box in my hands. "I was just going for a walk, and thought I'd drop some cookies off." Why did I always have to act like a fool in front of these guys? A walk, really?

Roman smirked, and his eyes smiled at me. Yes, I swear they smiled at me. They just sparkled, and looked, well, happy. Roman looked younger than the other guys, and he just had a way about him that made me want to tell him everything. I clamped my lips shut, praying I would not spew my verbal diarrhea about Kellan all over him.

"Well, I think I'll head over to the cafe for a bit and grab a cup of coffee. Kellan should be able to take those cookies off your hands for you." Roman winked and slid his sunglasses over his eyes. "Tell Kellan to call me." He sauntered around the building, and I watched him 'til he disappeared.

Well, that makes one of the Powerhouse guys I made a fool of myself in front of today.

Time to see if I was going to do the same in front of Kellan.

****

Kellan

Gum.

Fucking gum everywhere.

I was going to personally check every kid's mouth before they walked through the door. I had been pulling gum off the bottoms of the chairs the past half an hour, and I was slowly going insane.

One second, I was moving chairs around, moping the floor, and the next, I was on my hands and knees with a damn screwdriver scraping the bottoms of the chairs.

I managed to scrape a huge wad off, and I held it up. "And this is your life, Kellan." Gone were the days of bringing home trophies and chicks throwing themselves at me. Now, I was a kid wrangler and gum scraper.

I chucked it in the trash with the other pieces. Gum was now outlawed at Powerhouse.

It was half past two, and I still had the other half of the chairs to look over. Thankfully, Roman had said he would come in early to help clean. Little did he know he was going to be in charge of checking the rest of the chairs.

I stood up, arching to stretch my back. The damn mattress at the hotel had fucked up my back. I had meant to get to the chiropractor all week but never seemed to remember until I was in the middle of class, or they were closed.

Even bowing onto the mat made me cringe. I laid down on the edge of the mat, behind the half wall separating the chairs from the mat, and stretched my arms over my head.

I heard the front door open. "About time you got here, fucker. You get the honor of scraping the rest of the gum off of the chairs." His footsteps sounded on the floor, and I closed my eyes, ready for his smart-ass come back.

"I brought cookies."

My eyes snapped open, and Molly was standing over me, biting her lip. "Shit," I whispered.

"I always seem to make a fool of myself in front of you, so I figured I might as well start embracing my awkwardness." She held the box out to me. "Hi."

I grabbed the box from her hands and set it on the mat next to me. "Uh, hey. Sorry I called you fucker. I was expecting Roman."

"He's over at the coffee shop. I saw him on the way over here."

She was leaning against the half wall, and I couldn't stop staring at her. Molly was like no other woman I had ever met. She looked just like she had the first day she had walked over with cookies—her dark brown hair piled on top of her head, skin flush, and her gorgeous green eyes trained only on me. The only difference was she didn't have her usual apron on.

"Don't tell me you could hear me cussing all the way in the cafe," I joked.

She went back to biting her lip and shook her head.

"Need a new name for a drink? I'm sure the mocha-latte-whip-a-bullshit is your best seller."

A smile spread across her lips. "I think I have that covered. I don't think I can call all of my drinks whip-a-bullshits."

I gingerly sat up and leaned back on my arms. "I can keep guessing all day if that's what you want me to do."

She cleared her throat and looked anywhere but at me. "I thought I would just come over, and you know, talk," she mumbled.

"We got something we need to talk about? I thought everything got taken care of at the meeting Friday night." I was damn glad she had come over, but I had no idea where this was going.

Her hands were clasped on the wall, and she shook her head. "I actually wanted to talk about before the meeting." She pursed her lips, and finally looked at me. "If you want to," she added.

"Talk, cookie."

She sighed and reached up to tuck her hair behind her ear. "So, when Sage had called me out front when we were in the closet, um, you know."

"Kissing, Molly. I was kissing you." A blush flooded her cheeks at my words. I wasn't going to act like it didn't happen. I'm sure she was here to make sure I didn't mention anything to Gavin when he was in class. Finding out the chick you just started dating had been making out with some other guy probably wasn't a good start to a relationship.

"Yeah, you were. But when I came back, you were gone."

I shook my head and laid back down. "Are we really going to do this, Molly? I was gone because you agreed to go out with Gavin. I promise I won—"

"What?" Molly gasped. "I did not agree to go out with Gavin." She wrinkled her nose in disgust.

"That's not what I heard."

"What do you mean? I'm pretty sure I know what I said to Gavin. The man asked me out two times, and each time I told him no. The last time at the cafe, he finally got the hint that I'm not interested."

"Molly, I heard you say that you would love to."

She shook her head and leaned over the wall. "I told him I'd love to, but I have to wash my hair every night for the rest of my life. If that's not saying no, then I don't know what is."

What? That did sound like something Molly would say. She was a bit awkward, but it was cute as fuck. At least, to me, it was. "That's not what I heard."

"How long did you stick around for?"

"I heard you say you'd love to, and then I booked it out the door."

Molly rolled her eyes. "You probably should have stuck around for the rest. He got pissed off and left without paying for his coffee."

Holy fuck, how did I get that so wrong?

"So, is that why you left? I was five seconds away from letting you take me right there on the storeroom floor. You really think I could do that with you, and then agree to go out with someone else in the next breath."

I ran my hand through my hair. Now, I looked like a complete ass. Did I think Molly could kiss me then go out with someone else? No. But I didn't know what else to think when I had heard her talking to Gavin. "I'm an ass."

Molly laughed. "Yup, I think we established that before."

"So, this whole time, we could have been doing a lot more kissing instead of avoiding each other, huh?"

Molly pushed off the wall and headed towards the door.

"Molly, wait!" I shouted as I sprung up. "Don't leave." I had been a fucking idiot before. I didn't want to make the same mistake again.

She laughed and looked over her shoulder. "I'm not," she whispered. She slipped off her shoes and pulled off her socks. "I can't come on the mat with my shoes on, can I?" She shouldn't, but at this point, I would let her do anything as long as she didn't leave. She slowly walked back to me, her hips swaying side to side. "I don't want to piss off the karate gods."

And that right there was a perfect example of what drew me to Molly. She said what she wanted, and didn't care if she sounded like a nut. Although, from the cringe on her face, she might care a little bit about what people though. "Karate gods?"

She flitted her hand around. "You know, karate gods."

I chuckled and reached my hand out to her. "No, I think you're going to have to explain that one to me."

She gently rested her hand on mine, and a blush rose on her cheeks. She slightly bowed and stepped on the mat. "Sometimes, it's just best to go with whatever comes out of my mouth."

"I'll have to remember that, cookie." I pulled her close, rested her hand on my chest, and wrapped my arm around her waist. "So, you forgive me for being an ass?"

She quirked her eyebrow and shook her head. "I think there might be some groveling in your future. You did, after all, think I was some hussy kissing you and going out with Gavin."

"I didn't think you were a hussy."

She smirked and shook her head. "Mmhmm."

I leaned in and pressed a kiss behind her ear. "So, tell me what I need to do to make it up to you," I whispered.

She hummed and tilted her head. "I think maybe you could start with a date. Dinner?"

I trailed my fingers up and down her back. "Are you asking me out, Molly? I thought I was supposed to be the one groveling here."

She smacked me on the chest. "I wasn't the one doing the asking. You asked me what you needed to do to make it—"

I pressed a finger to her lips. "Shh, cookie. I'm just giving you hell." She gave a little growl, and a grin spread across my mouth.

"Gee, I never noticed that you liked to give me shit. I had a stray straggler come in the other day wondering if I still owned my sailboat."

I scoffed and buried my face in her neck. "I really need to delete that dating profile."

She wrapped her arms around my neck and leaned back. "Please do. I think that will be step one on your path to redemption."

"Path of redemption, huh? I think you might be enjoying this idea of groveling more than you should."

"I promise it won't be a long path. Just a couple steps."

I cradled her face in my hands and looked down at her. "And this path ends with you?"

She closed her eyes and leaned into my hand. "If you're lucky."

"I'm feeling damn lucky, cookie." I pressed my lips to hers, and she melted into me. Her arms tightened around my neck, and she delved her fingers into my hair. This was what I fucking needed. I had been planning on going over to the cafe tomorrow, because I was desperate to see her, even if she was dating Gavin.

She moaned against my lips, and my tongue slipped into her mouth. Molly responded to my touch, her body yielding to me. "Wrap your legs around me," I mumbled against her lips.

"The last time you said that, you left two minutes later."

I grabbed her ass, and she lifted her legs. "It's gonna end a whole lot differently this time."

****

Molly

I landed on the couch in the office, and Kellan covered me with his body. "What if someone comes in?" I gasped as his mouth assaulted my neck.

"We'll hear the door open."

I didn't know how true that was. If Kellan was touching me, all I could focus on was him. Once I had laid my hand in his, I knew coming over here today was the best decision I had ever made.

"Where's your apron?"

His teeth tugged on the lobe of my ear, and I gasped. "My apron?"

"Yeah, Cookie. I've been dreaming of taking the damn thing off you and having my way with you."

I giggled and ran my fingers through his hair. "You do know, if you take my apron off, I still have clothes on."

He lifted his head and looked down at me. "My fantasy was more of you wearing only the apron."

I mentally made a note to bring an apron home. "Fantasy? About me?"

He smirked, and his eyes heated. "Mmhmm, that one, and then there's this one we're working on right now. You and me, breaking in the couch." His hands went to the hem of my shirt, and he slowly raised it.

"I didn't have this on the path to redemption."

He leaned down and pressed a kiss to my stomach. "Detour, Cookie."

A shiver ran through my body, and I gasped as he lifted the shirt higher, exposing my bra. "Kellan, I don't think—"

His head came up, and he licked his lips. "Just a taste, Molly. I just need a taste to hold me over."

His tongue circled my navel, and his hands went to the button on my pants. All thought fled as the button slid from the hole, and he worked the zipper down. "Lift," he ordered.

I raised my hips, and he slid my pants down, exposing my panties. I frantically searched my mind, trying to remember what panties I had put on today.

"Is that...are those...My Little Pony?"

Oh, sweet heaven above, today had to be the day I wore *these* panties? I closed my eyes and wished I would sink into the couch and disappear. Kellan's body shook with laughter, and I knew my disappearing act wasn't working. "Can we just move on from this and never talk about it again?"

His hand cupped my pussy, and he pressed a kiss to the inside of my thigh. "Not likely. Although, it makes me wonder what other panties you have." He hooked his fingers in the waist of my questionable underwear and worked them down my legs. "I'm really more into what's under them."

Kellan sat back on his knees and pulled my legs up. "Kellan," I gasped.

"Drop your legs open."

I opened my legs and set one foot on the ground. "Are you sure?" I whispered. This was exactly what I wanted to be doing, but I didn't picture it would happen here.

"Shh, just a taste, Cookie." His hands trailed up my thighs, and he leaned down. "A taste will never be enough, though." He hooked his hands under my thighs and tilted my hips up.

Anticipation surged through my body as he parted the lips of my pussy, and I felt his breath on my skin. I threaded my fingers through his hair and held on as his tongue found my clit.

He rolled the bud around on his tongue, my hands gripping his head. He wound his arms around my thighs and held me down. "Easy, baby," he whispered.

"Kellan, please," I begged.

"You taste so sweet," he mumbled. He buried his face between my legs, licking, sucking and tasting me.

He flicked my clit with the tip of his tongue, and my hips rocketed off the couch. Holy fuck, did Kellan have a talented tongue? "Holy fuck," I breathed out.

"You like that, baby?"

I moaned my appreciation, and put my arms behind my head. Kellan's hand snaked up my body and pushed up my bra. The cold air drifted over my skin, and my nipple puckered under his attentive fingers. He sucked my clit into his mouth and swirled his tongue over it.

"Sweet mother Mary." My hands grasped the arm rest under my head, and my fingernails dug into the fabric. "Kellan," I gasped, feeling my release approaching.

His palmed my breast, squeezing as he nipped my clit with his teeth. "Are you going to come for me, Molly?" His voice was low and vibrated against me.

I bucked my hips up, yearning for his mouth to touch me again. "Kellan, please," I begged. This man was driving me insane, and I swear to God, he just laughed at me.

"God damn, baby. I love when you beg." I felt his lips smile against me for a brief second, and then his tongue flicked my clit. I slammed my eyes closed, feeling a full-body tremor rock through me.

I bit my lip, arching my back, never wanting Kellan to stop. "More," I purred.

His hand skated down my body, sending goosebumps along my skin. His tongue sped up, flicking my clit, while two fingers drove into me.

Stars exploded behind my eyes as my orgasm slammed into me. I chanted Kellan's name over and over as he continued to thrust his fingers in and out, drawing out my ecstasy.

One last tremor coursed through my body, and Kellan laid his head on my thigh. "Holy fuck, Molly."

I opened my eyes and looked down at Kellan. "Is that a good holy fuck?"

Kellan's eyes crinkled around the edges, and a smirk crossed his lips. "Your pussy milked my fingers so fucking hard, I swear to Christ, I was close to coming myself."

Relief swept through me, and I laid my head back. "Thank God."

"You need to stop doubting yourself, Cookie. That was the most amazing thing I've ever seen."

I laughed and sat up, leaning back on my elbows. "Think they'll make me the eighth wonder of the world?"

"You damn sure deserve it." Kellan glanced over his shoulder. "Fuck, I have class in twenty minutes. Kids are going to start showing up any minute." Kellan grabbed my bra and shirt and pulled them down.

"What?" I shouted. "Kellan, I'm half naked. Get off of me." I bucked my hips, trying to shove him off. The man was acting like it wasn't a big deal that twenty kids were about to see me naked with their teacher draped over me.

Kellan rolled off me and stood up. "Relax, Cookie. I'm the only one who gets to see your gorgeous body." He held his hand out to me and pulled me off the couch.

"Well, that's not going to happen if I don't get my pants back on."

"Yo, Kellan?"

I dropped down to the floor and slapped my hand over my mouth.

Kellan walked to the door and leaned out. "Give me five minutes, Ro." He shut the door behind him and leaned against it.

"Kellan, I'm half naked," I whispered. "And *he* is right out there."

Kellan grabbed my pants and sat down on the couch. "Come here."

I shook my head and reached for the pants. "No. I'm not touching you. My clothes seem to start falling off when that happens."

He held my pants behind his head and crooked his finger at me. "Come here, and I'll help you put them on."

I rolled my eyes but gingerly stood up. My legs were still a bit jello-y, and I stumbled over to Kellan. I put my hands on his shoulders, and he wrapped his arms around my waist, my pants now behind me. "Can I see you tonight?" he asked, looking up at me.

"Can we discuss this after I put my pants on?"

He shook his head no and tossed my pants behind the desk. "Not until you tell me I can see you again."

This man was absolutely crazy. Did he not care that one of his friends was not even ten feet away? "You can see me right now." I tried to pull out of his arms, but he tugged me into his lap, and I straddled his waist. "Kellan, I don't have any panties on," I protested, pushing at his chest.

His hands glided over my thighs, pushed up my shirt, and grabbed my ass. "I know, Cookie. That's how I like you."

"I'm starting to think you only have sex on your brain."

He shook his head and pressed a light kiss to my lips. "No, baby. I've got you on the brain. I haven't been able to focus on anything this whole damn week because no matter what I was doing, it was you I was thinking of."

I slid my hands up his chest and wound my arms around his neck. I guess if Kellan didn't care that I didn't have pants on, then why should I? "I think we both had the same problem."

"Oh, is that right? All along the cure to our problem was just next door."

I closed my eyes and leaned my forehead against his. "I really need to get my pants on, but you're not helping me."

"That's because I'm half tempted to lock the door, and not let you out until I've tasted every inch of your body. The hell with classes."

I pressed my body into him, wishing that were really a possibility. "Raincheck?" I whispered.

"Definite raincheck, Cookie."

I planted my hands on his chest, and his arms loosened around me. "And yes, by the way," I mumbled as I stood up and grabbed my pants from behind the desk.

Kellan ran his hands through his hair. "You're gonna have to remind me what the question was again."

My pants became my enemy as I struggled to untangle them. "I guess if you don't remember the question, then it wasn't important." I managed to work my pants up my legs and realized I didn't have underwear on. Son of a bitch.

Kellan had the offending My Little Pony panties hanging from his fingers with a smirk on his lips. "I think you forgot something."

"Do you have any idea how hard it was for me to get these damn pants on?" I complained.

"I guess I'll just keep these then."

My jaw dropped as he stood up and shoved them into his pocket. "Kellan, give me back my panties."

He shook his head and moved to open the door.

"Kellan, what are you doing," I protested. "I don't have my shoes on. Everyone is going to know what we were doing in here."

He looked over his shoulder at me and laughed. The damn man laughed at me again. "I hate to break it to you, Molly, but nobody else has shoes on out there, and I did just have my hands down their pants."

I crossed my arms over my chest. "I see we're back to being an ass. And I would hope you haven't had your hand down Roman's pants."

He winked at me and opened the door. "Try not to look like I just rocked your world, Cookie."

I snapped my mouth shut and glared at him. He disappeared out the door, and I heard him talk to Roman.

"Shit," I muttered. I dashed out of the office, not making eye contact with Roman and Kellan who were standing next to the front desk, and grabbed my shoes. I forgoed putting my socks back on and shoved them in my pockets. I didn't have underwear, so I might as well buck all undergarments. My feet slid into my shoes, the backs of them bent down under my feet, and I shuffled towards the door.

I was mid-shuffle of shame when Kellan called my name, but I decided escape was more important.

"Molly," he gripped my arm, but I managed to grab hold of the door, and pulled Kellan out with me.

"I need to get back to work," I mumbled.

He spun me around, wrapped his arm around my waist, and pulled me flush against him. "You gonna leave without telling me where you live?"

"403 Clarence Place. Apartment 278." My head was pointed at the ground, and I was trying not to die of embarrassment.

He hooked his finger under my chin and raised my head. "Now, kiss me goodbye."

My eyes frantically darted around, and I shook my head. "Are you crazy?" I hissed.

His hand stroked my cheek, and he leaned in, his lips a breath away from mine. "You're gonna have to get used to me touching you, Molly. I could care less who sees."

"Seriously, Kellan, this is a little too much for me right now." I could barely wrap my head around the fact that Kellan was talking to me, let alone what he had just done to me on the couch.

"Well, you've got about four hours to get used to it before my hands will be all over you again."

"This is actually happening, isn't it?" I whispered more to myself than Kellan.

He pressed a kiss to my lips, and I melted into him, wrapping my arms around his neck. His tongue swept through my mouth, and I figured four hours was enough time.

"I'll be there at seven," he mumbled against my lips.

I'm pretty sure I would have agreed if Kellan wanted to wage war against Mars and ride off in his rocket ship with him. "I'll be there."

The smile that was more than panty melting graced his lips, and he ducked back inside.

I closed my eyes and pinched my hand. "Well, that just happened," I sighed. I lifted my foot to head back to the cafe, and almost fell on my ass when I remembered I barely had my shoes on.

I continued my shuffle of shame around the building with a goofy ass smile on my face, because I had gone and got my man.

Bess and the Moaners would be proud as hell. I even managed to give him some pow pow.

****

Kellan

"So, I heard you finally got your head out of your ass."

I finished pushing the punching bag in the corner and wiped my hands on my pants. The last class of the day had just ended, and I was ready to get out of here.

Dante and Tate had shown up halfway through the first class, and apparently Roman had opened his mouth about Molly being here. I didn't care if they knew about Molly, but from the way she acted when she had left, she wasn't too keen on people knowing.

"We talked."

Dante chuckled and bowed off the mat. "I gathered that from what Roman said."

Tate was sitting behind the desk and slowly spinning circles. "So, does this mean we get free cookies for life now?"

Dante reached behind the desk and grabbed the box of cookies Molly had brought over. "It's already started, my man." He lifted the cover and held it out to Tate. "Not as good as those brownies she brought over, though."

I growled and bowed off the mat. I was still pissed those two idiots had eaten all of the brownies she had brought over when I was out of town. "That'll be the last of the cookies you get if you fuckers don't share them with me."

Dante chucked a cookie at me, and I grabbed it mid-air. "Fuck, these things really are good," I mumbled as I stuck it in my mouth, and headed to the bathroom. My bag was tucked in the corner, and I turned on the water in the shower. I had twenty minutes to get showered and head over to Molly's, and I didn't want to smell like a sweaty gym.

After a quick five-minute scrub down, I let the water run over me and looked down at my semi-erect dick. I couldn't stop thinking of how her body reacted to just a simple touch from me. The way her tight pussy milked my fingers drove me crazy, and I could still feel the vise-like grip she had on me.

I flipped off the water, toweled dry, and was out of the bathroom in record time.

Dante, Tate, and Roman were on the mat, sparring back and forth. Tate was sitting out, waiting to spar the winner. "You really fix shit with her?" he asked.

I grabbed my shoes and slipped them on. "Yeah. I was wrong."

"Kind of figured you were, but you're a stubborn bastard."

I couldn't really argue with that. I had bumped heads more than a few times with the guys because I wasn't about to budge. Mostly because I normally was right. "Yeah, but I figured it out."

Tate leaned back and looked up at me. "You gonna fuck it up again, or are you actually in it this time?"

I slung my bag over my shoulder and shook my head. "You know when we walked in this place, and we knew that this was where we were meant to be?" Tate nodded. "That's what I feel when I'm with Molly. I know that she's the one to call me on my bullshit, and also have my back. If I fuck this up, I know I'll be miserable without her."

"Pretty strong fucking words, man."

I slid my sunglasses on my face. "That's cause I'm not fucking around, man."

Tate raised his hand, and I slapped it. "Treat her right. You deserve each other."

Dante and Roman both tipped their heads at me when I hollered that I was leaving. Roman had decided he was going to get back on the circuit a bit, doing local tournaments, and Dante had decided his training would start tonight.

The door to Powerhouse closed behind me, and I looked at the setting sun. Pretty soon, it would be summer, and I couldn't help but think of spending time at the beach with Molly. Then, I thought about Molly's lush body in a bikini, and my dick came to attention.

I jogged to my car, tossing my bag in the backseat, and took off to Molly's. She only lived five minutes away from the studio, and before I knew it, I was parked outside her apartment.

"Don't fuck it up, Kellan," I murmured to myself as I jogged up the stairs, and then strode down the hallway to her apartment.

I knocked twice, and the door swung open to Molly looking fucking hot. Her long hair was framing her face, falling on her bare shoulders, while the black tank top she had on hugged her body, and the tight jeans she wore showed off her long, sexy legs I couldn't wait to wrap around me.

"Hey," she mumbled. She pushed her hair behind her ear, exposing the slight curve of her neck, and something snapped in me. I couldn't control myself.

I grabbed her around the waist, pushed her into her apartment, slammed the door shut behind me, spun her around, and pinned her against the door. "I fucking missed you," I growled as I buried my face in her hair. She smelled like a fucking field of flowers, and I never wanted to come up for air.

A moan escaped her lips as I pressed kisses along her jaw, my hands moving over her body, needing to feel her all at once. Her arms wrapped around my neck, and her lips found mine. Her tongue eagerly swept in my mouth, her need was as strong as my own.

"Kellan," she gasped.

"I need to be inside you, Molly," I confessed as my hands roamed over her ass.

A light flashed behind us, and I heard what sounded like a bag of chips crinkle.

Molly's eyes were closed, and I leaned my forehead against hers. "We're not alone, Kellan," she whispered.

Son of a bitch.

****

Molly

"Don't stop now, fella."

"I think I'll need my inhaler if he keeps going."

"Mama, who's that man kissing Molly?"

I kept my eyes closed and again wished I would disappear. Except Kellan could disappear with me, because I didn't want him to stop.

"I think we'll all just be going," Sage decided.

"But that man has Aunty Molly pressed against the door," Sam announced. "We can't leave."

The bag of chips Bess had been eating crinkled. "I'm okay with that. I told you these two were like a romance novel come to life," she proclaimed.

I peeked open my eyes and was greeted with Kellan's stunning eyes staring back at me. "Hi," I whispered.

"Shh," Gretchen hissed. "They might start going at it again."

"Hi, Cookie." His voice was light, and I could tell he was smiling.

"If you keep talking, they won't do anything," Bess snarled.

"Me?" Gretchen shouted. "I wasn't the one who took a damn picture. That's what spooked 'em."

Oh Lord, they were talking about us like we were some exhibit on display.

"I think we need to move," Kellan muttered. He pressed a kiss to my lips, and his hands left my body as he pushed off the door.

I leaned on the door, because I was pretty sure even though I was embarrassed, I was going to melt into a puddle on the floor from Kellan's kiss.

Bess pointed at me then clapped her hands. "That, right there," she marveled, "is the just been-fucked look, ladies."

Sage clapped her hands over Sam's ears and glared at Bess. "Do you think you could keep it PG for two seconds?"

Bess grabbed her purse off the chair. "Sorry, hon. I lose all sense when I see a man handle a woman like that. I need to head on home to Joe so he can, um," she glanced down at Sam and cleared her throat. "I need him to check my pipes."

Gretchen and the Moaners cackled, and Sage swatted her hand at them. "You guys are shameless," she scolded. She grabbed Sam's hand, shaking her head, but she had a smile on her face. "Call me later, Molly."

I nodded my head, unable to form a coherent thought. Kellan grabbed my hand and peeled me off the door. He tucked me under his arm, and Sage beamed at me.

"Much later," she muttered. She opened the door and tugged Sam behind her. "Move it, Moaners. The shows over," she called over her shoulder.

"Kids these days," Gretchen complained. "Always ruining my fun."

The Moaners filed out one by one with Bess bringing up the rear. She leaned into Kellan and crooked her finger at him. A smirk crossed his lips, and he tilted his head down to her.

"You should know that I also read murder mysteries. I know at least fifteen ways to get rid of a body without evidence. Hurt her, and no one will know where to look for you." She patted him on the cheek, winked, and strode out the door.

Kellan's head was still tilted, and he rubbed his cheek. "Did I just get threatened by a seventy-year-old?"

"I'm sixty-five!" Bess hollered.

I giggled and managed to swing the door shut.

"Throw the lock. Who knows if they might try to sneak in later," Kellan ordered.

I slid the lock and turned around. I leaned against the door and realized Kellan was in my tiny apartment. "Hi."

He shook his head and chuckled. "I think we covered that already, Cookie."

"Oh, yeah," I whispered.

"You look gorgeous, by the way."

My cheeks heated, and I ran my fingers through my hair. "I kind of figured you approved."

He grabbed my hand and pulled me to him. "More than approved," he whispered.

I wrapped my arms around his waist and looked up at him. "You look more than okay, too."

"More than okay?"

I licked my lips. "Sexy as hell?" I elaborated. Kellan was the most gorgeous man I had ever seen, and I couldn't find a word good enough to describe him. He was sexy, plain and simple.

He threaded his fingers through my hair and tilted my head up. "I missed you," he whispered before he touched his lips to mine.

The kiss started gentle, my lips loving the feel of his. His hands gripped my hair, gently pulling my head back. "Legs around me," he ordered.

"I think that's your catchphrase with me."

Kellan's body shook against me, and a smile curved on his lips. "I can't seem to get enough of you, Molly." He pressed a quick kiss to my lips and patted my ass. "Now, wrap your legs around me."

"So demanding," I whispered but did as he said. "Where are we going?" I asked as he moved through my apartment like he lived here.

"I wasn't lying when I said I need to be inside you. I couldn't think of anything but you and your sweet pussy all through classes this afternoon."

My breath hitched at his words, and I licked my lips.

"Stop doing that, or I'll fuck you right here against the wall."

I buried my face in his neck and inhaled his scent. "You smell good," I mumbled.

"Fuck me," he muttered as he opened the door to the bathroom.

"Keep going."

"I plan on it, Cookie, as soon as I find your damn bed." He slammed the door and stalked down the hallway.

I giggled and pressed a kiss to his neck. "I meant to keep going down the hallway."

He opened the door to the guest bedroom and tossed me on the single bed in the corner. "We're gonna have to get you a bigger bed."

I shook my head and sat up. "No need to. We're in the guest bedroom."

Kellan looked around. "Well, we can break this bed in first." He pulled his shirt over his head and tossed it on the floor. "Clothes off, now," he ordered as he unzipped his pants and pulled them down his legs.

I scrambled to pull my tank top off, and shimmied my pants down my legs. His eyes were on me as I reached around and unhooked my bra. "Stop," he commanded.

My fingers froze on the clasp, and I bit my lip. "Kellan?" I whispered.

"Do you know how fucking sexy you look right now?"

I felt more like a twisted pretzel at the moment, but I wasn't going to argue with the man. "Probably not as sexy as you do." He was stripped down to his boxers, and was stroking his dick through the thin fabric as he eyes traveled over me. Even though he still had his boxers on, I knew I wasn't going to be disappointed.

"Can I move now?"

"Only if you tell me one thing."

I nodded and wondered what he needed to know right now. "Okay," I whispered. I held my breath and waited.

****

Kellan

Her back was arched, her breasts thrust at me, waiting.

"If we do this, you know I'm not going to let you go."

She nodded.

"This is different, Molly. I've never felt this way before. I want you to know that after tonight, you're it. I don't want anyone else. It's you."

"Did I miss the question?" she whispered.

"After tonight, I belong to you."

Her eyes glassed over, and she sniffled. "I still don't see a question." She fidgeted, rubbing her thighs together. "Although I'm completely okay with everything you just said."

There was my Molly who said whatever she was thinking. "If I belong to you, then who do you belong to, Molly?" There it was. There was the question I needed an answer to. I was in so deep with Molly, and I needed to know she was right there with me.

Her arms dropped to her side along with her bra. She shrugged it off and slid off the bed. She grabbed my hand, and I pulled her to me. She rested her hands on my chest and looked up at me. "I belong to you, Kellan. I have since the day you kissed me in the cafe. You had me then, and I didn't even know you." She hooked her thumbs into the waistband of my boxers and pulled them down my legs. She kneeled in front of me and ran her hands up my legs. "I belong to you," she whispered.

I was speechless when she leaned in, grabbed my rock hard cock with one hand, and cupped my balls with the other. She licked her lips, her eyes connected to mine, and I knew this woman was going to be the final piece to my new life.

Her hand stroked my cock up and down, her fingers gently rolling my balls. "Was that the right answer?" she asked, her voice husky with desire. Her pink lips were wet, and all I could think about was watching them swallow my dick.

"Perfect, Cookie," I growled.

A seductive smile spread across her lips, and she licked them again. Her pretty pink tongue darted out and swirled around the tip of my dick.

"Mother fucker," I gasped.

Her hand continued to stroke me as she sucked on the tip. She slowly worked my cock down her throat with small moans. She was enjoying this as much as I was.

I threaded my fingers through her hair and guided my dick in and out of her sweet mouth. She looked up, her eyes meeting mine. "You're mine," I growled.

Her eyes flared, and she took me in as she relaxed her throat, and I reached a whole new level of belonging to Molly.

Her hand twisted and teased my balls, while her mouth devoured me. I felt the telltale tightening in my balls, and I knew it wouldn't be long before I would empty my load down her sweet throat.

I pulled out, her hand released my balls, and I hooked my hands under her arms. I hoisted her completely off the floor and tossed her back on the bed. "Your sweet pussy is going to make me cum the first time, Molly. Next time, it'll be your mouth." I grabbed my jeans off the floor and grabbed one of the five condoms I had brought. I had big plans for Molly tonight.

"Panties off." I ripped the corner of the condom off with my teeth and watched her scramble to comply with my demand. "No ponies on these ones?" I asked as I grabbed them mid-air as she tossed them. They were lime green with tiny black hearts all over them.

She blushed and shook her head. "I thought we agreed to never talk about the ponies again?"

I rolled the condom on and moved to the edge of the bed. "I have a whole new level of respect for My Little Pony after seeing them on your sweet pussy."

She rubbed her legs together, and sat up, leaning back on her arms. "Kellan," she whined. "Please."

I put one knee on the bed and crawled up her body. "That's all you have to say, baby, and you'll have me." I pushed her legs open and nestled my cock between her thighs.

Her arms wrapped around me, and she dug her heels into the bed. My hand parted the lips of her pussy—her wetness greeting me. "I haven't even touched you, and you're ready for me."

She arched her back, pressing her tits into me. "I liked tasting you," she whispered.

My inner caveman beat on his chest, and I slammed my mouth down on Molly's lips. This woman was mine, and I wasn't going to give her up for anything. My fingers flicked her clit, and her legs fell wide open as her tongue thrust in and out of my mouth.

I grabbed my dick, rubbing the tip up and down her wet pussy. "I need you, Molly," I growled.

"Then take me," she gasped.

I thrust into her, her mouth dropped open, and a groan ripped from my lips. "Fuuuck."

She wrapped her legs around me, hooking her heels behind my back, and her nails dug into my shoulder blades. I slowly pulled out, her pussy tightening around me on my withdrawal. "So mother fucking tight," I swore as I plunged back in.

"Oh, my God," she moaned. Her head was tossed back, and her eyes were clamped shut. That look of pure ecstasy was because of me. I was doing that to her, and I was going to be the only one to give that to her for the rest of my life.

I buried my face in her neck, sinking into her as deep as I could. I could die tomorrow, and I would be the luckiest damn man in the world. Her scent enveloped me, and I tasted her neck, running my tongue to her ear. I thrust in and out, her vise-like pussy squeezing and milking me. "Make me cum, Molly. Take me."

She tilted her hips, my dick driving even further into her. "Please, Kellan. Please make me yours," she pleaded.

"So fucking perfect," I growled as my hips pounded into her.

She chanted my name, "Kellan, Kellan…"

I reached down, flicked her clit, and she fell apart in my arms. Her mouth dropped open, as she screamed my name, her pussy clamping down on me.

"Give it to me, Molly," I grunted. I buried my face in her hair as I pumped my hips.

"Kellan," she gasped. Her pussy milked me, grabbing hold, and refusing to let go.

"Mine!" My load released as she ran her hands over my back, and I furiously thrust, giving her everything I had. I collapsed on top of her, unable to hold myself up anymore.

We were both panting, our breathing labored, and my heart was beating out of my chest. "Holy shit."

"You can say that again," Molly muttered.

"Holy shit."

Her body shook beneath me, and I looked up to see a huge grin on her face. "If I wasn't so worn out, I'd be concerned by the fact that you're laughing while my dick is inside you."

Her hands trailed circles on my back, and she pressed a kiss to the top of my head. "Didn't mean to bruise your ego."

I closed my eyes and hummed. I could have been hit by a truck at this point, and I wouldn't have cared. My ego could take the hit after the best sex of my life. "I'm a big boy. I'll make you pay for that later."

She combed her fingers through my hair. "How soon is later?"

I tilted my head back and opened my eyes. She was looking down at me, and I knew if she looked at me for the rest of my life, I would be one lucky guy. "Dinner, and then payback?"

"Can we order in?"

I rolled off her and tucked her into my side. "Yeah. You're not allowed clothes for the rest of the night, so takeout would be best."

"And next time, you think we can make it to my bed? It's only one more door down."

I reached behind me and nodded. "Yeah. I'm half an inch away from falling off this damn thing."

She giggled and wrapped her arms around me, pulling me further onto the bed. "I tried to warn you."

I hooked my leg over her hips, and she tilted her head back. "Is this where you tell me I never listen to you?"

She shook her head and buried her face in my chest. "No, because I'm pretty sure I couldn't have made it another step without having you inside me."

I slapped her ass, and she shrieked. "Get up, Cookie. I need to eat, and then I need to fuck you at least three more times tonight."

"Three?" she gasped.

I sat up, taking her with me. "Yup. You might want to get used to it. I don't see me ever getting enough of your sweet pussy." I pulled the used condom off and tossed it in the trash.

She blushed and slid off the bed. "I doubt that." She reached for her panties on the floor, and I grabbed her around the waist. "Kellan," she protested as I spun her around and pulled her into my lap.

"What happened?" I asked.

She looked around, everywhere but me. "I'm pretty sure we just had sex, Kellan."

"Yeah, we sure fucking did. I'm talking what just happened now." She put her hands on my chest and tried to pull away. "Your ass stays in my lap until you tell me what's going through that pretty head."

She rolled her eyes. "I don't need you to say things that aren't true, Kellan." Her eyes teared up, and she looked to the side.

I hooked my finger under her chin. "Cookie, I don't know what you are talking about. I haven't said anything that's a lie."

She scoffed and sniffled. A tear streaked down her cheek, and I wiped it away. "You'll never get enough of me?"

"That's what I said."

She shook her head, and more tears ran down her cheeks. "I'm so stupid," she mumbled. She pushed against my chest, trying to get away from me. I loosened my arms, and she scrambled off my lap.

I stood up and watched her rush to grab her clothes off the floor. "Molly, what is going on?" I snatched her panties out of her hand and held them behind my back.

"Kellan! Give me my panties!" she demanded.

"Not until you tell me what is going through your head. We just had the most amazing sex, and I was hoping for at least a couple more rounds tonight, but you're acting like I just told you to go to hell."

She threw her hands in the air. "This isn't going to work, Kellan. You and I are not two people who should be together. I'm all geeky, and awkward, while you're all…well…you're all macho, hot, sexiness."

I cleared my throat, trying not to laugh. That was the first time I had ever been called that. I grabbed her arm and pulled her to me. "We obviously need to get some shit straight."

"There is nothing to get straight."

I put my finger on her lips and shook my head. "It's my turn to talk, Molly." She rolled her eyes but didn't argue. "Did you hear anything I said while we were having sex?"

"Yes, I heard you."

"But you apparently didn't believe me." I dropped her panties on the floor and pulled her into my arms. "Wrap your legs around me."

"Kellan, we are not having sex. That isn't going to fix this."

I grabbed her ass and lifted her up. If she wasn't going to do it herself, then I would make her do it. She squealed as I lifted her, and she wrapped her arms and legs around me. "This isn't fair."

"We're gonna have sex, Molly. But first, I'm going to tell you exactly what I want, and then you're going to tell me if you want the same thing. I thought we were on the same page, but I guess I need to be more specific."

"Where are we going?" she asked. I walked to the wall and pressed her against it.

"I'm gonna fuck you against the wall after we talk."

"What if I don't want that after we talk?"

I looked into her eyes and saw so much uncertainty. "Then I've been wrong about you the whole time, but I know that's not true."

"Who I've been the whole time is the nerdy coffee chick next door who has no business being with a badass ninja."

I couldn't help it. I busted out laughing and buried my face in her neck. "Badass ninja?"

Her body tensed, and I tilted my head back to look at her. "Don't laugh at me," she whispered.

I pressed her against the wall with my body and brushed her hair from her face. "Cookie, I'm not laughing at you. You make me fucking happy, and I can't help but laugh when you call me a ninja. That was a first."

"Kellan, you're gonna get sick of me not thinking before I talk, and making a fool of myself. I mean, what would happen if I would call one of your friends a ninja? They would laugh at me and wonder what you are doing with me."

I shook my head. "Nope, I'm pretty sure Dante, Tate, and Roman would all think it would be badass to be called a ninja. Particularly by a smoking hot woman who means it in the best way."

Her eyes searched mine, looking for what, I don't know. "I'm going to embarrass you. I do it daily to myself, so it's only natural that I'll do it to you."

"You really think I fucking care, Molly? What you think is embarrassing, I see as you being you, and not caring what people think."

She tilted her head, and a small smile touched her lips. "You have a very odd way of seeing me, Kellan."

"Lock your arms and legs tight around me," I ordered. She instantly did what I asked, and I knew I was getting through to her. I delved my fingers into her hair and leaned in. "I see you the way the rest of the world sees you. You are the one who has an odd way of seeing yourself." She shook her head, and I cut her off before she could argue with me. "Dante. Tate. Roman. Gavin." She quirked an eyebrow at me, but I shook my head. "If I wouldn't have pulled my head out of my ass, and taken you tonight, all four of those sons of bitches would have fought to have you."

She scoffed and rolled her eyes. "Now, I think you're high."

I gently pulled her hair and tilted her head back to look me in the eye. "No, I've never been so sure of something in my life. You, Molly Rey, are a fucking prize to be won, and I'm the lucky bastard who gets to have you. Not Dante, not Tate, not Roman and sure as fuck, not Gavin. I wasn't lying, joking, kidding, or making shit up to get in your sweet pussy before. I fucking belong to you now, and you're not going to be able to get rid of me."

A tear streaked down her cheek, and I kissed it away. "Don't do that, Kellan."

"Do what?"

"Don't make me fall in love with you. You already drop-kicked my heart before, I can't take it again."

A grin spread across my lips. "I drop-kicked your heart? I like the way that sounds."

She shook her head and buried her face in my neck. "You hurt me when you walked away before. That was the best analogy I could come up with. I remember when I tried to dropkick, it hurt like a bitch. You made me fall for you, and then you went away."

"So, what happens if I make you fall in love with me and I don't go away?" I wasn't fucking going anywhere. Hell, I'd move Molly into my fucking house right now if she wouldn't think I was moving too fast.

"Then you're stuck with my awkward ass for the rest of your life because I'm pretty sure falling in love with Kellan Wright is something terminal I would never come back from."

"So, our love's terminal?" God damn, Molly was a fucking nut.

"Can we stop talking about this? I just realized how stupid that sounded."

"Only if you let me fuck you against the wall, and you never think we don't belong together because that shit is just that, shit."

She sighed and leaned back. "I thought you had to eat first?" And my sweet, awkward, and sexy as fuck Molly was back.

"I can fuck you quick, and then we can eat."

Her hand snaked between us and grabbed my cock. "I'm sorry," she whispered.

"Don't be sorry, Cookie," I gritted out. I wasn't interested in talking when her hand was stroking my cock. "Just know I'm not fucking going anywhere. I'm yours, and you are mine."

A sly smile spread across her lips, and she arched her back, pressing her pussy into me. "Okay," she whispered.

"Now, can I fuck you?" I asked, my patience running out.

"Please."

I reached down, my hand skimming over her skin, and stroked her pussy with my finger. She guided my cock inside her, and she sank down onto me. "Mother fucking son of a bitch."

She moaned and wrapped her arms around my neck. "My thoughts exactly," she purred.

I pressed her against the wall and thrust in and out of her warm pussy. "You would think since I just fucked you, this would take a while."

She hummed and closed her eyes. "You would think that."

"But your fucking pussy was made for me, and I'm pretty sure I'm ten seconds away from filling that pretty pussy full of my cum."

She stopped moving, and her eyes snapped open. "You don't have a condom on."

"No."

She looked down at my dick, and then back up at me. "I'm on the pill. Are you clean?"

"If I wasn't, I wouldn't be inside you right now."

She blushed and shook her head. "I'm sorry, I didn't think yo—"

"Stop. I would have been surprised if you didn't ask. You want me to get a condom, or can I keep fucking you?"

She bit her lip and eyed my pants on the floor. Her eyes cut to me, and she leaned in, pressing a kiss to my mouth. "Fuck me, badass ninja."

I shook my head and chuckled. "I'm gonna get cards with that on them. Kellan Wright, Badass Ninja." I pulled out, then slammed back into her.

Molly closed her eyes and threw her head back. "Make sure they say Property of Molly Rey," she added.

"Fuck yeah," I growled.

She ground her pussy into me, and I fucked her hard and wild against the wall. Molly was my perfect match, and I was never going to let her go.

A moaned ripped from her lips, her pussy gripping me as she fell over the edge and called my name. Her body sagged against me, her face buried in my neck, and I poured my cum into her, claiming what was mine, and vowing never to let her go.

"Mine," I shouted.

Molly Rey was mine.

****

Molly

"Ew."

"Ew? What do you mean, ew?" Kellan asked as he shoved a french fry into his mouth with a wad of mayo on it.

I curled my lip and cringed. "You just dipped your french fry into mayo."

He grabbed a fry and dunked it into the pool he had in front of him before shoving it in my face. "Ack! Get that away from me."

Kellan shoved it in his mouth and wagged a finger at me. "That's not what you were saying half an hour ago."

I ripped off a hunk of my burger and rolled my eyes. "I'm pretty sure if you were to dip your dick in mayo and wave it in my face, I would say the same thing."

Kellan's eyes bugged out, and he choked on the fry he was chewing. He took a sip of his soda and shook his head.

"Embarrassing?" I asked,

"No, funny," he chuckled. "Stop thinking you're embarrassing, Molly. I'm going to take you over my knee every time you think that."

Hmm, that was going to be something I was going to have to work on. Embarrassing and me go hand in hand. Although, from what Kellan said, I was just me. I mulled it over, thinking about everything Kellan had said, and then everything he had done to my body, and decided he must be telling the truth because honestly, that man had stamina like no other. If he wanted to spend his time with me, showing me just how un-embarrassing I was, then who was I to complain.

"Kellan Wright thinks I'm pretty cool," I sang out as I balled up the wrapper from my cheeseburger and walked to the garbage can.

The sexy as hell smile that made my panties melt spread across his lips. "He sure fucking does, and he plans on showing you all over again just who you belong to."

"Again?" I gasped. After he had fucked me against the wall, I had managed to order some burgers for much-needed sustenance, before Kellan decided I needed to be convinced again how un-embarrassing I was before the food even came. I had come all over his tongue again, and by the time the food arrived, I was a blubbering, bliss-filled mess.

"Still gotta break your bed in, Cookie."

Oh crap, Kellan Wright really did like me, and he had plans to fuck me into next week. "I can barely stand," I pointed out as I leaned against the wall.

Kellan smirked and dunked the last of his fries in the offensive mayo. "Then, it's a good thing you won't need to stand, and I plan on doing all of the work."

I sighed and wrapped my arms around me. "You don't fight fair, Kellan."

He winked at me, and my heart fluttered. "I never do, Molly. I wanted you, and now you're mine."

I certainly was, and honestly, I was damn happy Kellan didn't fight fair. He wanted me, and who was I to argue with a badass ninja?

Coming Soon

Love on the Mat
Book 2 in the Powerhouse M.A. Series

Hadley
Life isn't fair.
Hadley James learned early on in life the easy path was not in her future, and the past six months have been a testament to that. Losing her sister and getting guardianship of her nephew have knocked her world off its axis with no one there to help.
She takes the only job she can find to pay the bills, but it doesn't exactly make her feel like the motherly type. Slinging cocktails 'til two o'clock in the morning, then waking up four hours later to get her nephew out the door, leaves little time for anything but work and sleep.
Struggling to find a way to make ends meet, all Hadley wishes for is a normal life for her nephew, and a full night's sleep for herself.
Is that really too much for a girl to ask for?

Tate
Life is damn good.
Tate Holten co-owns a successful karate studio, has a gorgeous house, a brand new car, and the freedom to do whatever he wants, whenever he wants. Life couldn't have dealt him a better hand.
Although, spending most of his time at Powerhouse leaves Tate with little social life, and lately, he's been looking for something different.
Something or someone to share his life with seems to be the only thing he can't have.
Constantly searching for that one special thing leads Tate to Hadley, and he instantly knows she's what he has been looking for.
Tate just wants to save Hadley and give her everything she needs, but Hadley isn't looking for a handout from some stranger who watches her every night. Creepy much?
Tate is faced with his biggest challenge yet of convincing Hadley he isn't some creeper looking to land in her bed for one night. But will Hadley give him the chance, or will Tate have to take love to the mat to prove to Hadley he's just what she needs?

About the Author

Winter Travers is a devoted wife, mother, and aunt turned author who was born and raised in Wisconsin. After a brief stint in South Carolina following her heart to chase the man who is now her hubby, they retreated back up North to the changing seasons, and to the place they now call home.
Winter spends her days writing happily ever after's, and her nights zipping around on her forklift at work. She also has an addiction to anything MC related, her dog Thunder, and Mexican food! (Tamales!)
Winter loves to stay connected with her readers. Don't hesitate to reach out and contact her.
www.facebook.com/wintertravers
Twitter: @WinterTravers
Instagram: @WinterTravers
http://500145315.wix.com/wintertravers

LOVING LO
DEVIL'S KNIGHTS SERIES
BOOK 1

WINTER TRAVERS

Chapter 1
Meg

How did just stopping quickly to get dog food and shampoo turn into an overflowing basket and a surplus pack of paper towels?

"Put the paper towels down and back away slowly," I mumbled to myself as I walked past a display of air fresheners and wondered if I needed any.

"Oh dear. Oh, my. I… Ah… Oh, my."

I tore my thoughts away from air fresheners and looked down the aisle to an elderly woman who was leaning against the shelf, fanning herself. "Are you ok, ma'am?"

"Oh dear. I just… I just got a little… dizzy." I looked at the woman and saw her hands shaking as she brushed her white hair out of her face. The woman had on denim capris and a white button down short sleeve shirt and surprisingly three-inch wedge heels.

"Ok, well, why don't we try to find you a place to sit down until you get your bearings?" I shifted the basket and paper towels under one arm to help her to the bench that I had seen by the shoe rack two aisles over. "Are you here with anyone?" I asked, as I guided her down the aisle.

"Oh no. I'm here by myself. I just needed a few things."

"I only needed two things, and now my basket is overflowing, and I still haven't gotten the things I came in for."

The woman plopped down on the bench chuckling, shaking her head. "Tell me about it. Happens to me every time too."

"Is there something I can do for you? Has this happened to you before?" She was looking rather pale.

"Unfortunately, yes. I ran out of the house today without eating breakfast. I'm diabetic. I should know by now that I can't do that." My mom was also diabetic, so I knew exactly what the woman was talking about. Luckily, I also knew what to do to help.

"Just sit right here, and I'll be right back. Is there someone you want to call to give you a ride home? Driving right now probably isn't the best idea." I set the basket and towels on the floor, keeping my wallet in my hand.

"I suppose I should call my son. He should be able to give me a ride," the woman said as she dug her phone out of her purse.

I left the woman to her phone call and headed to the candy aisle that I had been trying to ignore. I grabbed a bag of licorice, chips, and a diet soda and went to the checkout. The dollar store didn't offer a healthy selection, but this would do in a pinch. The woman just needed to get her blood sugars back up.

I grabbed my things after paying and headed back to the bench. I ripped open the bag and handed it to the woman. "Oh dear, you didn't have to buy that. I could have given you money."

"Don't worry about it. I hope if this happened to my mom there would be someone to help her if I wasn't around."

"Well, that's awfully sweet of you. My names Ethel Birch by the way."

"It's nice to meet you, Ethel. I'm Meg Grain. I also got you some chips and soda." I popped opened the soda and handed it to Ethel.

"Oh, thank you, honey. My son is on the way here, should be only five minutes. You can get going if you want to, you don't need to sit with an old woman," Ethel said as she ate a piece of candy and took a slug of soda.

"No problem. The only plans I had today was to take a nap before work tonight. Delaying my plans by ten minutes won't be a problem."

"Well, in that case, you can help me eat this licorice. It's my favorite, but I shouldn't eat this all by myself. Where do you work at?" Ethel asked as she offered the bag to me.

"The factory right outside of town. I work in the warehouse, second shift." I grabbed a piece and sat down on the floor. If I was going to wait for Ethel's son to show up, might as well be comfortable while I waited for him.

"Really? Never would have thought that. Figured you would have said a nurse or something like that. Seems like you would have to be tough to work in a warehouse, sounds like a man's job."

I laughed. "Honestly, Ethel that is not the first time I have heard that, and it probably won't be the last. You need a certain attitude to deal with those truckers walking through the door. I have an awesome co-worker, so he helps out when truckers have a problem with a woman loading their truck."

"Sounds like you give them hell. My Tim was a trucker before he passed. I know exactly what you are talking about."

Ethel took another drink of her soda and set it on the bench next to her.

"Feeling better?"

"Surprisingly, yes. It's a wonder what a little candy can do. How much do I owe you?" Ethel asked as she reached for her purse by her feet.

"Don't worry about it. I'm just glad that I was here to help."

"Mom! Where are you?" Someone yelled from the front of the store.

"Oh good, Lo's here. You'll have to meet him." Ethel cupped her hands around her mouth and yelled to him she was in the back.

I started getting up off the floor and remembered I wasn't exactly as flexible as I use to be while struggling to get up.

"Ma, you ok?" I was halfway to standing with my butt in the air when his voice made me pause.

It sounded like the man was gurgling broken glass when he spoke. Raspy and *so* sexy. Those three words he spoke sent shocks to my core. Lord knows the last time I felt anything in my core.

"Yes, I'm fine. I forgot to eat breakfast this morning and started to get dizzy when Meg here was nice enough to help me out until you could get here." Ethel turned to me. "Lo, this is Meg, Meg this is Lo."

Oh, lord.

I couldn't talk. The man standing in front of me was... oh, lord. I couldn't even think of a word to describe him.

I looked him up and down, and I'm sure my mouth was hanging wide open. I took in his scuffed up motorcycle boots and faded, stained ripped jeans that hugged his thighs and made me want to ask the man to spin so I could see what those jeans were doing for his ass. I moved my eyes up to his t-shirt that was tight around his shoulders and chest and showed he worked out.

I couldn't remember the last time I worked out. Did walking to the mailbox count as exercise? Of course, I only remembered to get the mail about twice a week, so that probably didn't count.

His arms were covered in tattoos. I could see them peeking out from the collar of his shirt and could only imagine what he looked like with his shirt off. Tattoos were my ultimate addiction on a man. Even one tattoo added at least 10 points to a man's hotness. This guy was off the fucking charts.

My eyes locked with his after my fantastic voyage up his body, and I stopped breathing.

"Hey, Meg. See something you like, darlin'?" Lo rumbled at me with a smirk on his face.

Busted. I sucked air back into my lungs and tried to remember how to breathe.

Lo's eyes were the color of fresh cut grass, bright green. His hair was jet black and cut close to his head with a pair of kick ass aviators sitting on top of his head. He was golden tan and gorgeous. The man was sex on a stick. Plain and simple.

"Uh, hey," I choked out.

Lo's lips curved up into a grin, and I looked down to see if my panties fell off. The man had a panty-dropping smile, and he wasn't even smiling that big. I would have to take cover or risk fainting if he smiled any bigger.

"Thanks for looking after my ma for me. I'm glad I was in town today and not out on a run," Lo said.

Ok. Get it together Meg. You are a 36-year-old woman, and this man has rendered you speechless like a sixteen-year-old girl. I needed to say something.

"Say something," I blurted out. Good Lord did I just say that. Lo quirked his eyebrow, and his smirk returned.

"Ugh, I mean no problem. I didn't do that much. No problem." I looked at Ethel while Lo was smirking at me; Ethel had a full-blown smile on her face and was beaming at me.

"You were a life saver, Meg! I don't know what I would have done if you weren't here." Ethel looked at Lo and grinned even bigger. "You should have seen her, Lo. She knew just what to do to help me. I could have sworn she was a nurse the way she took charge. She's not, though, just has a good head on her shoulders and decided to help this old lady out."

"That's good, Ma. You got all your shit you need so we can get going? I got some stuff going on at the garage that I dropped to get over here fast."

I took that as my cue to leave and ripped my eyes off Lo and bent over to get my basket and paper towels.

"Yes son, that's my stuff right here. I just want to get Meg's number before she leaves."

"Why do you need my number?" I asked, as I juggled my basket and towels.

Ethel grabbed her purse off the ground and started digging through it again. "Well, you won't let me pay you back for the snacks you got for me so I figured I could pay you back by inviting you over for dinner sometime. So, what's your number, sweetheart?"

"I don't eat dinner," I blurted out. I was going to have to have a talk with my brain and mouth when I got home. They needed to get their shit together and start working in unison so I wouldn't sound like such an idiot.

"You don't eat dinner? Please don't tell me you're on a diet." Lo said as he looked me up and down.

"No," I said. Lord knew I should be.

Lo and Ethel just stared at me.

"So, no, you don't eat dinner?" Lo asked again.

"Yes. I mean no, I'm not on a diet. Yes, I eat dinner. I just work at night, so I meant that I wouldn't be able to come to dinner." I looked at Lo and blushed about ten shades of red. "Why is this so hard?"

"What's hard, sweetheart? Can't remember your phone number? I can barely remember mine too. Don't worry about not being able to make it to dinner; I can have you over for lunch. You eat lunch right?" Ethel asked with a smirk on her face. Lo had a full-blown smile on his face, even his eyes were smiling at me. That smile ought to be illegal.

I could see where Lo got his looks from. With Lo and Ethel standing next to each other, I could totally see the resemblance. Especially when they were both smirking.

I had to get out of here. I'm normally the one with the one-liners and making everyone laugh, now I couldn't even put two words together.

"Lunch would be good." I rattled off my number, and Ethel jotted it down.

"Ok, sweetheart, I'll let you get your nap. I'll give you a call later, and we can figure out a day we can get together." Ethel shoved the pen and paper back in her bag and leaned into me for a hug.

I awkwardly hugged her back and patted her on the shoulder. "Sounds good. Have a good day, Ethel. Uh, it was nice meeting you, Lo," I mumbled, as my gaze wandered over Lo again.

"You too Meg. See you around," Lo replied.

I gave them both a jaunty wave and booked it to the checkout. Thankfully there wasn't a line, and I quickly made my escape to my car. I threw my things in the trunk and hopped in. I grabbed my phone out of my pocket and plugged it into the radio and turned on my chill playlist, as the soothing sounds of Fleetwood Mac filled the car.

Music was the one thing in my life that had gotten me through so much shit. Good or bad, there was always a song that I could play, and it would make everything better. Right now, I just needed to unscramble my brain and get my bearings. Fleetwood Mac singing "Landslide" was helping.

I pulled out of the parking lot and headed home. All I needed was to forget about today. If Ethel called for lunch, I would say yes because she did remind me so much of mom, but I wasn't going to let Lo enter my thoughts anymore. A woman like me did not register on his radar, he was better just forgotten.

When I was halfway home, I realized I forgot dog food and shampoo.

Shit.

======

Lo

I helped mom finish her shopping and loaded all her crap into the truck. I looked around the parking lot for Meg, hoping she hadn't left yet so I could get another look at her. As soon as I saw her ass waving in the air as she struggled to stand up, I knew I had to be inside her.

It took all my willpower to not get a hard-on as her eyes ran over my body. Fucking chick was smoking' hot and didn't even know it.

"Thanks for coming to get me, Lo," Ma said as she interrupted my thoughts about Meg.

"No problem, Ma. I'll get one of the guys to bring your car to you later. Make sure it's locked." Ma dug her keys out of her huge ass purse and beeped the locks. We both got into the shop truck, and I started it up.

"Sure was nice of that Meg to help out. I don't know what I would have done without her."

"Yup, definitely nice of her." I shifted the truck into drive, keeping my foot on the brake, knowing exactly where mom was headed with this.

"You should ask her out." All I could do was shake my head and laugh.

"Straight to the point huh, Ma?"

"I'm old, I can say what I want. Meg is just the thing you need."

"I didn't know I needed anything." I pulled out of the parking lot and headed to Ma's house.

"You need someone in your life besides that club." My mom grabbed her phone out of her purse and started fiddling with it.

"We'll see, ma. Meg didn't seem too thrilled with me." She liked what she saw, but it was like she couldn't get away from me quick enough when she saw that Ma was going to be ok.

"Well, you are pretty intimidating, Lo. Thank goodness you didn't wear your cut."

My leather vest with my club rockers and patches was a part of me. "What the hell is wrong with my cut? If some bitch can't handle me in my cut, she sure as shit doesn't belong with me," I growled.

"Not what I meant Lo. That girl has been hurt, you can see it in her eyes. You'll have to be gentle with her."

My phone dinged. I dug it out of my pocket and saw my mom had texted me. "You texted me her number, ma?"

"Use it, Logan, fix her," she insisted.

I sighed and pulled into mom's driveway. "Maybe she doesn't want to be fixed, ma. Maybe she has a boyfriend."

"She doesn't. Call her, or I'll do it for you," she ordered.

I knew my mom's threat wasn't idle. She totally would call Meg and ask her out for me. Fuck. "I'll help you get your shit inside, ma."

"I'll make you lunch, and then you can call Meg," Ma said, as she jumped out of the truck and grabbed some bags.

I watched her walk into her house and looked at the message she had sent me. I saved Meg's number to my phone and grabbed the rest of Ma's shit and headed into the house.

Looked like I was calling Meg.

========

Take a ride with the Jensen Boys.

Meet Violet and Luke in the first chapter of DownShift!

DownShift
Skid Row Kings
Book 1

Winter Travers

Chapter 1

Violet

It was half past seven, and I should be on my way home already, but I wasn't.

I watched the lone girl who was sitting at the far table and sighed. She came in every day after school like clockwork, stayed till five forty-five then left. Except today, she didn't. The only way for me to get the heck out of here was to tell her the library was closing, but I didn't have the heart to.

She appeared to be well taken care of, nice clothes, good tennis shoes and well groomed. But she was never with anyone when she came in. Even when other kids would come in to work on homework or such, she stayed by herself at the far table.

I glanced at the watch on my wrist one last time and knew I had to go talk to her. All I wanted to do was go home, eat dinner, and take a nice long bath with my latest book boyfriend. Was that too much to ask?

After I skirted around the desk, I hesitantly made my way over to her, not wanting to tell someone they had to leave. I wasn't one for confrontation. "Um, excuse me."

The girl looked up at me and smiled. She couldn't have been more than thirteen, fourteen tops. Shiny braces encased her teeth, and black-rimmed glasses sat perched on her nose. "Yes?"

"The library closes at seven."

She glanced at the watch on her wrist and hit her hand on the table. "Crud. Luke was supposed to pick me up over an hour ago. I'm really sorry," she said, gathering her books and shoving them into her bag.

"Did you need to call him?"

"No, he probably won't answer the phone. He's only managed to pick me up once this week. He's busy getting ready for Street Wars. He's probably stuck under the hood of a car right now." She zipped her book bag shut and slung it over her shoulder. "I'm really sorry for keeping you here so late. I know the library closes at seven, but I was so into my book I didn't even notice the time."

"It's OK." I had totally been there before. That was the whole reason I worked at the library, I got to be surrounded by the things I loved all day.

"I'll see ya," she waved and headed out the door.

I quickly flipped off all the lights, making sure everything was ready for tomorrow and walked out the door. "Shit," I muttered as I got pelted with rain as I locked the door.

I ran to my car, looking for the girl but didn't see her. Was she really going to walk home in the rain? I glanced up and down the street and saw her two blocks up, huddled under a tree.

Whoever this Luke was who was supposed to pick her up was a complete douche monkey for making this poor girl walk. I assumed it was her father, but it was strange that she called him Luke.

I ducked into my car, tossing my purse in the back and stuck the key in the ignition. I cranked it up and reversed out of my spot. As I pulled up to the girl, all I could do was shake my head. What did she think she was doing? Standing under a tree during a thunderstorm was not a bright idea.

"Get in the car," I hollered over the wind and rain. That was one of the drawbacks of the library, there weren't many windows so I never knew what the weather was like until I went outside. "I'll give you a ride."

She shook her head no and huddled under her jacket. What was she thinking? It didn't look like the rain was going to let up anytime soon. "I'm not supposed to ride with strangers."

Well, that was all fine and dandy except for the fact me being a stranger looked a lot better than standing in the rain. "You've been coming into the library for months. I'd hardly call us strangers."

"I don't even know your name," she said, her teeth chattering.

"It's Violet. Now get in the car."

She looked up and down the street, and it finally sunk in that I was her only chance of getting home not sopping wet. As she sprinted across the street, I reached across the center console and pushed open the passenger door.

"Oh my God, it's cold out there," she shivered as she slid in and closed the door.

"Well, it's only April. Plus, being soaking wet doesn't help."

She tossed her bag on the floor and rubbed her arms, trying to warm up. I switched the heat on full blast and pointed all the vents at her. She was dripping all over, and I knew the next person who sat there was going to get a wet ass. "Which way?"

"I live over on Thompson, on top of SRK Motors," she chattered.

I shifted the car into drive and headed down the street. "How come your dad didn't come and pick you up?" I asked, turning down Willow Street.

"Probably because he's dead."

Oh, crap. Whoopsie. "I'm sorry," I mumbled, feeling like an idiot. She seemed too young to have lost her dad.

"You can rule my mom out, too. They're both dead." She pulled a dry sweatshirt out of her bag and wrapped it around her hair, wringing it out.

OK. Well, things seemed to have taken a turn for the worse. "So, um, who's Luke? Your uncle?"

"No, he's my oldest brother. I've got three of them. They all work at the garage together that Luke owns, he's in charge."

"So, your brothers take care of you?"

"Ha, more like I take care of them. If it weren't for me, they'd spend all their time under the hood of a car."

"What's your name?" Here I was giving this girl a ride home, and I had no idea what her name was.

"Frankie."

"I'm Violet, by the way, if you didn't hear me before," I glanced at her, smiling.

"Neat name. Never heard it before." That would be because my mother was an old soul who thought to name me Violet would be retro. It wasn't. It was a color.

"Eh, it's OK."

I pulled up in front of the body shop and shut the car off. It was raining even harder now, the rain pelting against my windows. "I'll come in with you to make sure someone is home."

"I'm fourteen years old. I can be left alone.'

"Whatever. Let's go." She was right, but I didn't care. I was pretty pissed off that her brother had left her all alone to walk home in the rain.

We dashed to the door, my coat pulled over my head, and I stumbled into the door Frankie held open. "Oh my God, it's really coming down," I mumbled, shaking my coat off. My hair was matted to my forehead, and I'm sure I looked like a drowned rat.

"I think Luke is in the shop, I'll go get him." Frankie slipped through another door that I assumed lead to the shop, and I looked around.

Apparently, I was in the office of the body shop. There was a cluttered counter in front of me and stacks of wheels and tires all around. Four chairs are set off to the side, which I assume is the waiting area, and a vending machine on the far wall.

The phone rang a shrilling ring, making me jump. I looked around, trying to figure out what to do when the door to the shop was thrown open, and a bald, scowling man came walking through. He didn't even glance at me, just picked up the phone and started barking into it.

"Skid Row Kings," he grunted.

I couldn't hear what was being said on the other end, but I could tell Baldy was not happy. I looked down at my hands, noticing my cute plaid skirt I had put on that morning was now drenched and clinging to my legs. Thankfully I had worn flats today, or I probably would have fallen on my ass in the rain.

"What can I help you with?"

My head shot up, baldy staring at me. "Um, I brought Frankie home."

He looked me up and down, his eyes scanning me over. "Aren't you a little too old to be hanging out with a fourteen-year-old? You're what, sixteen, seventeen?"

"Try twenty-seven." This guy was a piece of work. He was looking me over like I was on display and he thought I was a teenager.

His eyes snapped to mine, and his jaw dropped. Yeah, jackass, I'm older than you are probably. "What the hell are you doing with Frankie?"

"She works at the library. You know, the place you promised to pick me up from today?" Frankie said, walking back into the shop. She had managed to find a towel and was drying herself off. I would kill for a towel right now.

"Fuck," Baldy twisted around and looked at the clock behind him. "Sorry, Frankie. Mitch and I were tearing apart the tranny on the Charger."

She waved her hand at him and tossed the towel to me. Oh, thank you sweet baby Jesus. I wiped the water that was dripping down my face and squeezed all the water out of my hair into it.

"How the hell did you get so wet if she gave you a ride home?"

"Because I started walking home, Luke, until Violet was kind enough to stop and give me a lift."

He watched me dry my hair, confusion on his face. "Violet?" he muttered.

"That's me," I said, sticking my hand out for him to shake. "I didn't want Frankie to get sick walking home. Plus, it's getting dark and someone her age shouldn't be out then."

"She's fourteen years old," he sneered. "I was out on the streets when I was twelve."

"Oh, well. If that's how you want to raise her." Luke was a gearhead that was also an ass. I didn't have time for this. My bath was definitely calling my name now that I was soaking wet. I tossed the towel back to Frankie and pulled my jacket over my head again. "You're welcome for bringing your sister home."

"I didn't ask you to."

"I know," I turned to Frankie and smiled. "I'll see ya tomorrow." She nodded her head at me, smiling, and I turned to walk out the door. I twisted the handle, and the door blew into me, rain pouring in. I glance back at Luke one time, a scowl on his face, and figured the pouring rain was better company than he was.

I pulled the door shut behind me and sprinted to my car, dodging puddles.

Once I was safely in my car, I looked up at the two-story building and sighed. I wish I could say this was a hole in the wall garage, but it was far from that. The building itself was a dark blue aluminum siding with huge neon letters that boasted, Skid Row Kings Garage, also known as SRK Garage. There were five bay doors that I'm assuming is where they pulled the cars into and over the office part is where I believe they lived. It was monstrous. Everyone in town took their cars here, especially the street racing crowd.

I had never been here before, mainly because I have never really needed repairs done on my car. I always went to the big chain stores to get my oil changed and thankfully hadn't needed any major repairs.

I started my car, thankful to be headed home. I turned around, the big looming building in my review as I headed down the street.

Hopefully, that was the last time I would ever step foot in Skid Row Kings garage and never see Luke again. He seemed like a total ass.

= = = = = = = = = = = =

70371348R00160

Made in the USA
Columbia, SC
05 May 2017